UNTIL THE RAKE SURRENDERS

ROGUE RULES

BOOK FIVE

DARCY BURKE

Zealous Quill Press

UNTIL THE RAKE SURRENDERS

It will take nothing less than the promise of a heart-stopping, breath-catching, happily ever after to woo Lady Minerva Halifax into marriage, but that dream seems doomed. She only attracts money- and position-hungry rogues because she's the daughter of a wealthy duke. Then her friend's dashingly irrepressible brother, Evan Price, is injured showing off at a house party, and Min ends up caring for him. As unexpected sparks flash between them, she wonders if Cupid may finally be circling.

Evan foolishly falls for his reluctant nurse, but he knows he doesn't stand a chance of winning her hand without a title. Min is forced back onto the Marriage Mart by her parents, and Evan returns to filling the hollows inside himself with daring adventures and fleeting flirtations. He suddenly finds himself the most desired bachelor in Bath—except by the one person he really wants.

But when an absolute scoundrel swoops in to claim Min,

Evan must bare his heart and risk everything or chance losing her forever.

Don't miss the rest of the *Rogue Rules*!

Do you want to hear all the latest about me and my books? Sign up at <u>Reader Club newsletter</u> for members-only bonus content, advance notice of pre-orders, insider scoop, as well as contests and giveaways!

Care to share your love for my books with like-minded readers? Want to hang with me and see pictures of my cats (who doesn't!)? Then don't miss my exclusive Facebook groups!

Darcy's Duchesses for historical readers
Burke's Book Lovers for contemporary readers

Want more historical romance? Do you like your historical romance filled with passion and red hot chemistry? Join me and my author friends in the Facebook group, Historical Harlots, for exclusive giveaways, chat with amazing HistRom authors, and more!

THE ROGUE RULES

Never be alone with a rogue.
Never flirt with a rogue.
Never give a rogue a chance.
Never doubt a rogue's reputation.
Never believe a rogue's pledge of love or devotion.
Never trust a rogue to change.
Never allow a rogue to see your heart.
Ruin the rogue before he can ruin you.

CHAPTER 1

Wiltshire, September 1816

 ady Minerva Halifax stepped into the massive, wood-paneled great hall at Longleat and made a silent vow that she would *not* find a husband at this house party. Her mother, the Duchess of Henlow, sincerely hoped she would, but since she was not here, Min would not be pressured at every turn. Instead, that would happen when she rejoined her mother in Bath following the party.

Ellis Dangerfield, Min's companion for seventeen years—since Min was five and Ellis nine—entered alongside her. Min glanced around the cavernous great hall with its splendid wood beams decorating the high ceiling, her blue eyes shrewdly assessing, but did not seem overly impressed. Though, Ellis had mastered the art of being enigmatic.

"I'm still shocked my mother chose not to come," Min said softly as they moved into the hall. Her chaperone, Jane

Ogilvie, her mother's great-aunt's cousin, followed them and immediately found a chair on which to perch.

"Apparently, setting up the house in Bath was more important," Ellis replied. "Particularly since she plans to live there permanently."

That had been a surprising development. The duchess loved nothing more than presiding at Henlow House in London. So when she'd informed Min that she'd decided to set up a permanent residence in Bath, to say Min was shocked was an understatement. And she still didn't fully understand why.

It was no secret that her parents' marriage was fraught, but they'd tolerated each other for years. What had happened to force her mother to decide she no longer wanted to reign as one of Society's premier hostesses?

Min pushed the thought aside, for she would not find the answer here at Longleat. Instead, she would enjoy the house party and gird herself for the upcoming Marriage Mart in Bath. Her mother had indicated that Min's time was running out. If she did not wed this autumn, her chance to do so might well be gone. While Min didn't entirely agree with that dire assessment, she knew she was nearing the shelf. But the shelf was preferable to a loveless marriage and the risk of ending up in a perennial battleground like her parents.

For now, Min would enjoy the party at this gorgeous estate with Ellis. They would, no doubt, have little trouble evading the not-so-watchful eye of Min's chaperone. Mrs. Ogilvie was a pleasant woman of eighty years with warm hazel eyes and an upturned nose. She had a head of thick white hair due to the wigs she wore. They were neither embarrassingly antiquated nor were they fashionable. Widowed for nearly sixty years and without children of her own, Mrs. Ogilvie had been pressed into service—sometimes Min wondered if it had been willingly—as the family's eternal chaperone. Her only demand in return was that she not ever return to London. She'd left when her husband died and had never gone back.

Their hostess, the Marchioness of Bath, mingled about the great hall, greeting all the guests who were being held there. Min glanced at Ellis. "Do you suppose there is going to be an announcement?"

Mrs. Ogilvie answered before Ellis could. "That is what I expect. It is a trifle odd."

The marchioness came toward them with a bright smile. "Welcome, Lady Minerva, Mrs. Ogilvie, Miss Dangerfield." She focused on Min. "I'm so pleased you could attend our party, though I am sorry Her Grace was not able to accompany you."

Rather than address her mother's absence, Min returned the marchioness's smile. "May I offer my family's congratulations on the recent marriage of your daughter?"

"Thank you," the marchioness replied. "It has been busy dealing with that in London and then returning here for the party. But it is good to have one daughter wed," she added with a laugh. Her gaze lingered on Min somewhat expectantly. "I imagine you'll be hoping to make a match soon, and you are not the only one. Lord Ecclestone's daughter is also here."

Their hostess glanced toward the opposite side of the room where the young woman she'd mentioned stood with another young lady and their mothers. Min recognized them all from last spring in London. It had been Miss Ecclestone's first Season, and there had been many wagers on her betrothal. Only the ones who'd bet against her marrying had won.

The marchioness continued. "There will be several eligible men here, including the Viscount Claxton." He was heir to an earldom near York—Min's mother ensured Min knew who all the eligible bachelors were. "They are all young and robust with good fortunes," Lady Bath noted. "Indeed, you cannot make a poor choice."

Min doubted that most strenuously. She'd met most of the men who would be in attendance, and none of them met her standards. Every one could be described as a rogue or at least rogue-*ish*. It wasn't to say they were universally *bad*. She simply had no desire to wed someone who would not take the notion of marriage and partnership seriously.

And that was where she knew she was doomed. Very few men saw marriage as a partnership, with each person bringing specific skills and traits to the union that would benefit them both—and create a loving family. For that was what Min wanted more than anything else—a real marriage, not a strategic alliance. Nor would she settle because societal expectations dictated she should.

"Are you to play matchmaker?" Mrs. Ogilvie asked their hostess with a discerning eye, as if she were deciding whether the marchioness was up to the task.

"The Duchess of Henlow asked me to ensure Lady Minerva has ample opportunity to spend time with the bachelors at the party."

Min snapped her attention to Lady Bath. "She did?"

The marchioness nodded. "She sent me a letter. As a mother, I understand her…concerns. I do wonder why she has not come herself, however." Overall, her tone held an edge of condescension and disapproval.

Min was tempted to defend her lack of marriage thus far but decided there was no point. She would, however, provide a reason for her mother's absence. "My mother is busy setting up the household in Bath, where we will be going after the party. I don't plan to make any decisions regarding marriage until then. Surely you realize that a house party lasting a week is not a sufficient length of time for courtship." She gave their hostess a bland smile.

The marchioness's eyes narrowed ever so slightly. "Longleat can be very romantic. The grounds are beautiful. You may find yourself swept away and falling in love." Her gaze moved past Min. "You must pardon me, as I've another guest to greet."

After the marchioness had moved away, Mrs. Ogilvie said, "She's going to try to play matchmaker. It would be a coup for her to have your betrothal announced at the end of the party."

"But as neither of my parents is here, there will be no betrothal," Min replied. Even if they *were* here, there would be no betrothal. Min would not settle for anything less than love, and she was not going to find that in a week at Longleat, no matter how bloody "romantic" the gardens were.

"Not unless a betrothal becomes necessary." Mrs. Ogilvie chuckled. "Which, of course, it won't. You have been exceedingly careful when it comes to your behavior. Not at all like that friend of yours who was ruined, poor dear."

She referred to Pandora Barclay, who'd been ruined two years earlier by the Earl of Banemore during their annual holiday in Weston. Each August, Min and her brother, Sheff, the Earl of Shefford, along with Ellis, traveled to their father's estate, the Grove, near the seaside town of Weston. Several years ago, Min had befriended Persephone Barclay, who was Pandora's older sister. They had all become friends, along with two other young ladies who also visited Weston in August.

"Pandora fell in love," Min said quietly. "That clouded her judgment. She did not expect Bane would lie about loving her in return, nor did she have any idea he was already, apparently, betrothed." He'd left Weston after they'd been caught in a compromising position and married someone else, leaving Pandora's reputation in tatters. It was a cautionary tale about love and roguery. While love was a requirement for Min, she was exceedingly careful about falling in love with a rogue.

Ellis nodded in agreement. "That was a terrible situation, and one Min would never find herself in."

"Love is dangerous," Mrs. Ogilvie said sadly. "It leaves one completely vulnerable. Whilst that can be wonderful, it can also be devastating." For her, it had been the latter since she'd lost her husband, whom she'd loved, so soon after they'd wed.

The guest the marchioness had greeted strolled farther into the hall. He'd already removed his hat and likely given it to a footman, for his head was bare, inviting one to study the brown waves of his hair, which were particularly lush for a gentleman. It matched the thickness of the coal-black eyelashes framing his deep brown eyes, which were also notably attractive. Evan Price was objectively handsome— almost distractingly so. He was also Min's dear friend's brother.

Most important of all, he was a rogue.

Evan was, however, a safe rogue since he and Min were friends and would never be anything more. He turned his head and met her gaze. He appeared surprised, indicating he hadn't noticed her—or Ellis, whom he also knew well. Pivoting, he walked toward them with an affable grin.

"Good afternoon, Lady Minerva, Miss Dangerfield, and…" He looked at Mrs. Ogilvie with a faint air of panic. "Forgive me, but I don't recall your chaperone's name. Indeed, I don't even recognize her from London." He gave Min and Ellis an apologetic grimace. "Please tell me it's not the same person and that I haven't just made a complete fool of myself."

Min couldn't help laughing at Evan's self-deprecation. "In fact, this is not the same person. I have two chaperones—one in London and one outside town. Surely you recall Mrs. Ogilvie from the Grove? She is always there with us in August."

His eyes widened briefly, and he quickly bowed. "Of course. My apologies for not remembering you at first, Mrs. Ogilvie. I'm afraid I don't always recognize people. It's a rather embarrassing trait."

"You are Lady Somerton's brother," Mrs. Ogilvie said, referring to Gwen, who was Min and Ellis's friend.

Evan hesitated the barest moment. "Er, yes. Sometimes I forget she is Lady Somerton now."

"I think we are all surprised that Somerton wed," Min noted. He'd been a terrible rogue, and Gwen had been incredibly courageous to marry him—or so Min thought. Somerton did seem entirely reformed. They were deliriously happy.

Mrs. Ogilvie fixed Evan with an expectant stare. "Have you come to the party to find a bride?"

Evan quickly shook his head. "I am not ready for that. Yet."

"Is our esteemed hostess aware?" Mrs. Ogilvie pursed her lips. "She seems to be under the impression that the bachelors attending this party are in search of wives."

"I didn't ever say I was on the Marriage Mart," Evan said. He looked to Min. "Does the marchioness believe you are here to find a husband? I don't know that there will be anyone attending whom you will find…worthy."

"Why do you say that?" Mrs. Ogilvie demanded, as if it wasn't a well-trafficked rumor that Min's standards for a husband were so high, no man could meet them. She'd had several suitors and multiple proposals of marriage—all of which she'd declined.

There was also the fact that Evan, as a friend of Min's brother, likely knew the truth, that Min would not be wooed by anyone whose character was not above reproach. To Min, that was not setting her standards too high. It was respecting herself enough to expect what she deserved: a man who would honor her and himself with his behavior and, above all, who would love her beyond reason.

Actually, Evan wouldn't know that last bit, for Min did not speak about love. To do so would be to explain why the emotion was so important to her, and to do that would mean exposing her parents' loveless marriage. Though, that was likely no secret either. Especially now that her mother had decided to reside in Bath permanently.

Min answered her chaperone's question for Evan. "Mr. Price is aware I am not interested in marrying a rogue. I suspect rogues will be the only kind of bachelors in attendance."

Evan grinned. "Exactly so."

"Yourself included," Ellis said with a faint smile.

While Evan hadn't demonstrated roguish behavior as brow raising as Min's newly wedded brother or Evan's new brother-in-law, he did not comport himself as a gentleman in search of a bride. He was unserious and raucous, eager to impress others with his sportsmanship and gambling prowess at the tables.

"Shouldn't you be working in London?" Min asked. Evan was employed by the Treasury, where his father was one of the Lord Commissioners.

"Not at the moment," Evan said.

Min found it odd that he did not say more. However, she did not press him because three gentlemen entered the hall, their voices carrying loudly.

"Price!" one of them called. Min recognized him as Phillip Lambton, third son of the Earl of Alnwick. He was definitely not here to find a bride, despite what his parents would insist. According to gossip, he was supposed to be dedicating himself to the church and was only pretending to be interested in taking a wife first.

"Ah, the troops have arrived," Evan said wolfishly. He inclined his head toward Min, then Mrs. Ogilvie and Ellis. "Please excuse me. I'm sure I'll see you at dinner."

"Mmm, yes," Min murmured as Evan took himself off. The tails of his coat swayed with his brisk movement, allowing a glimpse of his rather attractive backside. The man really was too handsome.

Surely no good will come from that.

The observation was something her mother said about attractive gentlemen. Min was certain she referred to her own husband—Min's father—who'd been very handsome in his youth and still was, despite the paunch he'd developed through years of overindulgence.

"You are quite familiar with Mr. Price," Mrs. Ogilvie said with more than a hint of curiosity.

"He's a friend. Almost like family, really," Min replied. "His sister Gwen is one of my closest friends."

"Well, that is too bad. He's rather handsome," Mrs. Ogilvie said pertly before directing her attention to the gentlemen, now led by Evan, who'd moved to gawk at the huge paintings depicting the story of an orphan who'd been found on the estate. Evan pointed out the antlers, and their loud conversation turned to hunting. "They are going to be tiresome, aren't they?" Mrs. Ogilvie asked with a sigh.

Ellis laughed softly, and Min joined her.

The Marquess of Bath entered then, and the room gradually fell silent. The marchioness joined him near an incredibly long shuffleboard table. Indeed, it was so large that Min couldn't imagine how it had been moved into this room. Perhaps it had been built there.

"Welcome to Longleat," the marquess said loudly. "We have many entertainments planned for the next week, beginning with dinner tonight, followed by dancing and card games. There is also something very special for this party that Lady Bath will explain." He pivoted toward the marchioness.

She smiled at the assembly of guests, her dark eyes sparking with excitement. "There is great potential for a match to be made. If there is a betrothal, we will gift the couple with a golden rose." The marchioness smiled broadly.

Ellis leaned toward Min and whispered, "Does she really think that's going to entice any of these knobheads to wed?"

Min bit back a laugh. "'Knobhead'?"

"It fits," Ellis said with a shrug.

It did, indeed. But then another young gentleman stepped away from a group, his movement drawing Min's attention. She didn't recognize him and wondered if he was the Viscount Claxton. He was attractive, with auburn hair and strong features from his thick brows to his square chin. His gaze swept the room until it settled on Min. He smiled, slowly, deliberately, it seemed. Min's spine tingled as heat sparked in her chest.

"Do you suppose that's Claxton?" Ellis asked softly.

Min pivoted toward Ellis. "I was wondering the same thing."

"He's attractive," Ellis said with the hint of a smile.

A man's appearance held no bearing as to his character, and that was what Min cared about. "We shall see if he is one of Evan's 'troops.'"

Ellis glanced toward the man. "Does that mean you are going to give him a chance?"

"I suppose I must. If I'm to have any hope of marrying before I'm forced to accept someone my parents choose." Min didn't doubt that her mother would try to push her into a marriage. She'd agreed to allow Min to marry for love, but that hadn't come close to happening yet, and her mother was out of patience.

Min was less concerned about her mother's frustration than she was about her own. Perhaps she wasn't meant to fall in love. While she was encouraged by the recent love matches her friends had made, she couldn't help fearing it wouldn't happen for her. She'd never felt a special inclination for or a...pull toward someone.

She was beginning to wonder if she was incapable of experiencing that. Perhaps, after a lifetime of witnessing her parents' mutual animosity and resentment, she was simply broken.

~

*A*fter the ladies left the dining room that evening, Evan remained with the rest of the gentlemen, sipping their port. The Viscount Claxton, whom Evan hadn't met before, sat to his right. He seemed to be near the same age as Evan's twenty-seven years, with auburn hair and a handsome visage that, to Evan's eye, appeared tinged with arrogance, as if he knew he was attractive and wielded that to his advantage. The viscount was quick to make a jest, often at someone else's expense. At least that was what he'd done as soon as the ladies had gone to the drawing room.

Claxton had made a few crude remarks about a couple of the older gentlemen, including their host's godfather, who was perhaps the most senior guest. The man had a regrettable flatulence problem, and Claxton had made sure everyone in the room was aware.

"So which one of you gents is going to fall into the parson's trap?" Evan asked.

Lambton shook his head vigorously. "Not me. My money is on Barswell."

The dark-haired and dark-eyed Viscount Barswell gave Lambton a hooded look. "Why me?" he asked, before sliding a glance toward Claxton. "I think our money should be on the one with the need to wed."

Claxton narrowed his eyes at Barswell. "I would argue that we all need to wed at some point."

Even Evan knew that was true. He might not be a titled gentleman with a need for an heir, but his father was successful and had gained an important role in the government. He wanted a legacy and was eager for Evan to take a wife and have children to carry on the family name. Evan was, after all, the only son.

"Some sooner than others," Lambton said before sipping his port. He'd barely swallowed before adding, "Are the rumors about your finances untrue?"

The younger men sat at one end of the table, and every one of them swept their gazes toward Claxton. The older men at the head of the table, where the marquess was holding court, were not paying attention to the conversation at the other end.

Claxton frowned. "I don't know what you've heard, but I'm quite solvent, thank you." He tipped back the rest of his port, and a footman quickly refilled his glass.

Evan studied Claxton and tried to discern if the man was telling the truth, but it was impossible to tell.

"At least my teeth are straight," Claxton said to Lambton, confirming what Evan had already decided—that Claxton possessed a penchant for spite.

Lambton flushed before draining his glass. It too was quickly refilled.

Claxton turned his attention to Evan. "*And* I have a title, which can't be overlooked."

Was he trying to assert his noble dominance? Evan swallowed a laugh. "I am delighted to be free of the obligations that come with a title and dictate much of one's life."

"More time for your daredevil feats," another of the young men said. "Will you be conducting any of your riding tricks at the party?"

One of Evan's athletic pursuits was riding horses and performing tricks one might see at Astley's. "Who can say?"

"I think it's time we join the ladies," their host announced as he rose at the head of the table.

All the gentlemen stood and made their way from the dining room. The marquess spoke with one of the footmen and did not move toward the door until Evan was nearly there. They were the last two gentlemen to leave.

The marquess gestured at the doorway. "After you, Price."

Evan inclined his head and stepped over the threshold. Outside the dining room, the marquess moved to walk alongside him. "I'm glad you were able to attend the party. My wife is thrilled to have you here and is hopeful you will demonstrate your daring skills on horseback. Perhaps tomorrow after our ride?"

"I would be delighted," Evan said.

They stood facing one another, and the marquess studied Evan a moment. "Will you return to London after the party, or will you be spending the autumn away from Town?"

The man's assessing gaze made Evan tense. Had the marquess heard of the scandal that had driven Evan from London? "I will be spending a month or so in Bath," Evan replied evenly.

In fact, his father had instructed him not to return to London until the new year, to allow the gossip to dissipate. It was a major inconvenience to Evan, particularly since his role in the scandal was entirely fabricated.

The marquess nodded faintly. "A sound decision. I do

hope you'll be on your best behavior here. I'm not sure what happened specifically, but I would ask that you ensure my wife's party and reputation are not harmed by any…indiscretion."

Evan should have expected something like this since he was believed to have engaged in a liaison with a married woman whose husband also worked at the Treasury. The truth, however, was that he had not conducted an affair with Mrs. Dalton. That had been his good friend Roger Martin, to whom Evan owed a debt. He'd taken the blame, thinking he would weather the scandal far better than Roger, who was just starting a promising career as a barrister and who did not have the benefit of strong family or social connections to see him through.

Summoning a smile he hoped the marquess would believe, Evan inclined his head with a measure of deference. "I have learned my lesson, my lord. Please be assured my behavior will be well above reproach."

"I am relieved—and glad—to hear it," Bath said. "And if you are searching for a wife, the marchioness will be thrilled to assist you."

"I am not on the hunt, alas. And I think you may want to prepare her ladyship for the very real possibility that there will not be a match at this party. I don't think this particular crop of gentlemen is altogether serious about matrimony just now."

"You ought to convince them," the marquess said with a smile. "Marriage comes for us all, and there are several excellent bridal prospects here. One of you could very well procure the hand of Henlow's daughter. That man would be highly congratulated, his faults forgotten."

Was he trying to persuade Evan that he should wed Min in order to tidy his reputation?

"I'll point that out," Evan said. He didn't bother telling the man that Min wouldn't wed any of these rogues.

The marquess started toward the drawing room, and Evan fell into step beside him. "You should ask Lady Minerva to dance."

"I'm sure I will. She is a friend of my sister's, after all. And her brother is a close friend."

"One must wonder why the two of you aren't already betrothed," the marquess noted with a sidelong glance and a chuckle.

"We are friends, my lord. I am not sure Lady Minerva and I would be suited romantically."

"Sometimes it's enough to marry a friend –someone you respect and whose company you enjoy. It's certainly preferable to wedding a woman you barely know or with whom you have nothing in common." The marquess's gaze fixed on the doorway to the drawing room ahead.

Evan let the host of the party enter first, then followed behind. He sought out Min and saw that she was already dancing—with Claxton. She seemed to be enjoying herself, if her smile was any indication.

Ellis was standing in the corner, ever the wallflower. Evan joined her. "I have never seen you dance. Do you even know how?"

She laughed. "Yes, not that I have occasion to demonstrate my ability. I learned from watching Min—both in lessons and in practice at countless balls and assemblies."

"You did not partake in the lessons?'

"They weren't for me." Her tone seemed to indicate that didn't bother her, but Evan had to think she must have felt left out.

"You didn't want to learn?"

She shrugged. "I have always been Min's companion. While I received the same education from the governess, I was not given any training in comportment. The irony is that I am better at embroidery than Min."

Evan grinned. "How charming." They watched the dancing for a few moments before he said. "What will you do when Min weds?"

"*If* she weds."

"You think she won't?" He pivoted toward Ellis, whose evening gown was plain and whose blonde hair was coiled into a simple style, with only a ribbon to decorate it. Her appearance reinforced that she was subordinate to Min. Evan noted that regardless of the division, the two women appeared to be as close as sisters.

"I think she will only wed when and *if* she finds the right bridegroom. She will not settle, even if her parents demand it."

"She can always follow her brother's lead," Evan said. "When they demanded he marry, he found the most inappropriate woman possible."

Ellis turned her head to look at him. "And now they are happily wed. If that is the lead Min should follow, then I heartily agree. She deserves nothing less than true, abiding love and lasting happiness."

The dance ended, and Evan realized Ellis hadn't answered his question about what she would do when Min wed. Perhaps that was something Ellis didn't care to contemplate.

Min and Claxton parted as they left the small dancing area. Min went directly to a table bearing a Delft punch bowl. After helping herself to a cup, she took a few sips before making her way to Ellis and Evan.

Evan noted Min's pink cheeks and her rapid drinking of the punch. "I was going to ask if you wanted to dance the next set, but perhaps you would rather have a respite."

"There isn't going to be any more dancing," Min said. "We decided the space was too small. I'll dance with you at the ball on the final night, if you like. That will be in the ballroom."

"I'll look forward to it." He sent a look toward Claxton, who was now speaking with one of the other young ladies. Evan had no idea which one. If he was terrible at recalling faces, he was only marginally better at remembering people's names. It was damnably difficult to keep everyone straight, so he found it best to just be frank about his poor memory when it came to people.

"How did you find Claxton?" he asked Min, wondering if the man had revealed any of his venom.

"Quite charming, actually." She narrowed her eyes at Evan and edged closer, "Why, what do you know?"

He didn't want to tell her about Claxton's obnoxious behavior in the dining room. Perhaps the man had only been trying to show off since he didn't really know anyone. Evan could understand feeling nervous. He recalled the first time he'd met Min's brother and his friends more than a year ago in London and the first August he'd spent with them in Weston last year. He'd been somewhat intimidated by a duke, a viscount, and two earls, and even more so by their close friendship. He'd felt like an interloper until they'd welcomed him eagerly and sincerely.

"I don't know anything," Evan replied. "I'm sure you'll come to know him during the party."

"Can I count on you to tell me if you hear anything important?" she asked. "Particularly if he's a scoundrel."

"Yes, you can rely on me to deliver the truth if it is presented to me." He made a silent note to himself to keep a close eye on Claxton, particularly as his behavior pertained to Min. "I'm happy to play the role of brother during the party."

Min's brow creased. "I don't need another brother, but I appreciate your concern. I am looking forward to this respite from my family, so I would prefer if you didn't watch over me in that manner."

"I can understand needing a respite from one's family." Evan was glad to be away from his father in particular. He'd been livid when he'd learned of Evan's "indiscretion" and had promptly banished him from the Treasury and from London.

"Will you be performing any of your riding tricks at the party?" Min asked.

"In fact, the marquess asked me to demonstrate them tomorrow after the ride."

Min sniffed. "The ride the ladies aren't invited to?"

"Er, I suppose so," Evan said. "I am not as well versed in house parties as you, but don't the men typically ride separately?"

"Usually, but since the marchioness is playing match-maker, I thought she might allow the women to ride with the men. Instead, she isn't offering riding to us at all." Min made a sound of frustration.

"What will you be doing?" Evan asked.

"Reading or doing needlework, I would guess. Though, perhaps we will be invited outside to watch your perfor-mance." A mischievous glint lit her pale gray eyes. They were an astonishing color and never failed to draw his notice—and admiration. "If not, I think we shall happen to take a walk around that time." She looked to Ellis, who inclined her head in response.

"Then I shall attempt something extraordinary," Evan said with a smile.

Ellis arched a brow. "I shall hope you do more than attempt. We don't want anything unfortunate to happen to you."

"I haven't hurt myself yet, beyond the occasional bruise. I'm confident in my abilities." He leaned toward them. "You should be too."

"Well, if your arrogance is any indication, we shall be greatly entertained," Min said with a laugh.

Evan couldn't help grinning. "I shall do my best." He saw Min's gaze drift toward Claxton once more and had second thoughts about not telling her of his offensive behavior. "I'm sure I don't have to tell you to watch out for the handsome viscount since he is unknown to us."

"You do not," Min replied pertly. "There is no one more guarded when it comes to your sex than I."

That Evan believed.

CHAPTER 2

*A*s expected, the ladies were gathered in the drawing room late the following morning, either reading or working on embroidery. Min was doing neither and noticed there was another young lady who'd also eschewed the activities. She stood near the window looking out over the expansive gardens.

Min approached the young woman, who appeared to be slightly younger than Min's twenty-two years. She had dark auburn hair and bright blue eyes that were focused, rather wistfully, outside.

"I'm Lady Minerva. I didn't see you last night."

She turned her head toward Min. "I know who you are. I'm Iona Shaughnessy. We arrived late. One of our horses had a problem with his shoe."

"I'm sorry to hear that." Min looked out at the gardens. "Do you wish you were outside? Perhaps riding with the gentlemen? I do."

"It's certainly preferable to embroidery." Miss Shaughnessy wrinkled her nose. "Do you think it is worth telling the marchioness we would prefer to be riding?"

Min chuckled. "I'm not sure. The marchioness seems to have somewhat rigid ideas about what the men and women should be doing at this party. She's quite focused on whether someone will make a match." She slid a long look toward Miss Shaughnessy. "Will that be you?"

Miss Shaughnessy's eyes darted toward a dark-haired woman seated in a chair not far away. "My mother certainly hopes so. That's why she brought me here." She looked at Min. "Is that not why you are here?"

Min shrugged. "The marchioness would like it if I made a match, as would my own mother. However, my mother is not here, so I do not feel the same pressure as you do. My apologies, Miss Shaughnessy."

"Please call me Iona."

"Then you must call me Min, as all my friends do."

Iona smiled. "Are we friends, then?"

"I don't see why not," Min said. "We've already established that neither of us wants to be trapped in the drawing room under threat of embroidery. As it happens, I'm planning to steal outside shortly in order to watch Mr. Price demonstrate his feats of daring on horseback."

Iona's eyes took on a gleam of anticipation. "Do you mind if I join you?"

"Not at all."

"I've heard of Mr. Price's daredevil antics," Iona said. "My brother, Ruark, rather Wexford, is acquainted with Mr. Price."

"Your brother is the Earl of Wexford?" Min asked. "I know Lady Wexford. If she were here, she would no doubt be joining us outside."

Iona nodded. "She would indeed."

Min realized she'd heard of Iona Shaughnessy before, probably from Cassandra—Lady Wexford. The Earl of Wexford had four half sisters, one of whom was married to the owner of the Phoenix Club. Min had thought that the second oldest, which would be Iona, was betrothed, but apparently, she'd been mistaken.

"Forgive me," Min said, "I thought you were perhaps already engaged to be married."

Iona's lips twisted into a frown of disgust. "I expected to be; however, the gentleman did not make a formal offer, despite leading me to believe he would."

Min scowled. "The bounder! He sounds like a terrible rogue. I hate rogues. In fact, my friends and I have a set of rules we adhere to in order to avoid rogues at all costs. It can be very treacherous as a young lady, especially if she is on the Marriage Mart."

Iona pivoted toward Min, her eyes bright with enthusiasm. "Do tell me about these rules."

"They are somewhat common sense, but it is good to have a reminder and to have the support of one's close friends as we work to keep ourselves safe from scandalous men," Min explained. "They are: never be alone with a rogue. Never flirt with a rogue. Never give a rogue a chance. Never doubt a rogue's reputation. Never believe a rogue's pledge of love or devotion."

"I've learned that one," Iona interrupted with a harsh laugh. "Please continue, or is that all of them?"

"No, there are more. Eight in total," Min said. "Never trust a rogue to change. Never allow a rogue to see your heart. And when all else fails, ruin the rogue before he can ruin you."

"Oh, that is excellent advice," Iona said earnestly. "Do you and your friends have a club for avoiding rogues?"

"Not officially, but consider yourself a member of our group—a founding one, since you just came up with the notion to formalize ourselves into a club. We must stick together, especially as we navigate house parties such as this, where the field is rife with eligible bachelors we are supposed to consider."

"I've never been in a club," Iona remarked.

"Of course not. Nearly all clubs are for *men*." Min rolled her eyes, and they both laughed. "Will your mother force you to wed at some point?"

"Probably, but mostly she just wants to make sure my prospects haven't been ruined," Iona replied. "She's concerned my reputation has been damaged by my former suitor not proposing. But I don't care. I'm still young and have time before I'm consigned to spinsterhood. I'm in no hurry to find a husband after my recent experience."

"I don't blame you," Min said in commiseration. "It is very hard to find a gentleman who is not a rogue. Four of my antirogue friends have married, and their husbands were some of the worst rogues you can imagine. Love has somehow transformed them. I can scarcely credit it." She shook her head. "One of them is my own brother. It does give me hope, for if he can fall irrevocably in love and reform himself, then I think it's possible anyone can." Particularly since Sheff had perfected his roguish skills watching their father—one of the worst rogues Min knew. The difference between them, however, was that Sheff had been able to redeem himself.

"That's wonderful to hear," Iona said with a smile. "I did read that your brother recently married. Is his bride in your club?"

"Yes, Jo is absolutely delightful."

Iona's brow creased faintly. "Doesn't her mother own the Siren's Call? That's a gaming hell, isn't it?"

Min nodded. "Much to my mother's chagrin. Their happiness is proof that you can't let Society or even your mother dictate what's best for you."

"I agree," Iona said eagerly. "I have been thinking of ways

to placate my mother so that she will ease up on her management. She is hoping I might find a suitor here, but I confess, none of these gentlemen sparks my fancy."

"I completely understand and feel the same." Min lowered her voice slightly. "I have not been above making up pretend suitors to pacify my mother. But I've done so often enough that it doesn't work anymore. Perhaps it would work for you."

Iona seemed to consider the idea. "It might. Thank you."

Ellis approached them, and Min introduced her to Iona. "She's the newest member of our club."

"We have a club?" Ellis asked.

"The Rogue Rules Club," Min replied.

"I didn't realize it was a club," Ellis said with a laugh, her blue eyes sparkling.

"It was Iona's idea." Min sent her an admiring glance. "She asked if it was a club, and I wondered why it wasn't."

Ellis smiled at Iona. "Brilliant. Perhaps we all need something themed, perhaps embroidered handkerchiefs."

"I love that idea, but you and Pandora can manage that." Min chuckled. "Iona likes needlework as much as I do."

"Pandora and I will be *delighted*," Ellis assured her with just the faintest hint of sarcasm. "Shall we take our walk outside?"

Min looked to their new friend. "Iona will be joining us."

"Excellent," Ellis said with a nod. "I've already informed Mrs. Ogilvie that we will be taking a walk in the garden."

"Let me just inform my mother," Iona said.

"She won't want to come us, will she?" Min hoped not.

Iona made a brief moue of distaste. "I will make sure she does not. I daresay she will prefer to remain here gossiping."

Iona went to speak with her mother, a pretty woman with brown hair and a dazzling smile. As Min and Ellis made their way to the door, Min said, "Iona's brother is the Earl of Wexford."

"I knew that," Ellis said.

"Of course, you did," Min replied. "You know Debrett's even better than I do."

Ellis shrugged. "It has been useful over the years. To *you*, and I am your companion, after all."

While it *was* useful to Min, it wasn't for Ellis. She didn't have to navigate Society or consider family, and she did not have to worry about marriage or what connection she might make.

Iona joined them at the door, and they made their way outside. "What about hats?" she asked. "Or gloves."

"Min and I stashed ours in the yellow room near the door to the patio," Ellis said.

"Should I run upstairs to fetch mine?" Iona asked. She appeared slightly concerned, with fine lines crossing her brow.

"There may not be time. Wear mine," Min offered as they walked into the yellow room. "My mother isn't here to be annoyed with me."

Ellis hastened to the table where they'd set their accessories and handed her hat to Iona. "No, wear mine. I don't have a mother at all, nor does anyone expect me to be anything other than background furnishing." She grinned, which took the sting from her words. Still, Min could see that Iona didn't quite know how to respond.

"Ellis truly means for you to wear her accessories," Min said to Iona. "And she does not mind that we are treated differently than she is—even though *we* may mind."

"That is very kind of you, Ellis." Iona took the bonnet and set it atop her auburn locks. "But I refuse to take your gloves. I can manage without them, and this way, we are sharing."

Ellis smiled. "Fair enough."

They departed the house and stepped onto the patio. The day was bright and warm so that they did not need a wrap or spencer. The trees were still mostly green, but autumn was in the air. Longleat's gardens were extensive and stunning. They'd been designed by Capability Brown and offered a great many features.

The gardens did not beckon, however, as Min was eager to watch Evan's demonstration. They walked through the manicured gardens toward the stables. Min's maid had determined that the spectacle was to take place in the stable yard.

"We should probably watch from afar," Min said. "I don't want to cause a scene since we aren't supposed to be there."

"That's probably best," Iona agreed.

As the stable yard came into view, they searched for a vantage point and settled on standing beneath a tree on a slight rise. After a few minutes, the men rode into the yard. There was a flurry of activity as they all dismounted, and grooms took the horses away.

Not everyone dismounted; Evan was still atop his magnificent bay horse.

"Have you seen him perform these feats before?" Iona asked.

"By accident, I suppose," Min said. "He rescued a young woman from being trampled by a runaway horse in Hyde Park. It was most impressive. He was able to grab the bridle and pull himself onto the horse." Min exchanged a look with Ellis who had also witnessed the marvel. "I would not have believed it if I hadn't seen it."

Iona's eyes rounded. "That is astonishing."

The gentlemen gathered together to watch as Evan rode to the other end of the stable yard. He swept his hand wide and then kicked his horse into a full gallop around the circle of the yard. Just watching him ride was entertainment enough. He was incredibly skilled, his lean legs hugging the horse's flanks as they picked up speed. Horse and rider moved as one.

After a couple of laps, Evan let go of the reins and put his arms wide, casting his head back. The horse continued on its path and didn't slow. Min realized she was smiling. He was magnificent.

"Remarkable," Iona breathed. "That horse must belong to him."

"I would say so," Min agreed. "The animal would need to be as trained as he is. Any other horse would be bolting by now."

"It looks bloody terrifying," Ellis said. But then, Ellis rarely rode and not just because she hadn't been encouraged to, as Min had. Ellis did not care for it at all.

Evan retook the reins, and there was applause from the gentlemen spectators. After another lap around the stable yard, Evan bent low over his mount, his cheek pressed to the horse's neck.

Min held her breath in anticipation for what he might do next. He pulled his feet from the stirrups and brought his legs up. Again, the horse didn't so much as flinch. They continued speeding around the stable yard.

Then Evan twisted in the saddle, sitting sideways as he brought one leg over. He grinned and waved at the gentlemen, his hand still raised as he continued around the yard. He seemed to see Min and the others standing beneath the tree, as he casually flicked his wrist in their direction.

Min's pulse sped. "He sees us."

Evan turned again in the saddle and brought one leg up under himself where he planted his foot down. He swept his other leg to the side, crouching on the back of the horse.

"Is he going to stand?" Iona asked, sounding as breathless as Min felt.

"He can't," Ellis said, sounding horrified. But that was exactly what he did. He pushed himself up, one hand still on the reins. The horse slowed a bit, but not as much as Min would have thought. Her heart was racing as she watched him straighten and stand tall atop the saddle, both feet braced on the animal.

"He's going to fall," Ellis exclaimed. "I can't watch." She slapped her hand over her eyes.

"I can't look away," Iona cried.

Min was riveted. He completed one full lap standing atop the animal. Then he crouched down once more. The men watching applauded wildly and whooped loudly.

"He's back in the saddle," Min said, and Ellis peeked over her hand before dropping it to her side. She exhaled with relief.

But Evan wasn't finished. He tossed a handkerchief to the ground, then continued in his oval circuit of the stable yard. Min was entranced.

Taking one foot from the stirrups once more, he leaned over the other side of the horse and extended his arm to pluck up the handkerchief he'd dropped. As he grasped the white linen, the men cheered, and Min found herself clapping, a grin splitting her cheeks.

When he did not immediately right himself, Min's smile faded. Where all his previous movements had been marked by grace and precision, something was now wrong. His arm twitched, and he seemed to be fighting to bring himself up.

Time slowed as Evan tilted toward the ground. His body slipped from the horse while his foot was still stuck in the stirrup.

All three of them gasped. Min took two steps forward,

her breath frozen in her lungs. The horse was going to drag him if he couldn't get his foot free. But the horse was well trained, and it slowed quickly, just as Evan managed to pull his foot away. He fell to the earth.

Without thought, Min ran toward the stable yard.

CHAPTER 3

*E*verything was dark, just as one might expect it to be in the afterlife. It was also noisy, which was *not* what Evan had anticipated. Actually, Evan hadn't given much thought to what would happen when he died. Perhaps he should have done.

Or perhaps it was dark because his eyes were closed. The moment he realized that, pain shot through his head and ankle. He winced sharply.

"Are you all right?"

The question was called out several times. Evan blinked open his eyes and saw a circle of men standing above him. To a one, they stared down at him, their features concerned. Evan looked past them up at the blue sky, where a pair of clouds drifted overhead.

"Evan?" That was a woman's voice. He might be bad with faces and with names, but he knew voices, and that was Min.

She pushed through the circle of men and knelt down beside him. Stupidly, he worried that her pale-yellow gown would be immediately soiled from the dirt. She did not appear to care, however, her gaze fixed on him with gentle concern.

"So much for your arrogance," she murmured just loud enough for only him to hear.

Evan smiled and was rewarded with a jabbing pain in his skull. He closed his eyes again and felt Min—at least he hoped it was Min—touch his shoulder.

"We need to send for a doctor," someone said.

"Where do you hurt?" Min asked softly. Evan opened his eyes again and met her caring gray gaze.

"My head is pounding quite fiercely, but the pain in my left ankle is much sharper." He tentatively moved his foot and instantly regretted it.

She glanced at his foot. "That's the one that was stuck in your stirrup as you fell."

Evan winced, which only made his head hurt more. He wanted to argue that he hadn't fallen, but of course, he had. He didn't know what had gone wrong, but he would have plenty of time to consider that.

He gasped softly. "What about Merlin?"

"Is that your horse?"

Evan stopped himself from nodding as that would only bring more pain. "Yes. What happened to him?"

"He slowed down immediately, but I confess I was too concerned about you." Min looked up at someone. "Did a groom catch hold of Mr. Price's horse?"

"Yes." The response came from the marquess, Evan thought.

"And he's fine?" Evan tilted his head slightly, which hurt, of course, and saw the marquess standing behind Min.

"He is well," the marquess said. "You, on the other hand, need a doctor. And a bonesetter, I should think. We will need to fetch them from Frome, which will take time."

Min gently ran her fingertips across Evan's brow. Her

touch was instantly soothing. "We should get you inside. You can't very well lie here in the dirt until the doctor arrives." A faint smile teased her lips.

"Do not make me smile or, God forbid, laugh," Evan said. "It hurts too much."

"Then I shall only speak to you in a stern, commanding voice," Min replied, her brows pitching low over her stunning eyes.

"He needs some brandy," someone called.

"I definitely agree with that," Evan said.

Min gave him a nod before standing. She turned to the marquess. "Do you have anything that would serve as a litter to carry him inside?"

"I'm sure we can come up with something." The marquess strode away.

Min turned to someone else and told them to go inside to fetch brandy. Then she knelt back down beside Evan. "We'll get you inside very shortly," she said.

She turned her head and called for Ellis and someone named "Iona." Evan, of course, recognized Ellis, but the other young lady was unknown to him. He hoped he hadn't met her last night and already forgotten.

Min looked to her companion. "Ellis, will you go inside and arrange for a place on the ground floor to which Mr. Price can be carried? It must be somewhere the doctor and bonesetter can tend to him, and it must have a settee or some other piece of furniture on which he can put up his legs." She glanced back at Evan. "I think it's too much to carry him up the stairs."

He wondered why she didn't ask for his input but decided it didn't matter since he enthusiastically agreed with her. The thought of being jostled up the stairs and all the way to his small chamber in a distant corner was utterly repellent.

"I agree," Ellis replied, settling the matter for good—as if it had ever been up for debate. Ellis and the other young lady left with alacrity.

The weight of everyone's stares pricked at Evan, adding discomfort to his pain. He closed his eyes once more.

"What's wrong?" Min moved closer to his side and spoke quietly. "Are you going to lose consciousness again?"

"Did I lose consciousness before?" He did not open his eyes.

"I don't know. I wasn't here. Do you remember if you did?"

He tried to think through the sequence of events that happened. He'd plucked up the handkerchief, and he hadn't been able to right himself on Merlin. Then he'd looked toward the tree where Min and Ellis and the other young lady—Iona—were standing, wondering if they'd seen what he'd just done. That small distraction had made him lose his balance, and he'd slid from the horse, the weight of his body carrying him toward the ground. He hadn't been able to remove his foot from the stirrup before his ankle was painfully wrenched. Even thinking of it made his extremity throb in agony. At least Merlin hadn't dragged him, he supposed.

"Evan, did I lose you?" Min prodded him, pressing her hand against his upper arm.

He opened his eyes and met her concerned stare. "No, I was just thinking of what happened. Bloody humiliating," he muttered.

"I thought it was brilliant." Min smiled. "Right up until you fell, of course, but you even managed to make that look exciting."

Evan grinned, and once again, pain stabbed through his head. "Damn it, Min, I told you not to make me laugh or smile, and now you've made me curse in front of you."

"You know I've heard much worse at the Grove every

summer. Do you recall whether you lost consciousness or not?" she asked again.

"I think I must have," he replied. "At least for a moment or two."

"Well, I can't imagine this is how you'd hoped to spend your house party," she said with a sigh.

"Definitely not." He'd be cooped up in his tiny chamber far away from everyone. When he managed to make his way up there, and right now, he couldn't countenance it. Perhaps he'd just stay wherever they carried him to.

The marquess returned. "We've found a board that should support you. We're going to transfer you onto it and carry you inside. Move aside," the marquess said, waving at the men standing to Evan's left.

Min remained on his right side as a pair of grooms put a board down next to Evan.

Frowning, Min looked at the grooms in succession. "That isn't long enough."

"It will be sufficient," the marquess said, though Min hadn't been speaking to him.

She turned to address the marquess, one hand moving to her hip in a thoroughly managerial stance. "His left ankle is injured, as is his head. With that board, one of those appendages will be hanging over either end."

"My head is an appendage?" Evan asked.

Min tossed him a faint scowl. "You know what I mean." She returned her attention to their host. "They need a longer board, else Mr. Price risks further injury."

"I would rather not endure that," Evan put in, glad for Min's advocacy.

Frowning, the marquess looked at the board, and then at Evan, and then back to the board. "I didn't credit you for being that tall, Price. What are you? Six feet?"

"About that," Evan replied.

The marquess exhaled and looked to one of the grooms. "Find a longer board, please." As the grooms bent to pick up the board they brought, he added, "And take that one with you."

"Don't make too much of a fuss," Evan mumbled, hating to be a nuisance.

Min pursed her lips at him. "I'm in charge right now, and I will make all the fuss that is required to ensure your care and recovery."

"You're in charge?" he asked.

She nodded primly. "For now, someone has to be. Look around you. Nothing but useless men," she said quietly, her eyes darting from side to side.

Evan tought against another grin. "I am glad for your management." Without it, he would have been hauled inside with either his ankle or his head dangling over the board—or perhaps both. Neither of which sounded particularly pleasant.

"I brought brandy," someone said. Evan couldn't see who it was.

Min turned her head and looked up at whoever had spoken. "Did you not bring a glass?" she asked sternly. "You can't expect him to drink straight from the decanter."

Evan stifled another smile, which was only slightly less painful than actually smiling.

"That didn't occur to me," the man replied, sounding utterly nonplussed. "I'll fetch a glass."

"Please do," Min said.

"It's a very good thing you're in charge," Evan said. "How absolutely gauche to expect me to drink from the decanter."

She pressed her lips together and shook her head at his sarcasm. "How do you expect to drink at all, lying there in the dirt? I'm not sure why I bothered with a glass. If you open your mouth, I suppose I can just pour some down your gullet."

A laugh bubbled in Evan's throat, which lifted his head slightly. That also meant his head came back down on the earth. He winced. "I can wait until I get inside."

"Here comes another board. Let us hope this is an improvement." Min's gaze moved to his left. The same two grooms put another board down on the dirt next to Evan.

"Excellent," Min said with approval after assessing its length. Bizarrely, he wondered if she might provide the same quick judgment when perusing the lengths of other things. What a horribly indecent thought. Particularly involving Min.

"Who's going to move him onto the board?" Min asked, jolting Evan from his lewd meanderings.

"They can do it," the marquess said.

Min looked from one groom to the other and back again as she spoke. "Be very careful. Make sure you put your hands beneath Mr. Price's shoulders and lift him as gently as possible. Actually, try not to lift him much at all. It's best if you keep his left ankle as stable as possible, as it may be broken. Try to scoot him onto the board."

The grooms knelt, one behind Evan's head and one at his feet. He tensed, anticipating a burst of pain.

"Be very careful," Min repeated as the grooms slipped their hands beneath him.

Evan closed his eyes and braced himself. They picked him up and slid him onto the board, and as the groom who held his shoulders moved back, Evan's head dropped against the board, sending a new wave of agony through his skull. He heard Min suck in her breath.

"Now lift the board slowly and gently," Min instructed. "Can the two of you manage the board and Mr. Price alone, or will you need help?"

"They'll be fine," the marquess replied as if the grooms were mute.

Min stood and directed two other men to help with the board, one of whom was the Viscount Claxton. He gave her a charming smile. "It is my pleasure to do your bidding, my lady."

Evan steeled himself once more as they lifted him. The jostling was painful, but they made it into the house with only a slight bobble as they moved through the doorway.

Ellis was waiting for them just inside. "This way. We're taking him into the ladies' library."

They walked past the large main library into a smaller room with far fewer books and exponentially more pink, along with flashes of yellow. It was as if a bright summer garden had exploded inside the room.

"Set him down over by that settee," Min directed. "Carefully," she reminded them. They set him down on the floor, and as Claxton stepped around the makeshift litter, his boot grazed Evan's left foot. Evan gasped as pain tore through him.

Min was at his side once more. "What happened?"

"Claxton bumped into my foot," he growled.

She sent the viscount a surprisingly vicious glare that brought Evan far more glee than it should have. Served the man right for being an ass.

Claxton retreated as Min asked the footmen to gently lift Evan to the settee in the same manner they had moved him from the ground onto the board. This was far more painful, as they weren't just moving him in a parallel fashion. They had to lift him and set him down. He was now almost certain his ankle was broken.

He was thoroughly peeved at himself.

There was an influx of women then, led by the marchioness. The marquess also came in, along with a few retainers. Several gentlemen brought up the rear until the exceedingly floral ladies' library looked as if it were about to host a performance.

"Wonderful," he murmured. "I've become the party's entertainment."

"Being the party's entertainment is what delivered you here," Min pointed out.

"Can't you just make them all leave?" he whispered. "You're very good at ordering people about. I'm most impressed."

"I will do my best. But let me see about getting you that brandy first."

"Wait, I need to sit up instead of lying flat. Are there pillows you could put behind me?"

"Yes, in fact, one of the maids already has them," Min said, sounding pleased. She and the maid worked together to plump pillows behind him and get him situated on the settee.

"Brandy, if you please," Min asked the maid.

The marquess moved forward to the settee, along with his wife. "I'm dreadfully sorry this has happened. We'll make sure you are well cared for."

"I appreciate that," Evan replied. "Min is doing an excellent job. Lady Minerva, I mean."

The brows of the marchioness—and to a lesser extent the marquess—arched in silent question.

"We are well acquainted," Min explained. "Mr. Price's sister is a close friend of mine, and my brother is a close friend of Mr. Price's."

The maid arrived with a glass of brandy before anything further was said.

Min took the glass from the maid. "We shall need some cold compresses."

"Right away, my lady." The maid departed once more.

Min addressed their hosts. "While I understand everyone's curiosity, I think it's best if we let Mr. Price rest until the doctor and the bonesetter arrive."

"I agree," the marchioness said. "I shall have Marguerite sit with him to attend to his needs." She glanced toward another maid, who was rather dour faced.

"I will be staying with him," Min said firmly. "As I said, we are friends, and it will probably do him good to have someone he knows at his side."

Evan could find no quarrel with that. In fact, he didn't want Min to leave.

The marchioness frowned. "Still, Marguerite should stay in case you need assistance, or perhaps I should send Mrs. Ogilvie down."

Min exhaled. "Just what do you think might happen between me and Mr. Price in his current condition? Furthermore, he is like a brother to me. There is nothing for anyone to be concerned about with regard to propriety. Think of me as his sister providing care in his time of need."

"This isn't exactly a secluded place," Evan put in. "People are in the library all the time. I guarantee you, I'm in no condition to do anything but drink brandy and perhaps sleep, although I don't think the latter is possible in my current state of extreme pain."

Min sent him a concerned glance.

The marchioness seemed to consider their arguments, and ultimately, an expression of defeat passed over her features. "Very well. I shall still ensure a maid checks in regularly, in case you need something."

"That would be most appreciated," Min replied. "For now, if you could clear the room so that Mr. Price may rest until the doctor and bonesetter arrive. I think that would be best."

Min did not wait for their hostess to respond. She turned her back to the marchioness and held up the brandy. "Do you need my assistance to drink this?"

"I don't think so." He took the glass from her, his fingers grazing hers. A quick but wholly shocking jolt of awareness shot through him. First, the inappropriate thoughts outside, and now this. How hard had he hit his head?

Evan sipped the brandy, careful just to not down the contents. "I don't suppose the brandy bottle is nearby. I foresee needing that when the doctor and bonesetter arrive."

"Yes, that is probably true," Min replied. She turned to ask Marguerite if she could provide a bottle of brandy, or perhaps whiskey, if there was any to be found.

Marguerite slid a glance toward Evan and gave him the very slightest nod, her eyes narrowing in what appeared to be a commiserative manner. "I'm sure I can find some whiskey," she said in a quiet tone to Min.

Evan would not have guessed the maid with the sour expression might be his savior, proving that one should not judge someone based on their appearance or their demeanor.

After Marguerite left, Evan said, "We may have an ally in the household."

Min's brow arched. "Time will tell."

The room was soon empty of everyone save Min. Evan closed his eyes briefly with relief. "Thank you for doing that."

"Well, you need your rest," Min said. "Enduring the doctor and the bonesetter will be quite taxing, I'm sure."

Evan grimaced, which again reminded him that his head felt as though he'd been in a fight and lost. "Let us not speak of it. I'm trying not to think of my disappointment or how angry I am at myself. I confess I'm not looking forward to whatever comes next."

"We should perhaps try to remove your boot," she suggested, moving toward his foot.

"I'm not sure that's wise," he said.

"You may be right. The bonesetter will likely want to cut it off."

Evan moaned. "These are my favorite riding boots, and they were not inexpensive."

"Better to have a new pair of boots than to lose an appendage," Min said.

He blinked at her. "I'm not in danger of losing my bloody foot."

She lifted a shoulder. "I am not an expert in such matters, and neither are you."

"I changed my mind," he said. "You are far too depressing to stay. You should go as well."

Min shook her head with a faint smile. "My apologies. I am merely concerned. I'm sure everything will be fine. You don't even know if your ankle is broken. Let us not get ahead of ourselves. We shall wait for the doctor and the bonesetter to examine you. In the meantime, I will stay here, and we will not speak of such things."

That would be best. Evan already knew that he wouldn't be allowed on horseback any time soon. He scarcely went more than a few days without riding. He would miss Merlin and the feats they accomplished together more than he could contemplate.

Min moved back to his head, then pulled a chair next to the settee and sat down beside him. "What shall we discuss while we wait?" she asked.

Evan looked about the extremely floral room with its bright, feminine colors. "I suppose we could converse about the decor. There's plenty to say about it."

"I'm surprised to hear you say that." She looked about the room. "I wouldn't think this color scheme would be appealing to you, whereas I like it."

Evan turned his head despite the pain, to see if she was being serious. She was.

"I had planned to roast the décor." He wrinkled his nose and regretted doing so for the pain it caused. "It's awful."

"I beg your pardon." She sounded affronted. "Pink is a lovely color. My suite at Henlow House is decorated in pinks. Indeed, the sitting room is quite similar to this. I suppose I can see where it may not appeal to you. What would you prefer? Brown? Perhaps a dark, muted blue?"

"In fact, my bedchamber back home in Wales is decorated in blue and chestnut brown. I don't really know what chestnut brown is—and don't tell me it's the color of a chestnut. Who pays attention to such things? But that's what my mother calls it."

Min laughed. "So, you take issue with this room because of the color. The excess of flowers doesn't bother you?"

"Oh no, I find that equally appalling," he said. "I suppose you like them?"

"I do like flowers, but I'll allow that this is perhaps a bit too fussy. That is what it shares in common with my sitting room, which my mother decorated." She made a disagreeable face that somehow made her more attractive, not less. Yes, he'd definitely sustained a major head injury. The doctor could not arrive soon enough.

"Thank you." He sipped his brandy. "You are quite putting me at ease."

"I am happy to do it." Min clasped her hands in her lap. "If I can spend the remainder of the house party here with you instead of fending off rogues, I will count myself lucky indeed."

"Then embarrassing myself horribly and potentially breaking my ankle was all for a good cause," he said.

She gave him a smile that lit her eyes to an astonishingly silvery hue. "I think that is the best way for us to look at it, don't you?"

Evan could not disagree. He just hoped his ankle wasn't broken. It was bad enough that he'd suffered a mind-scrambling head wound that was causing him to look at his friend's sister in an altogether different light.

He needed to remember what she'd said—that he was like a brother. That reminded him of what he'd said to her last night. "Why is it I'm like a brother to you today, but when I offered my brotherly services yesterday, you declined?"

"Because *I* don't need your brotherly help. *You*, on the other hand, require my sisterly management." She gave him a stern but lively stare.

He wanted to argue, but the truth was she was right.

CHAPTER 4

$\mathcal{M}$in stepped gingerly into the ladies' library not long after the bonesetter left. The doctor had arrived first, and she hadn't stayed while he'd examined Evan. She had, however, lingered in the library and strained to hear what was happening, particularly when the bonesetter arrived. That was how she knew that Evan had sustained a mild concussion as well as a sprained—not broken, thankfully—ankle.

Closing the door behind her, Min walked toward the bed where Evan now rested, his head elevated by several pillows. She'd heard the commotion of the bed being brought down when the doctor had arrived. He'd decreed that the settee was not a sufficient place for an examination, particularly for the bonesetter. The doctor had also insisted that Evan have a bed in this room on which to recuperate, as he should not be transported upstairs.

"I know you're there," Evan said without opening his eyes.

"Do you know who it is?" Min asked as she looked down at him.

"Of course, I do."

Min couldn't imagine how he could. "And how is that?"

"You always smell like violets," he replied, his eyes still closed.

"How do you know what violets smell like?" She snorted. "You aren't even sure what color chestnut brown is."

His mouth lifted into a half smile. "I believe your brother once mentioned that you wore the scent of violets. I may not know what violets smell like, but I know what *you* smell like."

Shock and heat bloomed in Min's chest. She'd felt twinges of awareness around him earlier—a few charged moments that confused her—from something he said or the way he looked at her. It had made her wonder if Evan had done more damage to his head than he realized. She supposed he had, since he'd sustained a concussion. However, his concussion would not be responsible for *her* sudden and perplexing reaction to him. Min reasoned that was due to the drastic situation. He'd been in danger, and she was caring for him.

It was nothing but that.

"How is your head? Has the medicine helped?" Min asked. The doctor had provided a headache tonic as well as a salve that was to ease the pain in his foot.

"It's slightly improved," Evan replied. "But my ankle still throbs like the devil, even after three tumblers of whiskey."

Min's brows shot up. "Three? I should think that would help a little."

"Have you ever had whiskey, Min?" He opened his eyes and turned his head toward her.

"Once or twice." She shrugged. "Perhaps ten times."

"*Ten* times?" Surprise brightened his dark eyes. "Do you nick it from your father's study?"

"I used to," she said. "The last couple of glasses came from Sheff. I think we were lamenting about our meddlesome parents. Whiskey always helps those conversations."

Evan smiled. "I can imagine. Now that Sheff is married,

all their attention can be directed upon you and your matrimonial prospects. I'm surprised your mother isn't at this party."

"She's busy in Bath, and I don't mind her absence one bit." Min glanced at the round table that had been moved somewhat close to the bed. All the furniture had been rearranged to transform the library into a bedchamber. A bottle stood on the table, and she'd noted an empty glass on the smaller table next to the head of the bed. "Would you like another glass of whiskey?"

"Not until I eat something. Marguerite was going to bring me some biscuits."

Min noted his boots on the floor near the foot of the bed. One was in pristine condition, though muddy, and the other had been cut apart. "I'm sorry about your boot."

"It's a travesty," he moaned. "The marquess did offer to buy me a new pair since I sustained my injury entertaining his house guests, but I declined."

"That was nice of him to offer," Min said. "Who is your boot maker in London?"

"Those boots came from Cardiff, and they are my favorite. No one makes boots as well as Leather Davis."

"His name is Leather?"

Evan chuckled. "No, that is just what we call him. His name is David Davis, which, as you can imagine, is confusing."

"I should say so, but then you Welsh people, with your lack of a variety of surnames and unpronounceable language, are *very* confusing."

"I shall take that as a compliment," Evan said, closing his eyes once more and shifting his head so it faced upward instead of toward Min.

"How do you feel about your new lodgings?" she asked.

Evan made a noise in his throat. "It's better than walking up the stairs, especially if I keep my eyes closed. At least the bedclothes aren't pink or floral."

"Neither are they blue or brown," Min noted, eyeing the stitched ivory coverlet. "I shall find something in those shades to ease your discomfort."

He cracked another brief smile without opening his eyes. "That would be most welcome."

Marguerite entered carrying a tray with tea, cakes, biscuits, sandwiches, thick slices of bread, and a rather delectable-looking hunk of cheese.

"Here you are, Mr. Price," Marguerite announced as she set the tray down on a table. "I see your nursemaid has returned." The maid gave Min an approving nod.

Evan opened his eyes and regarded Marguerite. "She has indeed. Min, would you mind pouring out?"

"Not at all," Mins replied, moving to the table." I see there are two cups. I think Marguerite must have expected me to be here." She smiled at the maid.

"You did say you would return," Marguerite replied. "Not that you went far. Weren't you in the library while the doctor and bonesetter were here?"

"I was." Min cast a glance toward Evan, who was looking at her.

"You were?" he asked.

"I wanted to know what was going on," Min admitted as she poured out the tea. "I don't know how you take your tea."

"Milk and just a hint of sugar."

Min made his cup as directed, then added milk and twice as much sugar to hers. She turned to Marguerite. "Thank you. Where will you be if we need you?"

"Not far," the maid replied. "I'll come back and check on Mr. Price at regular intervals. Lady Bath has assigned me to his care, in addition to you, of course, Lady Minerva." She turned and left the library.

Min transferred one of everything from the tray onto a plate and brought it to the small bedside table along with his tea. "There we are. Do you need any help eating or drinking?"

"I think I can manage that, since neither activity requires my foot." He glanced down at his left ankle, which—though covered by the bedclothes—appeared to be surrounded by a box of some kind.

"May I look?" Min asked. She was most curious as to what the bonesetter had done. Evan's grunts, and occasional yelps, of pain had been rather distressing to hear. However, Min did not want to point that out for fear he would be embarrassed.

"Certainly, but I must caution you that my leg is bare. They had to cut off my stockings and the lower portion of the leg of my breeches."

His warning gave her pause, but her curiosity won out. She carefully lifted the bedclothes and moved them to expose his ankle. Evan's lower leg was strapped into a wooden box contraption that surrounded his calf and foot on three sides, as well as the bottom of his foot. Bandaging was wrapped tightly around his ankle.

She looked up and met his gaze. "Is it uncomfortable?"

"Not being able to move is difficult, but I'm to keep my ankle as still as possible for the rest of today and all of tomorrow."

"And what happens the day after that?" she asked.

"I am still to wear the box, but I can move. With help, of course," he added. "The bonesetter will send a wheelchair as soon as he can."

Min imagined how Evan might do certain…activities

until he could move. "But you're going to have to move before then. How will you take care of your…needs?"

He arched a brow at her. "What needs are those?"

"Changing your clothes. And other…things." She pulled the bedclothes back over his foot. "I refuse to elaborate."

"Marguerite is to help me with clothing and my other requirements. But it is kind of you to ask." A smile teased his lips. "I would not have asked you to help with such things."

"Well, no. That would not be appropriate. Even for a sister-friend," she murmured.

"Definitely not for a 'sister-friend,'" he agreed. "Whatever that is."

Min picked up her teacup and saucer from the table and returned to Evan's side, where she perched on the chair. She sipped her tea as Evan reached for his cup.

Setting her cup and saucer down hastily, she moved to assist him. "Let me help you with that." Rising, she handed him the cup and saucer and stood nearby as he sipped the brew.

He looked up at her. "You needn't hover."

"I suppose not." She sat down. "When will you be allowed to walk?"

"In a week—so at the end of the party." He exhaled with disappointment. "Even worse, I can't ride for a month."

She arched a brow at him. "I'm surprised you're eager to ride again after what happened. You aren't afraid? Or nervous?"

"Not at all. I'm worried Merlin will miss me or that we'll forget how to do something since we aren't practicing." Evan would miss riding Merlin. He looked forward to when he could walk to the stables and at least spend time with him.

"I'm glad you can walk in a week's time. That's much better than if you'd broken bones."

Evan couldn't disagree, but it was a bloody inconvenience. "I will need to use a walking stick for a fortnight. At that time, I should seek another physician's evaluation—wherever I am, since I will no longer be here—and determine if I'm ready to walk without assistance."

She frowned at him. "You don't think it's better if you just stay at Longleat until you are completely healed? Lady Bath told me she hoped you might do that. She feels terrible that this happened."

"She did make that offer to me, and the marquess also encouraged me to stay as long as I like. However, I don't know that I want to be cooped up here after the party is over." He looked about the ladies' library with faint distaste. "Being stuck in here during the party is bad enough."

"Where would you go after this?" Min asked.

"I'm supposed to go to Bath."

"Are you?" Min hadn't known that. "Why not London? Don't you have a position with the Treasury you ought to return to?"

He sipped his tea. "My presence is not required at the moment."

She narrowed her eyes at him. "Why is that?"

"My father has asked me to consider standing as MP for a vacant seat."

"A member of Parliament," Min said. "Does that interest you?"

"Perhaps," he replied somewhat enigmatically before sipping his tea again. He moved the cup toward the table, and Min reached to take it from him and set it down. He picked up the plate of food without her assistance.

Min found it odd that he was away from his position at the Treasury for so long—first in Weston last month, now here, and then he would be going to Bath. "Why *are* you going to Bath? Not for the Marriage Mart, surely."

He replied between bites. "My mother has taken a house

there for the autumn." He took another bite and swallowed before continuing. "She asked if I would join her for a while."

"It sounds as though she may want you to participate in the Marriage Mart," Min teased. "Are you prepared for that?"

After swallowing another bite, he gave her a rather devilish grin. "Always. But she knows I am not ready for matrimony. Particularly if I'm to focus on taking a seat in Parliament."

"That sounds like an excuse my brother would have made before he met Jo," Min said with a low laugh.

"Call it an excuse if you like, but it's the truth. I am not ready to wed, and to do so would be…irresponsible. Or at least disingenuous to a bride looking for a groom who is utterly devoted to her." He popped the last bite of bread and cheese into his mouth and made an expression of pleasure. His eyes closed briefly, and his lips curled into an almost sensual smile. Heat coiled in Min's belly, much to her consternation.

She focused on their conversation instead of her inane reactions to Evan. "It sounds as though you're saying you aren't currently capable of devotion. Marriages don't necessarily require that. Just look at my parents," she noted wryly. While she'd observed that many marriages lacked a truly deep, romantic connection, Min knew that such a union would not be sufficient for her.

"You are correct about the first part. I am not prepared to fall in love." He set his empty plate on the table next to the bed. "I don't know the details of your parents' union, but I know enough from Sheff's comments and from rumors that they, ah, detest one another." He gave her an apologetic look.

"Don't feel sorry for me. Direct your pity at them. They are the ones living in an unhappy situation." Her shoulder twitched.

Evan stared at her. "Is that why you've hesitated to wed?

It is, isn't it? You keep every suitor at bay—rogue or not—because you're afraid you'll end up like them."

Min felt as though someone were standing on her chest for the barest moment. How had he seen through her when no one else had? Save Ellis, who knew Min almost as well as she knew herself. Recovering, Min managed to take a deep breath. "I haven't 'hesitated.' I've refused every suitor because they were all rogues or roguish."

"Isn't your father a rogue?" he asked.

"I would describe him as such, yes." She abruptly turned, hoping to end this conversation. "Shall I fetch a book to read to you?"

Evan snagged her elbow, his warm hand closing around her bare skin. "I didn't mean to upset you."

Min faced him, but he did not immediately release her. The moment stretched as they looked at one another. She was wholly aware of his touch. And not just where his flesh met hers.

This was becoming inconvenient. She could not develop an attraction to her patient, let alone her friend's brother who was a known rogue. Or at least had roguish tendencies.

As if he had come to the same conclusion, he let go of her arm and withdrew his hand to his side. He then picked up her new topic of conversation. "What book?"

Good. This was better.

"What would you like?" Min moved to the nearest bookcase and opened the glass door.

"Whatever you choose will be brilliant, I'm sure."

"Do you like horror novels?" she asked. "There are quite a few here."

"I don't think I've ever read one," he replied. "You must promise to read it with a gloomy pitch."

Min laughed softly as she plucked a book from the shelf.

"*The Mysteries of Udolpho* is quite entertaining. Utterly far-fetched and dramatic. Truly horrible."

"That sounds perfect."

As Min returned to the chair, she met his gaze once more. Again, she was besieged by a fluttery feeling in her belly.

This was an unusual situation, she reminded herself. There was nothing more to it than that.

∾

*L*ess than twenty-four hours had elapsed since Evan had been confined to the pink floral hell, but he was already miserable. His head felt better this morning, but his ankle was still paining him terribly.

He realized he was cranky, and why wouldn't he be, for he hadn't slept well. It wasn't even that he'd tossed and turned, because, of course, he could not. Instead, he'd been forced to try to slumber on his back with the box strapped to his lower extremity. Evan preferred sleeping on his side. He hadn't realized how much.

The worst part was hearing the sounds of the house party well into the night. Guests—mostly the bachelors—walked past on their way to the dining room or probably the billiard room. They'd stopped in after dinner on the way to the drawing room, but only for a few minutes. At least they'd brought him a bottle of port and a glass.

Min had already been there following dinner, having come straight from the dining room when the ladies had gone to the drawing room. She'd read another two chapters of *The Mysteries of Udolpho* before Ellis had come to tell her that she *had* to join the others to appease their hostess as well as Mrs. Ogilvie.

The lads had seen the horrid novel and laughed at Evan's

choice of literature. That was when he'd told them to leave because their presence was making his head throb.

Marguerite had brought him breakfast this morning, and Min had come in briefly on her way to the breakfast room. The marquess had also visited to check on his recuperation. He'd then apologized for the overwhelming femininity of Evan's quarters.

"Morning, Price," Lambton called as he and three of the other bachelors entered the ladies' library.

They were dressed rather sportingly, and Evan wondered what they were up to. He also didn't want to ask. He hated the feeling of exclusion when something exciting or diverting was happening and he was not able to attend. It was almost like a fear that he was missing something.

Barswell sauntered toward the bed. "How are you feeling this morning?"

"My head hurts marginally less," Evan replied. "Where are you off to?" It seemed he couldn't help asking.

Claxton glanced toward the windows, where Marguerite had opened the curtains. "The weather is quite fine, so we are paddling boats on the pond. Shame you can't join us." He smiled rather acidly, and Evan didn't believe the viscount found it a shame at all.

Had the man sensed that Evan didn't care for him? *Good.* Evan didn't suffer fools, and he read Claxton as an absolute bounder. Still, he would gladly have tolerated the man's company if it meant he could go boating.

"What did I miss last night in the drawing room, after dinner?" Evan apparently wasn't able to keep himself from hearing about all the amusements he was missing.

"Miss Ecclestone graced us with a lovely performance on the pianoforte," Jarvis replied. He was the youngest of the set, and Evan had only met him a few times before.

"Mostly, Barswell and Claxton fought over who got to

stand closest to Miss Shaughnessy," Lambton added with a laugh.

"What's so special about Miss Shaughnessy?" Evan asked.

Claxton's mouth curved into a smug smile. "Did you not have a chance to meet her yesterday before your fumble?"

Evan bristled at his use of the word "fumble." "I did not."

"She's very pretty." Lambton sent sly smiles to both Claxton and Barswell. "Dark red hair, stunning blue eyes. Large...well, you know." He looked to Evan. "Surely you noticed her after you fell from the horse. She and Lady Minerva and that companion were there."

Evan thought back. Of course, he recalled Min being there, and he remembered Ellis. Lambton's description of her as "that companion" annoyed Evan. "You mean Miss Dangerfield."

"She's the companion." Lambton shook his head at Evan. "I forgot you have a concussion."

"I was informing you of her name," Evan said, barely concealing his irritation. "I realize there was a third woman there." He couldn't conjure her image, however, which was unsurprising.

"She's Wexford's sister," Barswell put in. "Not the one who married Lord Lucien Westbrook."

Claxton snorted. "Of course she's not. This is *Miss* Shaughnessy."

Evan looked at Barswell and Claxton. "Let me understand. You're fighting over who gets to stand next to a pretty young lady whom neither of you have any intention of marrying?"

"That's not entirely true," Barswell said defensively. "I am not as opposed to marriage as some of you."

"I'm not opposed to marriage," Evan said. "I'm just not in the mood yet."

This provoked laughter, notably from Claxton.

Lambton shot the man a pitying look. "Claxton is going to have to wed. He likes to pretend that he isn't in need of an heiress, but we know the truth."

Claxton scowled. "You know nothing."

"I don't think Miss Shaughnessy qualifies as an heiress," Lambton said. "Her father was the steward at the Wexford estate in Ireland. When Wexford's father died, his mother married the steward. Miss Shaughnessy would be better suited for Price or Jarvis. Their families don't expect them to marry someone from the nobility."

"Well, surely she's almost nobility, since her half brother is an earl," Barswell argued.

Lambton shook his head. "My father would say, 'It's not in the blood.' Not like Lady Minerva, who is the blue-blooded daughter of a duke."

"None of us has a chance with her," Jarvis said, looking around at everyone, including Evan. "At least that's what I've heard." His gaze lingered on Evan.

"Why are you looking at me?" Evan asked.

Jarvis shrugged. "Because you know her. Isn't she nursing you?"

"She's keeping me company." Evan didn't like the characterization that she was his nurse. That implied something more…intimate. "That's because my sister is a dear friend of hers, and her brother is a good friend of mine. We are like family."

"Well, there's family," Lambton said. "And there's *family*." He waggled his almost invisible blond brows.

Evan hated looking up at all of them. "What is that supposed to mean?"

"There's blood family, and there's married family. Isn't it obvious?" Lambton blinked. "She is not your blood family, so that leaves the other."

"That's ridiculous. I said she is *like* family. Obviously, she is not my wife," said Evan. "Nor will she be. Shouldn't you be off to the pond?" Their visit had done nothing to improve his mood. In fact, he felt even more sour than before they'd arrived.

"Come, lads, we'd best be on our way," Claxton said airily. "Enjoy *The Mysteries of Rudolph*," he added with a laugh.

"*Udolpho*," Evan muttered as they departed. He glowered at the book on the table next to his bed, then looked to the window. It was indeed a fine day, marvelous for a boat ride. Alas, he couldn't even see the pond from his floral dungeon.

He scowled at a particularly offensive floral-patterned chair near the hearth

"Evan, I brought a visitor," Min said from the doorway in a singsong voice.

Glad for the diversion, he turned his head and saw that Ellis was with her. Their arms were full: Min carried a vase with a very odd arrangement of flowers and twigs, as well as a coverlet, while Ellis brought a painting.

Min set the vase down on the table next to his bed. "Let's put these on the settee." She placed the coverlet on one side of the cushion as Ellis deposited the painting on the other.

"You brought me gifts?" he asked.

Moving back to his bedside, Min said proudly, "We brought you blue and brown—not chestnut brown, but brown just the same." She gestured to the painting depicting brownish cliffs and the ocean, which was blue enough. The coverlet was a very light brown stitched with blue, and the vase contained blue flowers and twigs.

He laughed, and Min glanced at the vase. "I didn't realize you would laugh, though I do agree that the arrangement is somewhat sad. However, there are no brown flowers, so I put in twigs instead. Aren't the forget-me-nots pretty?"

"They're lovely," he said as he collected himself. His head was now throbbing from the laughter, but it had been worth it. "You've quite cheered me. Thank you, both of you. Wherever did you find those things?" He gestured toward the settee.

"The painting came from the sitting room outside my chamber," Min replied. "Marguerite found the coverlet. I daresay one of the other gentlemen is missing part of his bedclothes."

"I do hope it's Claxton," Evan said with a grin.

Ellis narrowed her eyes with amusement. "I think that is who Marguerite said. Why were you hoping it was him?"

"Because he's nearly insufferable."

"Only nearly?" Ellis's brow arched, and Evan chuckled again.

"While I do appreciate your visit, you must stop provoking me to laugh. Anything beyond a faint smile makes my head hurt." He put his hand to his brow.

"Apologies." Ellis grimaced. "I'm afraid I forgot about your head. You don't look like an invalid."

"Not from the waist up," he said. Marguerite had dressed him as well as his valet in London—above the waist.

"Goodness, what about beneath the bedclothes?" Ellis asked as pink stained her cheeks. She looked away. "Never mind. Please forget I asked."

Evan chuckled. "I don't mind telling you there is nothing beneath the coverlet or the bedclothes. It is far too difficult to get dressed when one's foot is stuck in a box." The marquess had sent the valet, Thompson—who'd been assigned to Evan upon his arrival—to cut away the remainder of his clothing below the waist. He'd also bathed Evan as well as possible, for which Evan was grateful.

Too late, Evan realized he should not have told them about his nudity. Ellis was still blushing—and not looking at him. Min, however, was staring at him. He could not tell what she was thinking and feared he'd completely offended her.

Before he could apologize, Ellis spoke.

"I'm sorry you can't come to the pond with us." She'd regained her normal color.

"You're going?" he asked, glad for the awkwardness to pass.

Ellis nodded. "Iona needs protection from the rogues."

"I think that's a good idea," Evan said.

"Why?" Min crossed her arms over her chest. "What have you heard?"

"Only that she's very pretty, and it seems Claxton and Barswell were competing for her attention last night."

"Well, she *is* very pretty," Min said. "I'm surprised you didn't notice that."

"I don't recall meeting her yesterday," Evan replied with a slight grimace.

"Of course you wouldn't. You had just hit your head." Ellis shook her head at Min.

"I suppose that's true." She gave Evan a rueful smile. "Iona is more than a pretty face. She is delightful, and we've already befriended her."

"Then you should go to the pond too," Evan said. "The more protection for her, the better."

Min swept the book up from the table. "I'm afraid I couldn't possibly tear myself away from whatever happens next at Castle Udolpho."

Ellis started toward the door. "I shall be on my way, then. Enjoy your reading. I'll stop in after the boating if there is any exciting gossip to share."

"You are never one to gossip," Min said in mock horror.

Turning at the door, Ellis said, "I will make an exception for Evan, given his current sad state." She waved at them and departed the library.

Min brought the chair close to the bed and sat. She opened the book.

Evan held up his hand. "Before you begin, would you be terribly upset if we read something else? I'm afraid I just can't continue with the melodrama."

Min exhaled and set the book back down. "I confess I was only pretending to be enthusiastic because I thought you were enjoying it. I'd forgotten *how* horrid it was. I read it years ago."

He stifled a smile. "And I was pretending to like it because I thought you were enthralled. Your reading was rather zealous."

Min laughed. "Well, I've always enjoyed a dramatic reading or playacting. I was hoping the house party would include a play of some kind, but I can't see the other bachelors partaking in such an entertainment."

"I don't see why not," Evan said. "They're all fools, and what are fools if not entertainers?"

"Perhaps I will suggest to Lady Bath that we put together a play that can be performed in here for your entertainment."

Evan shook his head and instantly regretted it. Someday, he would remember that he had a concussion. Likely not until the pain had faded. "Not in here. It's far too small. And too pink. Though the additions you brought today have greatly improved the space."

She inclined her head. "I am a very good sister-friend. The best you will find, I think."

She stood from the chair and took the book back to the shelf from which she'd taken it the day before. "What shall we read then?"

"The marquess thought I might enjoy *Waverley*." Evan nodded toward the book on the table where the tea set had been the day before. "It's about a young soldier in the Jacobite Rising."

Min went to fetch the book and gave him a skeptical look. "That doesn't sound terribly intriguing to me, but I will read whatever you like."

"That is generous of you," he said. "But you must be honest and tell me if you don't care for it."

"Then you must promise to do the same. My job is to keep the boredom from worsening your condition, and I can't do that if you pretend to enjoy something."

"Fair enough." He held out his hand. "Let us make a gentleman and lady's agreement. We shall be perfectly forthright with one another."

She took his hand, and they shook. The moment they touched, their eyes locked on one another. Evan was suddenly very aware of his nudity beneath the bedclothes. And that Min was also aware of his naked state. Was she thinking about that too? Heat flushed his body, and he hoped his face didn't flame.

Min looked away first and withdrew her hand from his. She settled into the chair and flicked a look toward his legs. "Are you truly wearing nothing underneath the bedclothes?"

The earlier awkwardness returned tenfold. She *had* been thinking about it. In truth, it wasn't awkwardness he felt, but a shocking wave of desire. Evan was suddenly afraid of what might happen beneath the damned bedclothes. "Why would you ask me that?" Did his voice sound strained?

"Because I'm curious, and you did just promise to be forthright. So are you?" she asked, apparently unaware of the physical battle Evan was waging to keep the bedclothes from becoming a bloody tent.

When he did not respond, she waved her hand. "Never mind that I asked. I was just thinking it must be odd to be only half dressed, even if you are covered up. But don't worry, I am just your sister-friend, and I won't pay it a second thought." She said that, but did her gaze linger on his groin?

Evan was now painfully aware that he was nude from the waist down, and he was barely keeping something very untoward from happening below his waist. Something shocking and unsettling. Min was his sister-friend, and such reactions were not to be borne.

He closed his eyes and prayed for *Waverley* to be a massive distraction from the beautiful and thoughtful young woman beside him.

CHAPTER 5

*M*in was thrilled to inform Evan that the wheelchair had arrived at last. A footman called Vargas wheeled the chair as he accompanied Min and Ellis to the ladies' library. Evan sat in a chair near the windows, his boxed ankle propped on a footstool. Min was pleased to see that he was fully dressed. Yesterday, he'd worn a dark green banyan.

"Surprise!" Min called as they moved toward him. "Today, you will make your escape from your floral dungeon."

Evan smiled brilliantly. "The wheelchair has finally arrived! I feared the bonesetter had forgotten."

Min took in his fully clothed state. "How convenient that you are dressed and ready to depart your convalescence chamber."

"Prison cell, more like," he said sardonically. "Where are we going?"

"Since it's raining, everyone has gathered in the drawing room for card games," Ellis replied. "I heard mention of a potential whist tournament."

"Splendid." Evan grinned, looking happier than he had since his injury.

Min gestured to the footman holding the wheelchair. "This is Vargas. He's been charged with pushing you about."

"I'm most grateful," Evan said with great enthusiasm. "I shall need your help to move into the chair."

"Of course, Mr. Price," the footman said as Ellis moved to hand Evan the walking stick that the marquess had provided the day before.

Lord Bath had sent someone to Frome to purchase it. The stick was quite elegant, with a carved wooden top in the shape of a horse's head, which was both thoughtful and ironic. Evan had found it most amusing.

Evan took the walking stick from Ellis as Vargas positioned the wheelchair next to where Evan sat. The footman then moved to clasp Evan's free arm and helped him rise. Evan also used the walking stick to push himself up. After taking one tiny step, Evan pivoted so his back was to the wheelchair. Vargas helped him sit down and guided his boxed ankle on the footrest that was affixed to the chair.

Ellis took Evan's walking stick and set it against the chair he'd just vacated.

"Ready, Mr. Price?" Vargas asked.

"More than," Evan said eagerly. The footman pushed him toward the door.

Min and Ellis followed Vargas as he pushed the chair. When they entered the drawing room a few minutes later, Evan was met with applause and cheers.

"Thank you, everyone," Evan said loudly. "I am happier than I can say to be in a different room."

Min leaned down to ask him, "Where would you like to be parked?"

He turned his head, and the movement brought his

mouth quite close to hers. She hadn't intended for that to happen. Surprise flickered in his gaze, indicating he hadn't expected that either. Min pulled back slightly and glanced away.

"Wherever is convenient," he replied. His gaze moved to the refreshment table and narrowed with purpose. "I see those delicious almond cakes I've become quite fond of."

The marchioness approached them with a smile. Min straightened.

"Mr. Price, it's wonderful to see you outside the ladies' library," Lady Bath said. "Do come sit with us."

Evan inclined his head. "I would be delighted. Vargas, if you don't mind?"

"Not at all, Mr. Price."

Before Vargas could wheel Evan away after the marchioness, Min bent down once more, careful to keep a more respectable distance. "I'll fetch you those almond cakes."

Evan turned his head and gave her a dazzling smile that made her toes curl. *Why are my toes curling?* "What would I do without you, Min?"

"Aren't you glad you don't have to find out?" She smirked at him.

He met her gaze. "Quite."

Min's breath snagged before she whirled about and moved toward the refreshment table.

Ellis went along with her. "He seems cheered." She looked down at the walking stick she carried. "What am I to do with this?"

"Use it to bat away the rogues?" Min quipped.

As they arrived at the table, Ellis whispered, "Speaking of rogues, Mr. Jarvis is coming this way."

"Is he a rogue?" Min asked.

"He's certainly associating with them. He follows Claxton and Lambton around as though he were their foundling puppy." Ellis gave her an apologetic look. "He actually seems nice enough."

"He does indeed, but your point is well taken. Perhaps he just wants an almond cake."

"Perhaps." Ellis sent her a skeptical look. "Though I think it's more likely he's coming to speak with you, particularly since he made a point of sitting near you in the drawing room last night after dinner."

"You're probably right," Min said with a sigh.

For all that he accompanied the rogues, Mr. Jarvis was indeed the least roguish of the bachelors at the party. However, that didn't mean Min was interested in spending more time with him. She had not come to this party to make a match, and since Evan's injury, she'd become entirely focused on keeping him entertained. She realized it was as much for her as it was for him, since it allowed her to avoid the rogues as well as Lady Bath's matchmaking endeavors. That made her feel somewhat selfish.

She also had to admit she was enjoying the time she spent with Evan. More than she'd expected to. Because she hadn't expected anything.

"Good afternoon, Lady Minerva," Jarvis said.

Min wasn't sure of his exact age but wondered if he might even be a year or so younger than she was. He was certainly not much older. He had a youthful face and a mop of dark hair. His brown eyes gleamed with eager intention.

"Good afternoon, Mr. Jarvis. Have you come for one of the delectable almond cakes? I was just fetching some for Mr. Price." Min put three of them on a plate. Ellis moved to the other side of the table.

"I don't care for almond," Jarvis said.

"Perhaps the lemon cakes, then?"

Jarvis wrinkled his nose. "I'm afraid I don't like lemon either. Do you see any of the ones with currants? I found those quite tolerable."

Min looked about the table. "I don't see any, but I'm sure you could ask a maid to fetch some for you."

"Ah, well, it doesn't matter," Mr. Jarvis replied. "I wasn't looking for a cake. I wanted to ask if you'd care to promenade with me."

Min looked toward the windows where rain was falling in a steady rhythm against the glass. "I daresay a promenade would earn us a soaking," she said with a laugh.

Mr. Jarvis's cheeks turned a faint shade of pink. "I didn't mean outside. I thought we could circuit the drawing room or perhaps take a jaunt to the orangery."

Min was fairly certain they would have to walk outside to reach the orangery, but decided not to point that out, lest the poor man blush again. She did not wish to make him uncomfortable.

"I do appreciate the invitation," she said kindly. "However, after I deliver these cakes to Mr. Price, I'd thought to participate in the whist tournament. Will you play?"

"I will. Perhaps we will be fortunate enough to sit together." Mr. Jarvis glanced toward Evan, who was now holding court with most of the ladies at the party. "You have been most dedicated to Mr. Price. If I should divert my attention elsewhere, I would hope that you would tell me plainly." The young man fidgeted briefly with his hands.

"My focus on Mr. Price is that of a friend helping another friend after a grievous injury," she explained. Perhaps grievous was a tiny exaggeration, but he *had* suffered a concussion in addition to the sprained ankle.

There was a tinge of relief in Mr. Jarvis's answering smile. "That is encouraging to hear. I am sorry we have not had a chance to become better acquainted during the party, but I will be in Bath next month. Perhaps we could take our promenade then."

"That would be lovely," Min said, somewhat doubting that would come to pass. But if it did, she would accept. She would not assume he was a rogue simply because he was communing with other rogues at the party. It wasn't as if he had much choice. Furthermore, since she was attending to Evan, wasn't she just as guilty? For Evan was absolutely a rogue.

"I shall look forward to it." He smiled broadly. "Now, I think I *will* go see about finding those currant cakes. You've quite put me in the mood for them."

"Good luck to you." Min took the plate to Evan. She saw that Ellis had made her way to a seating area with Mrs. Ogilvie.

Evan was still surrounded by several guests, most of them young and female. Some were seated and others stood. Min held the plate rather than interrupt. Lady Bath announced that the whist tournament would start soon. This scattered the group, and Min finally handed Evan the plate of cakes.

"Thank God," he said rather dramatically. "I feared you meant to keep them for yourself." He devoured one cake in two quick bites.

"I didn't wish to interrupt your assembly," she said wryly as she perched on the chair nearest him.

He chuckled as he swallowed, then picked up the second cake. "You may always interrupt with an almond cake in hand."

"Everyone missed you," Min noted. "And you seemed to enjoy holding court."

He swallowed the last of the second cake. "I saw you had a court of one for a few minutes with Mr. Jarvis. What was that about?"

"He asked me to promenade in the house because of the rain. I declined."

"That was why he appeared disappointed," Evan said with a nod before taking a bite of his last cake. He took his smallest bite yet, as if he meant to savor it.

"I didn't mean to disappoint him, but I had already put together your plate," she explained. "I did agree to promenade with him in Bath next month."

"And that is when he looked delighted." Evan eyed her thoughtfully. "I'd say Jarvis has taken an interest in you."

"We hardly know one another," Min said.

"You would know him better if you weren't spending so much time with me," Evan remarked.

She blinked at him. "Are you saying you don't want my company anymore?"

"Not at all," he answered quickly. "You are the reason I have retained my sanity."

Min gave him a sheepish look. "I'm glad to hear it, because I'm not too ashamed to admit that caring for you has kept me from having to fend off Lady Bath's attempts at matchmaking. They have been most egregious. I didn't tell you, but yesterday, she tried to send me on an errand with Barswell to fetch apples from the orchard. Thankfully, I'd already promised to play chess with you."

"Why didn't you mention that when you came for chess?"

Min shrugged. "I don't know. It didn't seem important. Anyway, I'd much rather lose to you at chess for the third time than fend off Barswell's flirting."

"He can't be as bad as Claxton," Evan observed. "Unless… Has something happened?" He leaned toward her, his gaze hardening. "Has Barswell done something untoward?"

"Not to me," Min said, wondering at Evan's sharp reaction. "But he's still a rogue, and I've no desire to spend time with him. I heard he's lost twenty pounds to Sir Rodney and another ten pounds to Mr. Harris during the party."

"Is it gambling that makes him roguish, or being bad at it?" Evan asked with a hint of a smile.

"Gambling. Although, if you *must* indulge, you may as well be good at it." She gave him a pointed look. "I know you gamble. Or so I've heard."

"I do indeed, and though it makes me sound arrogant, I *am* good at it," Evan said. "Did you know, there are wagers at this party about the matches being made?"

Min stared at him. "I did not know that. How did you learn that?"

"Lady Bath just told me, in confidence."

"And what do these wagers conclude?" Min asked.

"First and foremost, that you will leave the party without a betrothal or even a suitor. But the odds on that are quite high. The most interesting wager is whether Claxton will snare Miss Ecclestone in the parson's trap. The rumor is that he needs an heiress."

Min shook her head. "Miss Ecclestone's dowry is respectable enough, but she isn't an heiress."

"That was my understanding. However, she does come from a noble family, and that may be enough. Especially since you are not available," he added.

"What do you mean by that?"

"No one thinks you are seriously going to make a match here. You have said for some time—years, I suppose—that you are interested in marriage, but most have deduced you really aren't."

Min made a face. His statement wasn't wrong, but she felt the need to defend herself. "I would be for the right man, though I'm beginning to think he doesn't exist." *Beginning* to think? She was all but convinced.

"You could give Jarvis a chance," Evan suggested. "But

perhaps you can't, since he isn't nobility. Like me. I imagine your parents expect you to marry a title, especially since Sheff has so recently wed the daughter of a gaming hell owner."

Min grimaced. Her brother's marriage had been a great disappointment to their mother. Bizarrely, it seemed their father was now in favor after his initial opposition. "I suppose I do feel a bit of pressure to marry well, whatever that means. But I won't settle."

"What will you do if the right man, as you called him, isn't nobility? What if he's the son of a gaming hell owner or a tradesman…or a *groom*?"

This conversation was treading precariously close to things Min did not wish to discuss. Namely, what mattered most to her, and it was nothing to do with a title. She wanted love and trust, and, perhaps above all, peace. Thankfully, Lady Bath returned and asked if they were going to join the whist tournament that was about to begin.

"I cannot refuse, especially after my confinement," Evan said. He looked at Minerva and arched a brow. "What do you say?"

Min saw Iona enter with her mother and smiled in her direction. "Let us play."

Vargas came forward to wheel Evan to one of the tables. Minerva went to greet Iona, and together they sought chairs at the same table.

Her mind turned to her conversation with Evan. She was still open to marriage, regardless of what people said. Was it wrong for her to have specific requirements? Was it wrong to want love and to feel secure in that love? And was it wrong for her to steer away from anything that wasn't that?

As it happened, she sat across from Mr. Jarvis. Perhaps she ought to give him a real chance. She'd always tried to become acquainted with suitors, unless their reputation was beyond the pale. Mr. Jarvis was good-natured and seemed genuine. She did not think he was a rogue disguised as a kind, unassuming gentleman.

However, he didn't stir anything within her. She froze because that had never stopped her from spending time with suitors before. How else would something spark if she didn't give it time?

For some reason, her assessment had changed. There was no spark with Mr. Jarvis, and she knew there wouldn't be. What had changed to give her such certainty?

She realized it was because she *had* felt stirrings of late and, for the first time, little inexplicable flutters and flashes of heat. Her gaze darted to the next table, where Evan laughed at something Miss Ecclestone said to his right.

He was the source of those stirrings. Evan bloody Price.

~

*L*ate the following evening, Evan contemplated reading another chapter of *Waverley* before retiring. He wore a banyan over his nightshirt and was ready for bed, thanks to the valet. Now that Evan had reentered polite company at the party, he required Thompson's assistance, rather than Marguerite's, once more.

Evan credited the wheelchair with being able to rejoin the party. He no longer had to stay holed up in the pink flower dungeon. Vargas had wheeled him to dinner last night and this evening, and even out onto the patio that afternoon to watch the other guests play badminton. It wasn't as fun as if Evan had been able to play, but it was better than sitting in the florid library wondering if he ought to try reading *The Mysteries of Udolpho* again to stave off the boredom.

At dinner, Evan had used the walking stick to transfer himself from the wheelchair to a chair at the table. His ankle had been rather tender last night, but was improved today. He hoped he might try walking with the stick tomorrow instead of using the wheelchair at all.

A light rap on the door from the library drew his attention. He had no idea who it might be. It was rather late for Min to be visiting.

"Come in," he called.

The door was pushed open, and Min stepped inside. Though it was late, she was still dressed as she had been for dinner in a stunning dark coral gown. A pearl necklace shimmered at her throat, and matching earrings dangled from her ears. Her sable hair was styled elegantly and affixed with a pearl and diamond comb. She far outshone everyone at the party, including their hostess.

He made the assessment objectively—anyone could see and appreciate Min's beauty. However, there was perhaps more to it than that, not that he was going to spend time thinking about it.

"I'm not intruding, am I?" She came toward his chair. She hadn't closed the door behind her, but it had a habit of swinging almost closed.

"Not at all, though I'm surprised to see you this late," Evan replied. "Is aught amiss?"

She shook her head. "The younger set was up late playing charades, and I was finally able to make my escape."

"How so?" he asked.

"I pleaded a headache." She put her finger to her lips as she sat in her usual chair, which was angled toward his. "Don't tell anyone."

Evan chuckled. "You do not have a headache."

She arched a brow in a sardonic fashion. "My head aches from the endless flirting from the rogues."

"I do understand," Evan said. "But why have you come

here? I'm surprised you didn't just retire." He cocked his head. "What about Ellis? Did you leave her there?"

"Goodness, no. Ellis had the intelligence to retire nearly two hours ago. And Iona followed shortly thereafter. Unfortunately, I think she actually had a headache."

Evan thought of Min playing charades with the other bachelors and young ladies. "I didn't realize you were playing charades. I might have stayed in the drawing room."

"Why didn't you?" Min asked.

"I needed to take my shoe off." He glanced toward his ankle. "It's too tight with the bandage."

"I still can't believe no one had a shoe larger than yours that you could borrow. I see you're already prepared for bed." She eyed his banyan. While it covered him completely, he felt a twinge of awareness at being garbed this way, which was silly, because he'd been sitting with Min while half nude underneath the bedclothes. And he was not nude beneath the banyan, so this was surely better.

"Shall we play chess since you are here?" Evan asked. "You were close to beating me this morning."

She laughed. "I wasn't really, but that's kind of you to say." Standing, she went to fetch the chessboard from the larger table and brought it to the small table between the arms of their chairs.

The pieces had jostled a bit as she'd moved the board, so they set about righting them. "Perhaps I should play black this time," she said.

"You can if you like." Evan moved the pawn in front of his king.

"That was fast," Min remarked. "I wasn't ready to start."

"You can take all the time you need to move. You know that." Indeed, she'd taken nearly a quarter hour today on her final play before he'd moved his queen into checkmate.

It was only a moment before she moved her queen pawn.

Evan barely hesitated before moving one of his knights. Min studied the board a moment and moved her knight.

"You're getting faster," he said. "And better."

"I *have* played chess before this week. It's just been a while. I used to play with my father when I was younger."

Evan saw his next move—his bishop would pin the knight Min had just moved. However, before he could lift the piece, she turned her head toward the door to the main library.

"Did you hear that?" she asked.

"No, what did you hear?"

"I thought I heard someone in the library." She whispered as if they hadn't just been speaking in regular tones.

"You might have," Evan said with a shrug. "People go in there all the time. In fact, very late the other night, somebody made a noise in there that woke me up."

A creaking sound came from the other side of the door. "That exact noise," Evan said.

She glanced back toward the library. "What do you suppose it is?"

"It sounded like furniture creaking." Evan had made that deduction the other night, just as he'd assumed the purpose for it—someone having a romantic tryst.

"Could someone be moving the ladder to fetch a book that's too high to reach?" she mused.

He hadn't considered that. What did it say about him that he assumed the noise had something to do with a sexual encounter? "That could be it."

There was another sound, as if someone were moaning. Evan was now certain that whoever was in the library was not looking for a book.

Min stood and walked toward the library door.

"What are you going to do?" he asked, hating that he couldn't just jump up and intercept her before she barged in on a potentially intimate situation.

She looked back at him over her shoulder. "Do you think someone might be in distress?"

Did she not realize what was happening? "No, I don't think so." He grasped his walking stick as she reached the door.

"Careful, Min, don't just walk in unannounced." Evan pushed himself up and gingerly tested his left foot before taking a halting step. There was only the faintest bit of pain —not enough to stop him—but Min had already opened the door. Thankfully, she hadn't thrown it wide. Instead, she cracked it and peered through the small opening. He watched her features twitch and her gaze fix on something. She suddenly closed the door and turned, her eyes widening as she saw that he was approaching.

"What are you doing?" she asked, keeping her voice low.

"Coming to see what you were doing. What did you see in the library?"

Her cheeks blazed with color. "Just—oh, never mind. Let's finish our match. You shouldn't be walking."

"I was going to try tomorrow anyway. Tonight is close enough," he said. "It barely hurts."

"Still, you don't want to reinjure yourself." She moved to his side and took his arm. "Lean on me if you need to."

"I don't, but thank you. I can guess what you saw in the library, Min."

She darted a look at him as they made their way back to their chairs. "You can?"

He smiled. "The creaking of the furniture together with the moaning leads to a reasonable conclusion, and your reaction confirmed my suspicion."

"Oh." She blushed again. "Well, now I feel foolish for not knowing."

"Don't. Your concern for someone who perhaps needed help is wonderful. Who did you see? I won't tell."

"It was Claxton."

"And who was he with?" Evan wondered if there would be a betrothal announcement tomorrow before the party concluded.

Her brow arched. "You assume he was with someone?"

Evan grinned to keep from laughing. "I suppose he could have been pleasuring himself. Though, I would hope he would keep such activities to his bedchamber."

"I didn't mean that." Her face flamed once more.

"Who was he with?" he prodded.

"One of the housemaids."

"What were they doing?" he asked.

"Kissing...and...never mind." She did not meet his gaze. "This is a highly inappropriate conversation."

She let go of his arm as they reached their seating area. But Evan did not sit. He was enjoying being vertical for the first time in several days. He pivoted to face her.

"Did what you saw unsettle you?" He could see she was uncomfortable, which he found surprising. He hadn't ever thought of her as easily flustered. She was Sheff's sister, and he was somewhat debauched. She'd always seemed to have an air of sophistication, but perhaps it did not extend to matters of sex. And why should it? She was the unmarried daughter of a duke. She ought to be innocent. That he hadn't presumed her to be said more about Evan and *his* state of debauchery.

"Well, I had never seen anything like it," she said. "Dallying with a maid proves Claxton is a rogue."

Evan frowned toward the library as he had an unpleasant thought. "Was she there of her own accord?"

"Ah, she seemed to be...enjoying the encounter. She wasn't pushing him away or anything like that."

"I'm glad to hear it, else I would intervene. Sometimes the line between rogue and blackguard is rather thin."

"Would you really?" She sounded surprised and perhaps even impressed.

"I would." Evan didn't think he would mind having to trounce Claxton if the need arose.

She narrowed her eyes slightly. "Is there a chance you aren't a rogue?"

Evan laughed. "Perhaps roguishness is in the eye of the beholder." He sobered, thinking he should not be making light when she may have been uncomfortable with what she'd witnessed. "I'm sorry if what you saw upset you. I was going to try to stop you from opening the door, to keep you from intruding on someone's interlude. I did not think of how it might affect you."

"And why should you?" She took a deep breath. "It's fine. I'm fine. We should continue our match."

"Have you never been kissed, Min?" The question leapt from his mouth before he could censor himself. She'd been right—this *was* an inappropriate conversation, and yet he could not seem to keep himself from pursuing it.

She hesitated, but only briefly. "Once, several years ago, in Weston. I was young. He was young. He was Welsh, actually."

"Was he?" Evan asked with a laugh. "We Welshmen do know how to kiss. Should you ever decide you would like to try it a second time, I would happily offer my services."

Bloody hell. Had he really just offered to kiss her? Why would he do that?

Because they were talking about kissing, and for some reason, it had seemed a natural thing to suggest. Also, wholly improper.

Nevertheless, he did not rescind the offer, nor did he regret making it.

She stared at him, her lips parting. "Don't be silly. I'm your sister-friend." She laughed nervously.

Evan sensed an energy swirling within and around her. It wasn't just nervousness. Her gaze held an edge of anticipation. He suddenly knew that he *wanted* to kiss her. All during their time together, he'd felt moments of attraction and even desire. He'd tried to ignore them or attribute them to some other reason—gratitude for her assistance, perhaps, or appreciation for her care. But right now, standing before her, staring at her mouth, he realized there was more to it than that. He was curious to see if she felt the same.

"I dislike that description," he said softly.

"What description?" she sounded nearly breathless.

"Sister-friend. I have a sister, and she's not you."

Color rose in her cheeks once more. "But we are friends, at least."

"We are more than that, I think." He edged toward her.

"It is kind of you to offer to kiss me, Evan, but I don't need your pity." Her eyes flashed with pride. "I am not a lady rogue who goes about wondering when she may be kissed again."

"No, you are not a lady rogue," he said, though his body heated at the idea.

"It's not that I don't want to kiss someone," Min went on. "I just know that I need to marry first."

"And what if the man you wed is a terrible kisser? That would be a tragedy."

She sucked in a breath. "Yes, it would. Though surely, he could learn."

"Who would teach him?" Evan ached to touch her, though he should not. "You, with your vast experience?"

She narrowed her eyes at him. "There's no need to be unkind."

He held up his free hand. "It is not my intent to be cruel. I am merely stating the truth. If you decide you should like to increase your experience, my offer stands, whether it's tonight or at some point in the future." He could not seem to stop himself from persisting with this madness, or hoping that she would accept his offer. Preferably now.

She put her hand on her hip. "Are you making the argument that I should kiss every man I might consider marrying?"

"It's not the worst idea." Wasn't it, though? She was the daughter of a bloody duke and the sister of one of his good friends.

She scoffed. "You're trying to turn me into a rogue. I will not be infected by your debauchery."

He laughed. "Roguishness is not a disease. Do you not even flirt, Min? I would argue you have flirted with me plenty this week."

"That has not been my intent," she said, looking horrified.

"Nor has it been mine," he said quietly. "I apologize for being carried away by this inappropriate conversation. We have perhaps become too familiar this week."

Except he wouldn't change a thing. Injuring himself and Min's subsequent care had completely changed the casual friendship they'd once shared. "I can't be sorry. Perhaps I am a rogue after all." He searched her face. "I know your primary reason for spending so much time with me this week was to avoid the other bachelors, but I am grateful for every word you read, all the almond cakes you brought me, and especially the blue and brown gifts."

Her eyes were bright as she regarded him intensely. "That may have been one reason I chose to care for you," she said softly. "But it was more than that. Nobody ever needs me. It felt...good to be useful."

"You were far more than useful, Min. I don't think I could have endured this without you. I have a terrible time being still—just ask my mother. Or Gwen. You made it bearable."

She moved closer until they nearly touched. Evan's breath

caught. She put her hand on his chest. His heart beat hard and fast beneath her palm.

"I think… I would like you to kiss me, Evan. Provide me with the experience I apparently lack."

"You're certain?" he murmured as desire swirled in his belly—and lower.

"I insist."

Triumph sang through his veins as he lowered his mouth to claim hers.

CHAPTER 6

*M*in had been utterly unprepared for the overwhelming sensations Evan's kiss aroused within her. This was nothing like the one experience she'd had years ago. And thank goodness for that. This exceeded her imagination and altered everything she believed. Kissing wasn't terrible after all.

His warm hand cupped her neck, making her feel both safe and hungry for something she couldn't explain. He stroked her jaw with his thumb and deepened the kiss, his mouth gently opening against hers.

She braced herself for what would come next. She knew that much, at least, except this was, once again, completely different from what she'd known before. He coaxed her mouth with his lips, urging her to open, but she did not feel pressured or invaded. Instead, she was swept away on a tide of thrilling curiosity. She opened her mouth against his and felt an instant jolt of pleasure.

His other hand was against her lower back, and he pressed more firmly, bringing their bodies more tightly together. She was surprised but did not mind. Rather, she gloried in the contact.

Then his tongue slipped past her lips, and she felt emboldened, meeting him with her own. The intimate exchange was not at all distasteful. On the contrary, the heat curling inside her expanded and spread. This was passion. She'd never expected to experience it. But she *had* hoped.

Evan moved slowly, his hands caressing her with gentle precision while his mouth did the same. When their tongues met more fully, a shiver raced through her. She clutched at his shoulders, and he held her tightly, and she was both overwhelmed and desperate that this embrace should never end. What if this was the only time she would feel like this?

Min copied what he did, sliding her tongue along his and angling her head. She clasped the back of his neck and twined her fingers in the thick hair at his nape. Pressing herself against him even more, she felt his arousal just above her own sex. She became aware of sensation there. It began as a faint throb of desire, but she felt it in every part of her body.

Evan made a sound deep in his throat and lifted his head from hers. "That is probably as far as we should go," he said softly.

Min released him and took a step back as reality reclaimed her. "We should forget this happened."

He looked into her eyes and, never appearing more serious, said, "I shall not ever forget this, Min."

She wouldn't either. Averting her gaze, she mumbled, "Good night," as she moved past him, fleeing the library. She practically raced for the staircase hall.

As she ascended, she wondered if she ought to return and help Evan to his bed, but he seemed to be managing all right with the walking stick. She didn't think she could go back. In fact, she wasn't sure how she could ever face him again after what had just happened.

She slowed as she reached the top of the stairs and pressed her hands to her warm cheeks. She needed to grab hold of herself before she reached her bedchamber. If Ellis was still awake, and she almost certainly would be, she would see Min's face and know something had happened.

Was Min not going to tell her?

Blowing out a breath, Min considered whether she wanted to reveal the kiss. There were very few secrets she kept from Ellis. In fact, they were only the secrets that she, in many ways, kept from herself.

By the time Min reached the bedchamber, she felt a little more herself. At least, her cheeks were thankfully not as warm as they had been. Opening the door, she slipped inside and closed it softly behind her. She still wasn't sure what she would say, if anything.

A small cot had been provided for Ellis, but Min had invited her to share the large bed, since it was far more comfortable and there was plenty of room for them both. That was what they usually did when they shared a room for whatever reason.

Ellis was already in bed reading. She looked up from her book as Min entered. "Did you finally win at chess?"

"No," Min replied. "I kissed Evan instead."

So much for not sharing what had happened. But that had never really been a possibility. Of course, Min would tell Ellis about the kiss.

Ellis set the book on the table next to her side of the bed and slid from beneath the bedclothes. Min moved toward the armoire and kicked off her slippers.

"That's all you're going to say?" Ellis asked, coming to stand beside Min.

Min shrugged as she pulled the pearl comb from her hair.

"There's nothing *to* say." She didn't dare look at Ellis, but she could imagine her expression of astonishment.

"You can't just say that and nothing else," Ellis said. "What happened?"

"It was nothing." Min glanced toward Ellis, who was staring at her with her lips pursed.

Ellis crossed her arms over her chest. "You kissing Evan is not nothing. You kissing *anyone* is not nothing." She paused. "Should I ask *him* what happened?"

Min turned to face her. "No, you're never to speak of it to him or to anyone. We're going to forget it happened." Except he'd explicitly told her that he would not. And Min knew she wouldn't either. Moving past Ellis, she went to the dressing table and set the comb atop it.

"But it *did* happen." Ellis had turned and followed her partway to the dressing table. "If you don't want to talk about it, I won't force you, but I'm here to listen if you want to share."

"Thank you." Min let her shoulders dip with relief. "Will you unfasten my gown?" She presented her back to Ellis, who immediately set to work.

In a few minutes, Min had stripped away everything but her chemise. Ellis stood near the dressing table, her gaze wary.

Min couldn't stand it any longer and threw her hands up. "I'm so confused. He asked me if I'd ever kissed anyone."

Ellis went to one of the two chairs near the hearth and sat. "Did you tell him about Samuel in Weston, all those years ago?"

"I did." Min joined her and perched on the other chair. "I suppose that's what prompted me to ask him to kiss me."

"You asked him to?" Ellis's pale brows climbed her forehead.

"Yes." Min shivered. There was a low fire in the hearth,

and she held out her hand for a bit of warmth. "For so long, I thought that maybe I wasn't made for kissing—or for marriage. I hated that kiss with Samuel."

"I knew you didn't care for it." Ellis's brow pleated. "I didn't realize you'd *hated* it. Some people are just bad kissers. Not you, but Samuel," she clarified.

"What if it is me?" Min hadn't shared that fear with anyone before. "I had assumed there is something wrong with me."

Ellis leaned forward and reached out to touch Min's hand. "Oh, Min, there's nothing wrong with you. Why would you think that?"

"I know you've kissed someone, and you enjoyed it. Persephone had kissed someone before she met Welles-bourne, and she enjoyed it. Why didn't I?"

"Like I said, it could just be that Samuel was an awful kisser." Ellis patted Min's hand before sitting back in her chair. "It's nothing to do with you."

"Except, wouldn't you think that I would have wanted to try again with someone else so that I could experience a good kiss?" Min asked. "Instead, I've avoided it. Honestly, I didn't even really want to kiss Samuel, but I thought I would try it. I didn't like it, and I didn't care to try again."

"It makes sense to me that you might choose to avoid kissing anyone again until the right person came along. Is that what happened with Evan?"

"Yes." The answer surprised Min, but it shouldn't have. She'd *wanted* to kiss him. She'd felt a tingling anticipation she'd never experienced before. "I've started to feel different around him the past few days. My heart pounds, and I have a fluttery feeling in my belly." She brushed her hand over her midsection.

"It sounds as though you're attracted to him at least," Ellis said with a smile. "Could it be more than that?"

Min snapped her gaze to Ellis's. "Are you asking if I'm falling in love?" Min shook her head. "We are *friends*. I can't imagine being married to Evan. He's Gwen's brother."

"But you *are* attracted to him," Ellis said. At Min's nod, she added, "I confess I'd wondered if maybe you might be attracted to women instead."

Min blinked at her. "I did consider that, because when I would listen to you and the others talk about kissing or how our friends feel about their husbands, I just couldn't understand. I've never felt anything close to that. Not even an inkling." Min blinked at her. "You know what I mean, don't you? You've kissed one or two young men."

"Two," Ellis replied.

"I remember the cobbler's son that one summer we were at Beacon Park," Min said. "You kept going into town to see him. You seemed smitten. What did that feel like?"

"Much like you describe." Ellis smiled, her gaze warming. "Flutters and a racing pulse, a wonderful heat coupled with excitement when I would go to see him. Is that how you feel with Evan?"

That tingling anticipation Min felt in his presence. "Yes. What does that mean?"

"I'm describing lust," Ellis said frankly. "In hindsight, that is what I shared with Jacob. It wasn't love."

"This isn't love with Evan either. I suppose it could be lust."

"Perhaps you've simply had an awakening," Ellis suggested with a wave of her hand. "For whatever reason, Evan has stirred something within you. And since you are friends, I think it's brilliant that you felt you could ask him to kiss you, if only to see what it was like." She looked at Min intently. "And how was it?"

Min chewed the inside of her lip. She was afraid to say. "It was nice," she said quietly.

Only, nice didn't begin to describe the tumult of feelings that were still churning inside her, and the excitement that Ellis spoke of simmered within Min. But the house party was nearly over, and while she might see Evan in Bath next month, they could not—they would not—continue as they had here at the party.

"I can see you're worried," Ellis noted. "Why?"

Min lifted a shoulder. "I suppose I don't know how to act with him now. We agreed to forget that it happened." They really hadn't.

"But you can't."

"Not immediately, at least." Min exhaled. "I'm glad the party's almost over—one more day. Evan is well enough to move around on his own, so I needn't spend time with him tomorrow. He doesn't need me to distract him or entertain him."

Ellis arched a brow. "One might argue he never needed that. But you provided companionship just the same. Have you considered why?"

"I was being a friend," Min said, thinking she sounded a trifle defensive. A voice in the back of her head suggested there was, perhaps, something more to it. But no, there couldn't be—Evan was her friend's brother, as well as a rogue and uninterested in marriage at this juncture.

"I have one last chance on the Marriage Mart," Min said with determination. "I must give that my full attention in Bath."

Ellis cocked her head, her eyes narrowed slightly. "You haven't just declined suitors because they were rogues, have you?"

"No," Min whispered. "The ones who weren't rogues didn't stir anything within me. I didn't want to be trapped in a marriage without love or…passion."

"That is not only understandable, it's admirable." Ellis

gave her an encouraging smile. "I know my opinion on the matter counts for very little, but there you have it."

"Your opinion will always be important to me," Min said fiercely.

Ellis smiled briefly. "Do you really expect to find a husband in Bath?"

"No," Min replied honestly. "However, I do have the faintest hope. I'd given up, but now that I know I can feel passion, I think it's possible the right man is out there. And if I fail to find him in Bath, I'll enter a convent."

"If you don't find him, it won't be a failure, Min."

Min knew what her friend was trying to say—that Min's inability to find a husband was through no fault of her own. Not wanting to accept a marriage without love or passion was not a failure. In fact, marrying someone for whom Min felt none of those things would be the ultimate failure to her.

Ellis rose. "You can't go to a convent. We're supposed to start a school for girls, if you recall."

"Oh, yes, of course." Min grinned as she stood and went to the dresser to fetch her night rail.

They'd talked about opening a school for some time now, but the truth was that Min, as the daughter of a duke, would not be allowed to do such a thing. Or would she? Her father had changed of late. He was no longer pressuring her in the same ways as her mother.

Min changed into her night rail and walked to the bed, where Ellis was standing.

"Whatever happens, I will be your companion as long as you want me to," Ellis said.

Min hugged her tightly, grateful for her support and love. There was no one in the world she trusted more. "Thank you, Ellis. I don't know what I would do without you."

"Then it's a good thing you never have to find out."

CHAPTER 7

*M*in had arrived in Bath just over a week ago at her mother's house, a charming stone-fronted terrace in the Circus. It was strange to think that this was her mother's new permanent residence and that the duchess would not be returning to Henlow House in London or Beacon Park in Bedfordshire. But it was for the best. Though her parents avoided each other if they happened to be in residence at the same time, it was still a stressful environment for everyone. Having completely separate households would guarantee peace.

Not *peace*, exactly. At least Min wouldn't have that, not with her mother's marriage demands becoming more strident than ever. She was particularly frustrated with Min for how things had gone at the Longleat house party.

Lady Bath had written a letter to Min's mother, explaining how Min had spent much of the party caring for Evan. The duchess had been displeased and had harped on missed opportunities with potential suitors at Longleat. Today, however, it seemed her mother was ready to change her focus. Probably because tonight was the first ball of the Season.

The duchess had come into Min's bedchamber to select the gown Min would wear that evening. They stood surveying the three new evening gowns that had just been delivered from the modiste. Min's mother always insisted she have new garments for every Season, and these three were only the beginning. Her mother had purchased a subscription to the Upper Rooms, which meant Min would be attending two balls each week, one on Mondays and one on Thursdays. The fancy ball was held on Thursdays, which was tonight.

There would be dozens of evening gowns, since Min's mother would not want her to wear the same one twice. It was too much, but Min's attempts to convince her that she could surely wear the gowns she'd just worn in London in the spring had been shut down.

Ellis was lucky in that her presence was not required—not in choosing what to wear nor in attending the balls, apparently. In a break from the past, the duchess had announced that the subscription to the Upper Rooms did not include Ellis. Min was livid; however, her protests had been as successful as her complaints about the unnecessary wardrobe enrichment.

Min's mother had never made a secret of her disapproval of Ellis, which had always grated on Min. The duchess hadn't wanted Min's father to take Ellis in after her parents had died. It didn't matter that Ellis's father's family and the duke's family had been friends for generations.

Not that Min had known of her mother's attitude at first, because she'd been all of five years old when Ellis had come to live with them as Min's companion. Indeed, Min could barely remember a time when Ellis hadn't been in their household. And that made Ellis like a sister to Min, even if her mother treated Ellis as if she were an interloper.

"I think you should definitely wear the ivory," her mother said, gesturing to the gown that hung in the center. It was flanked by a dark pink and a daffodil yellow. Seeing the colors together reminded Min of Evan's floral dungeon at Longleat. She quashed a smile.

Min preferred the pink, but she'd learned long ago to choose her battles with her mother. In the end, Min didn't care what dress she wore tonight.

The duchess went on, "The color says you are serious about marriage. It denotes purity and innocence and a readiness to become a wife. I truly believe the time has finally arrived, Min. I know how important it is to you to find the right bridegroom, and I think you will find him here in Bath."

"I wish I shared your confidence, Mama." Min was just glad that Jo was in Bath and would attend at least some of the balls since Ellis could not. It was too bad that none of their other friends had been able to come to town. Persephone and Tamsin were at their country estates, and while Gwen had planned to be there with Somerton, she'd sent a letter saying she was ill.

"You should." Her mother gave her an earnest look. "Tonight, I want you to pay special attention to the Viscounts Barswell and Spilsby. It will be the battle of the viscounts," she added with a laugh. "Do stay away from the Viscount Claxton, however. He's a fortune hunter."

"I met Claxton at Longleat," Min said. "I can assure you, I have no interest in him. Who is Spilsby?"

"That is Mr. Eberforce. *Was* Mr. Eberforce," her mother corrected. "He inherited his uncle's viscountcy over the summer. Isn't that wonderful?"

Min was familiar with Eberforce, and he was a

jackanapes. He'd humiliated Min's friend Gwen, Evan's sister, at Almack's in the spring. Again, Min chose not to start an argument with her mother. Instead, Min would do her best to steer clear of Eberforce. Or Spilsby. She suddenly laughed.

Her mother's eyes narrowed. "What?"

Spilsby was the most perfect title Mr. Eberforce could ever have inherited, for he'd made a spectacle of poor Gwen when she'd tripped at Almack's and spilled orgeat on Eberforce's garish waistcoat. Honestly, it was the best use of Almack's terrible drink as it transformed Eberforce's equally horrid garment into a more tolerable color.

"I was just recalling something humorous that Mr. Eberforce, rather Lord Spilsby, said last spring," Min lied. Her mother would not appreciate the irony of Spilsby's new title. Min could not, however, wait to tell Ellis, who would be greatly amused.

"That's encouraging," her mother said with enthusiasm.

"I met a pleasant gentleman at Longleat—Mr. Jarvis," Min added. "I told him I would dance with him in Bath."

The duchess frowned. "I have no idea who that is. Don't dawdle with him. You must focus on the men who are worthy of you."

"Those are the men you mentioned?" Min asked, thinking Spilsby was no more worthy of her than a slug. Actually, she would find a slug far more tolerable.

"Yes," her mother replied, somewhat impatiently.

"And what makes them worthy?" Min shouldn't prod her like this, but it was as close to defiance as she would dare this afternoon.

"Their titles and their social standing," her mother said with a hint of exasperation. Then her eyes lit, and she clapped her hands together. "I don't know if he will be coming to Bath this autumn, but you might also consider the Earl of Banemore."

Min kept her jaw from dropping. There was no situation in which she would *ever* consider Bane. He had thoroughly ruined her dear friend Pandora Barclay. Min hoped he would not be coming to Bath, since Pandora lived here with her aunt. Pandora did not participate in the Marriage Mart— Bane's treatment of her ensured that she had no prospects, despite being the daughter of a baron and the sister of a duchess. That Min's mother would suggest Bane as a match for Min was shocking, though it should not have been. The duchess would overlook his extraordinary shortcomings because he was heir to a dukedom.

"He will be looking for a new wife," her mother said with confidence. "His father is ill, and everyone expects Bane will inherit the dukedom soon. Taking a new wife and begetting an heir will be top of his priorities, I'm sure."

One should not presume to know what Bane's priorities were. He'd carried on with Pandora in Weston two years ago while he was already apparently betrothed to the woman he'd eventually wed. His *priority* had clearly not been Pandora. Sadly, Bane's wife had died in childbirth, as had the child. Min detested the man but would never have wished such a tragedy upon him.

As Min once again considered whether to oppose her mother, she realized she often took the path of least resistance with her. It simply wasn't worth the aggravation to do anything else. In this case, however, Min believed it was.

"Mama, I must tell you that I would never consider the Earl of Banemore. Since you mentioned unworthiness, I would argue that he is absolutely *not* worthy of me, given his past behavior."

The duchess waved her hand. "If you're referring to that

tiny scandal with that silly chit in Weston, that is ancient history."

A wave of anger swept through Min. "That silly chit is sister to the Duchess of Wellesbourne. She's also a very dear friend of mine whom I will be seeing while we are in Bath. It is not ancient history to her or to any of us who were witness to his perfidy. She believed they were to wed. He misled her. I am sorry for what's happened to him, but he's horrible, and I would never marry him, so just put that from your mind."

Narrowing her eyes at Min, the duchess set a hand on her hip. "My dear, you are past the point at which you may be selective. The reason your choices are these two viscounts and anyone else we might hunt up here in Bath is because no one believes you are serious about marriage. Better prospects have moved on. Indeed, some of them even married this past Season, and you missed out entirely. I daresay you're going to have to accept the next marriage proposal that is offered."

"Even if it's Mr. Jarvis?" Min asked sweetly.

The duchess blew out a breath and threw up her hands. "Don't be ridiculous. You must choose someone with a title."

Min was saved from further discussion by the arrival of the housekeeper.

"I'm sorry to interrupt," Mrs. Barker said. "Lord and Lady Shefford have arrived. They are waiting downstairs in the library."

"Thank you, Mrs. Barker." The duchess grimaced faintly before glancing at Min. "We'd best go welcome them." She departed the bedchamber.

Min followed her mother, eager to see her brother and his wife. Jo was also Min's good friend and was expecting a child in the new year. The prospect of becoming an aunt was most exciting, especially since Min doubted she would marry and have children of her own.

She followed her mother into the library. Jo sat in a chair, and Sheff stood beside her.

"I'm so pleased to see you," Min said. She hurried over to hug Jo, who stood as Min approached. As they embraced, Min felt Jo's bump against her belly and glanced down between them. "Are you feeling well?" she asked with a smile.

Jo nodded. "Quite, thank you. Your brother makes sure of it." She looked over at Sheff, who, though he wasn't smiling, possessed an air of pride and joy that was unmistakable, at least to Min. She'd never seen her brother so happy and was very glad for him.

"Did you just arrive in Bath?" the duchess asked.

"Yesterday," Sheff replied. "We've taken a house in Portland Place," Sheff replied. "It's well-appointed, and the butler keeps an organized household."

"That is most satisfying," the duchess said. "I have finally rounded out the retainers here, and I do hope things will begin to move more smoothly now that we have a full complement. Will you be attending the ball tonight?" She glanced at Jo's midsection.

Sheff edged closer to Jo. "No, but I did purchase a subscription. I want to support Min." He smiled at his sister.

Their mother inclined her head. "That is very kind of you, Sheff. Your sister needs all the support she can get. I'm afraid she's run out of time on the Marriage Mart. This is her last chance. Unfortunately, the options here in Bath are not extensive. Alas, it will have to suffice. I am confident she can find someone who is worthy." She gave Min a pointed look before her gaze drifted toward Jo. The unspoken message was clear: Sheff had not chosen someone who was worthy, and Min must not make the same mistake.

"You must excuse me," the duchess said. "I've a meeting with the new cook." She swept from the library, and it was as if the air in the room lightened.

"My apologies," Min murmured to Jo. "You needn't come here anymore. I can visit you."

Jo gave her a smile. "It's all right, I can put up with your mother."

Sheff looked to Min. "We were hoping you might take a walk with us to call on Father. His house is just over in Catharine Place."

Min was surprised. She knew her father was coming to Bath, but she wasn't sure when. Her mother would be angry, but hopefully, their paths wouldn't cross. It was perhaps too much to hope, as Bath was not large.

"Let me just fetch my hat and gloves," Min said. "And Ellis —if she wants to come."

"Actually, could you not invite Ellis?" Sheff asked. His expression seemed uncertain or perhaps tinged with discomfort.

Min found his request odd. "Why?"

"You'll understand why when we get to Father's."

Frowning slightly as she tried to puzzle why Ellis's presence wouldn't be wanted, she quickly fetched her hat and gloves. A few minutes later, they left the house and walked from the Circus onto Brock Street toward the Crescent, where Pandora's aunt lived. However, they would turn right before that to make their way to Catharine Place.

"Now don't be shocked," Sheff said. "Father is not living alone here."

Min's eyes rounded briefly. "Mrs. Welbeck is with him?" That was his new mistress, whom he'd met in Weston this summer. Sheff had said their father was smitten.

Min hadn't met her yet. "I still can't believe he has a mistress who has lasted more than a month."

"Mrs. Welbeck appears to be different." There was a sparkle in Sheff's eye. "But Father is also different."

"So you've said," Min replied.

"He hardly drinks at all anymore," Sheff continued. "He and Mrs. Welbeck like to take rambling walks about the countryside. With her dogs."

"*Our* father does that?" Min was agog.

Sheff chuckled. "I know it's hard to believe."

As they neared their father's house, Jo gently touched Min's arm. "We have something important to tell you when we arrive, and I just want you to know that you must have whatever reaction you feel, and I am here to support you."

Min grew alarmed.

"Don't worry," Sheff said. "It's nothing terrible—well, I mean, it is somewhat awful, but we'll all manage."

Stomach clenching, Min stopped. "Father is going to divorce Mother, isn't he? Has he found proof of adultery?"

"We are not aware of any divorce plans." Sheff's brow darkened. "Though, I see why you would think that. I do wonder if Father has considered divorce." He frowned slightly, his features contemplative. "He could... I won't say more until we go inside. The house is just there." He gestured to the next terrace.

A friendly butler called Jurgens greeted them and showed them to the drawing room upstairs. Min's father, the Duke of Henlow, rose from a chair as they entered. He looked very well. His nose had lost its typical redness, and his midsection appeared to have diminished somewhat.

"My dear Minnie," he said with a smile and held his arms open for her. He hadn't done that in years. She walked toward him and stepped into his embrace. She closed her eyes as she leaned her cheek against his chest. For a fleeting moment, she was eight years old again.

They separated, and he surveyed her a moment. "You look well. How was Longleat?"

"It was quite tolerable, Papa." She didn't want to exchange pleasantries when there was a revelation of import hanging in the air. "What is this critical thing you must tell me?" Min looked from her father to Sheff and back to her father again.

"Let us sit." Their father went back to the chair he'd vacated while Sheff and Jo sat together on a settee. Min perched on a chair near her father, across from Jo and Sheff.

The three of them looked at each other, and Min began to grow frustrated. "You're starting to worry me."

"This concerns Ellis," her father said slowly, almost hesitantly. "We've learned some information about her that is vital and surprising. It concerns her parentage."

Min's pulse picked up speed with the mention of Ellis's parentage. The parents who'd raised her until she was nine when they'd died had adopted her. The identity of her true parents was not known—at least not to Ellis or to Min.

Over the years, many people suspected the duke was Ellis's father because of the way he'd welcomed her into their household when she'd been orphaned. The duchess's disdain for her presence supported the suspicion, but the duke had always maintained he was not Ellis's father. And since he'd just said what they'd discovered was surprising, the information clearly didn't involve him.

"What have you learned?" Min asked, her body rigid with tension.

Jo exhaled. "There's just no easy way to say this. Ellis is my half sister."

Of all the things Min might have expected, that was not it. She stared at Jo and tried to make sense of it. "I have many questions."

"I'm sure you do," Sheff said. "Let us try to explain. I think many have assumed that Ellis is our father's by-blow."

Min nodded and looked to her father. "But she is not your daughter."

"No, she is not, as I have always said." The duke's face creased with concern. "She is, however, your half sister too."

That only left one explanation… She gaped at Sheff. "Our mother is *Ellis's* mother?"

Sheff pressed his lips together as he inclined his head.

Min's jaw dropped completely, and she made an incoherent sound as words failed her for a long moment.

What Sheff had said about their father being able to consider a divorce made sense. If Ellis was their mother's daughter, the duchess would have had an affair while married to Min's father. And since Jo was Ellis's half sister, that meant the duchess had conducted a liaison with Jo's father. To think her mother had the nerve to lecture Min about the worthiness of people based on their social standing! By Mother's own measure, Jo's father wasn't "worthy," yet she'd betrayed her husband with him and borne a child.

Min sagged back against the chair as she finally snapped her mouth closed. This was going to take some time to comprehend. She thought of Ellis. What would she think? What would she *do*?

Whenever Ellis heard the oft-repeated rumor that the duke was her father, she denounced it immediately. He had told her years ago quite firmly that he was not her father, and she'd believed him, regardless of what anyone said. Min believed it was because he'd always welcomed Ellis into their family, whereas the duchess—Ellis's actual mother—had treated her horribly. Ellis felt a strong loyalty to him.

Ellis would be devastated.

But there was also a sense of joy, for Ellis was Min's half sister. That made her smile.

"That is not the reaction I was expecting," Min's father noted, his brow furrowing as he studied Min.

"I was just thinking it's nice to know that Ellis doesn't just feel like my sister. She *is* my sister. That will be the only thing about this that will make her happy," Min added. She narrowed her eyes at all of them. "Why are you telling me before her?"

"We thought it best you know in advance so that when we —all together—do tell her, you will be able to anticipate what's coming," Jo explained. "If I were Ellis, I would be grateful to have someone at my side who I know cares about me."

Min nodded. That made sense. "Who else knows?"

"No one," Sheff replied. "That includes Jo's father and our mother. Well, Mother knows, obviously, but she doesn't know that *we* know."

Jo grimaced faintly. "My father isn't even aware there was a child, let alone who it could be."

"How awful," Min said softly, shaking her head. "I'm struggling to reconcile the mother who raised me with this person who committed adultery and had a daughter and has treated her so poorly."

In recent years, the relationship between Min and her mother had deteriorated as the duchess had become increasingly demanding with regard to Min's duty to marry. Still, Min had loved her and believed her mother had wanted the best for her. Now, however, Min felt nothing but anger and betrayal, primarily for how she'd treated her own flesh and blood. To think she'd had two daughters in her household and treated them so differently was unconscionable to Min.

There had been so many things over the years—the vast differences in their wardrobes, that Ellis's chamber wasn't just much smaller than Min's, it was located on the same floor as the servants, or even, most recently, not purchasing a subscription for Ellis. In every way, Ellis had been excluded, and why? She could very easily have been accepted into their family and been given the same opportunities as Min. She should have been Min's "adopted sister" rather than her companion.

"Why does she hate Ellis so much?" Min whispered.

"Because I made her accept Ellis into the household," the duke said.

Min blinked at him. "You knew Ellis was her daughter?"

"I did. I did not know the identity of her father until recently, but I knew your mother had a child and that she wasn't mine. We'd stopped sharing a bed after your brother was born."

Min froze. "Does that mean you are not my father either?"

"No, no," her father assured her. "After Ellis was situated with her adoptive parents, which I coordinated, your mother felt beholden to give me another child, and I am delighted she did, because that is you, my beautiful Minnie."

"Why didn't you make her accept Ellis as a member of the family instead of just the household?" Min demanded. "She should have been given everything I was."

Her father's face fell. "I could not convince your mother to do that. I should have insisted. Instead, I made a bargain— that Ellis could stay so long as she was your companion and nothing more."

"Why would you agree to that?" Min was so angry at him.

"I was still hopeful your mother and I might find a path to reconciliation." His mouth curled into a brief, sad smile. "I loved your mother far longer than I should have."

"You had a terrible way of showing it," Min snapped.

"Min, you don't know everything about their marriage," Sheff interjected.

She turned her head toward her brother. "Then tell me."

Sheff glanced at their father, and it was he who responded. "I married your mother because I loved her beyond reason, Minnie. However, she did not reciprocate my affections. She married me for my title, and once we were wed, she made that quite plain. She hated my rakish behavior, all while pretending to be enamored. Still, I tried to woo her—with no effect. I was lonely, and I decided that once a rake, always a rake. I am not proud of how I've acted over the years, but my heart was broken for a long time."

Min was shaking now. In the span of a quarter hour, everything she knew had completely changed. She could scarcely believe all that had been revealed. And she could not imagine how Ellis was going to react.

"We need to tell Ellis as soon as possible," Min said. "But we're going to the ball tonight at the Upper Rooms."

"We'd thought to tell her and my father together," Jo said. "He is here in Bath. We invited him to come so that we could tell them, and they could get to know one another."

"What if Ellis doesn't want that?" Min didn't want Ellis to be put into any position she didn't agree to. "We mustn't force her to do anything."

"I agree." Jo looked at Sheff. "Perhaps we shouldn't tell them together."

"I think that would be for the best," Min said. "We need to tell Ellis tomorrow."

She didn't really want to wait at all, but there wouldn't be time before Min would need to start preparing for the ball. And she agreed that they needed to all tell Ellis together, away from their mother's house. "We should do it here."

"Yes, of course," Sheff agreed. "Tomorrow afternoon."

Min's mind was churning. She didn't know how she would keep the secret from Ellis until then. Whenever she thought she could not tell Ellis something, she invariably did, just as she had last week at Longleat after kissing Evan. Keeping this secret in particular from Ellis would be torture.

Min rubbed her hand over her brow. "I don't know how Ellis is going to react to this."

"She's going to be upset," Jo said gently. "But we will be here for her."

"I expect she won't want to stay in your mother's household anymore," the duke noted. "She's welcome to come here."

Min's gut twisted. "No, she won't want to stay with us," she said softly, which meant Min would be alone. The life she had loved and had taken for granted was now over. She thought of what Ellis might want. Would she still wish to run a school for girls?

Min looked to her father. "You must give her whatever she wants. She deserves that."

He nodded. "I agree. However, I don't think she can have a Season or seek a husband on the Marriage Mart. That would raise too many questions after she's been your companion for so long."

Min doubted Ellis would want either of those things, and not just because people would assume—definitively—that the duke was her father.

"The truth of Ellis's parentage cannot be revealed beyond our family," Sheff said. "No one can know that Ellis is the child of Jo's father and our mother. She must continue as your companion who was orphaned by friends of our family."

"I don't think she'll want to continue as my companion. I imagine she'll want to be as far away from our mother—*her* mother—as possible." Min wanted that for herself too.

"I can settle a dowry on her," the duke said. "It's very possible she could find a husband, if that's what she wants. Do you know what she wants, Min?"

"I can't possibly," Min said. "This changes everything. I'm not sure she'll know what she wants. I don't think I would."

But Min wasn't in Ellis's position. She was dealing with the expectation that she wed. And now more than ever, especially after hearing her father's heartbreaking revelation, she didn't want to marry someone whom she did not love completely, and who did not love her in return.

However, now that she knew she could at least feel passion, she'd begun to accept the notion of marrying for that, if nothing else. The only person with whom she felt that, though, was Evan. She pushed him from her mind. Now was not the time to think about him.

"What is our plan for tomorrow, then?" the duke asked.

"We'll meet here tomorrow afternoon," Sheff replied. "Early, before the social hour in Sydney Gardens."

Min wanted to laugh. As if she or Ellis would want to walk in the gardens after what Ellis would learn.

"Are you all right, Min?" Jo asked tentatively, her face full of concern and love.

"Not entirely," Min replied. It would be difficult to be with Ellis and not tell her the truth.

Tomorrow could not come soon enough.

CHAPTER 8

*E*van loved Bath, with its sweeping hillside views and the winding, beautiful River Avon. He only wished he were able to ride Merlin. The poor horse clearly missed their outings, but no more than Evan. Merlin was now ensconced in the mews that came with his mother's house, where Evan was staying. Located in Catharine Place, she'd leased it the past few years.

Tonight, Evan escorted her to the Upper Rooms for the first ball of the Season. He would not be dancing, since he was still relying on the walking stick, but he was moving around quite well after the setback he'd suffered the last day of the house party. He'd overdone it and had needed to convalesce for a few more days at Longleat before coming to Bath.

"It's strange attending this ball without your sister," Evan's mother said as they departed the carriage and stepped toward the entrance.

Evan looked toward his dark-haired, elegant mother. Catriona Price was a popular hostess in Society from Cardiff to Bath to London. "Just so long as you don't expect me to make a match now that Gwen is married off."

They paused to wait as others entered before them, and she gave him a playfully scolding look. "Of course I expect you to marry. You are your father's only son, and you must carry on the family name. I do not, however, anticipate you will be doing so anytime soon." There was an edge of disappointment in her tone, but also of resignation.

Though Evan's father did not have a title, his position as Lord Commissioner of the Treasury was admirable. And there was always the chance that a title or knighthood might be bestowed upon him at some point. Regardless, Evan's father took family legacy very seriously. His own father and grandfather had been MPs before him.

Evan wondered if his mother wasn't being entirely honest about her expectations. "Why did you bother with a subscription to the Upper Rooms since you no longer need to find a match for Gwen?"

"I enjoy the Upper Rooms," she replied as they edged forward. "And I enjoy presenting my handsome son to everyone."

"*Presenting* me?" That did not sound as though she wasn't expecting something from him. "What are you hoping to accomplish, Mama?" he asked softly so no one could overhear.

"Your reputation could use a bit of polishing," she replied in a whisper. "Do promise me you will not engage in any scandalous behavior while you are in Bath."

Evan stiffened. She had every right to make such demands since he was staying with her. Not to mention the fact that everyone believed he'd engaged in scandalous behavior in London. He should have expected she would want to rehabilitate people's perception of him.

The urge to defend himself and confess the truth was great, but he'd wanted to help Roger, both to repay a debt and because they were friends. Evan would be fine, whereas Roger might have been ruined. Some would say he deserved that, but Evan didn't like to judge people. Everyone made mistakes, and what Roger deserved was the chance to learn from his.

But perhaps Evan wasn't as immune as he'd thought he'd be. "I will behave with the utmost decorum, Mama. Is my reputation truly damaged?"

"I can't say as we are not in London. Your father's last letter indicated there is gossip." She pursed her lips and gave her head a slight shake. "Let us not speak of it."

Evan regretted his mother's discomfort. It was one thing for him to take accountability for something that might harm him, but he'd never wanted his mother to be affected.

They moved into the entrance hall, where the master of ceremonies greeted them. After his mother deposited her wrap with the cloakroom, they made their way into the ball-room, where the first set was already underway.

Evan surveyed the ballroom and realized he was searching for Min. It took him a moment to find her, but there she was, dancing with Barswell, of all people. He was surprised to see that since she hadn't seemed to want to encourage his suit at Longleat.

"It's a shame you can't dance," Evan's mother said. "How soon will I lose you to the cardroom?"

Evan laughed. "Definitely after the tea, and perhaps a bit before." Since the supper interval in the tearoom was nearly two hours off, Evan didn't want to make any promises.

"I suppose that will do," she replied just before they were besieged by several mothers and their daughters.

When the next set started, Evan and his mother were alone once more, as the young ladies all found partners for the next set. Evan watched as Min partnered with Eberforce, a thoroughly despicable fellow who'd insulted Evan's sister. Evan was affronted that Min would dance with him, but reasoned she hadn't much choice if he'd asked.

"Did you hear that Eberforce is now the Viscount Spilsby?" Evan's mother asked, evidently following Evan's line of sight.

"*Spilsby?*" Evan turned his head toward his mother and laughed. "What a hilariously appropriate name since Gwen spilled orgeat all over him at Almack's." Evan was still angry that he hadn't been there to defend her. Though, his friend Somerton to whom Gwen was now married—had done an admirable job.

Evan's mother laughed. "I hadn't thought of that. You're right. It's quite fitting. I must say, I do not care for him at all."

"Because you are a woman of taste." Evan tried not to scowl as he watched Min in the scoundrel's arms. Min was also a woman of taste, just as she was a young lady being pressured to wed.

Evan was sorry he couldn't dance, because he would have asked Min. Then he could demand to know why she was spending time with bloody Spilsby of all people. Evan sniggered as he thought the man's name and wondered if he would do so forevermore.

He shouldn't care who Min was dancing with—they were friends and nothing more. In fact, he wondered if they were now not even really friends. Things had been awkward since their kiss, the day after which had been the end of the party.

He'd taken advantage of his newfound mobility that day to visit with his horse, play billiards, and even indulge in lawn bowling for a short time. Looking back, he wondered if he'd kept himself busy so he wouldn't notice that Min had not come to visit him after breakfast, as she'd done every day before. In fact, they'd only exchanged a few brief words before dinner that evening, and he hadn't seen her the next day before she departed Longleat.

Perhaps she was angry with him. He hoped their friendship wasn't ruined. It was good she was here, for he could speak to her tonight. He didn't want things to be bad between them.

"I do think I need to sit, Mama," Evan said.

His mother pivoted toward him, her forehead pleating with concern. "Yes, you should probably have done so by now. If you want to go to the cardroom, I won't deter you."

"I shall meet you in the tearoom for supper," he said, then departed the ballroom after one final look at Min.

Outside the ballroom, Evan plotted how he might approach Min and speak to her privately. He had to assume she would be dancing every set, which meant his best chance would be during the tea. There would probably be two more sets before then, so he would bide his time in the cardroom.

Near the end of the last set before supper, Evan left the cardroom—despite being quite ahead—and made his way to the ballroom. He wanted to catch Min as she left.

However, it wasn't easy to spot her in the ivory gown, as many other young ladies wore the same hue. Finally, he saw her leaving the dance floor with Jarvis. Instead of going to her mother, she went toward the other doorway.

Evan had to hurry to catch up to her. He moved as quickly as his injured ankle would allow, which was probably faster than he should have done. But he couldn't let this opportunity pass. He managed to reach the other doorway just after she stepped through it into the corridor.

Taking a large step that sparked a flare of pain in his ankle, he reached for her with his free hand and tapped her arm. She swung around, her brows dipped into a V, and looked ready to snap at him.

"Evan," she said, sounding a trifle breathless as her brow smoothed.

But it was Evan who felt as if the breath had been knocked from his lungs. Had he forgotten how beautiful she was? No. He'd forgotten—or perhaps not realized—the extent of his reaction to her. She was stunning, from the rich sable of her hair to the arresting gray of her eyes to the elegant sweep of her neck as it met her collarbone.

Suddenly, Evan was right back in the florid pink ladies' library at Longleat with Min in his arms as they kissed until he could hardly see straight. "Good evening, Lady Minerva. Might we take a short promenade?" He was proud that he managed to sound normal and not flustered by her presence. Which he shockingly was.

She appeared briefly surprised, and he held his breath, waiting to see if she would accept. At last, she took his arm. "You seem to be moving around well."

"Doing my best. I'm afraid I overdid it that last day of the party and ended up staying at Longleat four more days to recover."

She grimaced. "You had to spend four more days in the pink dungeon?"

He laughed. "I did, and without your company, it was even more horrible, if you can imagine."

She smiled, and he felt immense relief, but she sobered quickly. He sensed tension in her—her mouth was tight and her body was rigid. They walked into the vestibule, and he took her into a shadowy corner.

She frowned at him. "This seems inappropriate. I need to go to the tearoom before my mother realizes I'm missing."

"You aren't missing," he said. "We're just having a short conversation." Her demeanor was cool, icy even. He never should have kissed her and ruined their friendship. "I'm so sorry, Min. I never meant to upset you or cause disruption to our wonderful friendship, which I value so much more than I could have ever imagined. In a matter of days at Longleat, you became my dearest friend."

She blinked at him, appearing slightly confused for a moment. "You don't need to apologize. What happened between us is in the past. We both agreed to forget what happened, and that's what I'm doing."

Except she was clearly agitated. And he didn't exactly remember them agreeing to anything. In fact, he recalled telling her he would remember their kiss forever. "I hoped we would still be friends."

"We are."

He edged closer to her, keeping his voice low. "Then why do you seem upset?"

She exhaled. "I am not upset with you. There is something else going on. I can't discuss it." She looked over her shoulder, and Evan frowned.

"You're sure it's not me?" he asked. "You can tell me the truth. I hate thinking that I might be the cause."

"You aren't," she snapped, the ice in her eyes melting as anger sparked.

"I see." While he was glad it wasn't him, he was still eager to determine the cause of her irritation. "Can I be of help? I don't like seeing you this upset. Something seems greatly amiss."

She wiped her hand against her brow. "I shouldn't tell you, but I cannot bear the burden. I learned some distressing news earlier today from my father and brother." She spoke very quietly.

"Your father is here?" Evan had known Sheff and his new bride, Jo, would be in Bath, but he wasn't aware that the Duke of Henlow would be as well.

"Yes, he's taken a house in Catharine Place. With his mistress," she added with a slightly arched brow.

"That's where I'm staying. My mother's house is in Catharine Place."

"I'd forgotten that is where she leased a house," Min murmured. "Well, I was there this afternoon with Sheff and Jo and learned the most shocking news. I really shouldn't tell you. No one must ever know. I haven't even told Ellis, and she's the one person who *needs* to know."

Evan realized he hadn't seen her in the ballroom. "Where is Ellis?"

Min pressed her lips together as anger darkened her gaze once more. "My mother did not buy a subscription for her. She did not want Ellis distracting me during the balls. She is intent that I will find a husband by the end of the month, if possible."

"That can't be pleasant."

"No, it is not. And it is even worse than that because I learned this afternoon that my mother is actually Ellis's mother too."

Evan gripped his walking stick. That was major news indeed. "I take it Ellis is not also your father's daughter." If she were, she would not be Min's companion but her sister.

Min explained—very quietly—how her mother had an adulterous affair with Jo's father, of all people, and bore a child. Min's father had known of the child, of course, but not who the father was, and had arranged for the child's adoption with family friends. That was how His Grace had become so involved in Ellis's life and why many people, Evan included at one time, assumed she was his by-blow, particularly given His Grace's penchant for extramarital affairs.

Min had grown more anguished as she'd related the tale. Evan gripped his walking stick to keep from pulling her into his arms. She finished by telling him that they would reveal the truth to Ellis tomorrow.

"I can see why you don't want anyone to learn this information. Rest assured, I will not breathe a word of it." He met her gaze as a surprisingly warm feeling washed over him. "I am honored that you would trust me with this, and I'm glad I can be a friend to you. It's the least I can do after your care at Longleat. I would have been lost without you." That was all true. Here, he'd been worried their friendship had been ruined, but it seemed the bond they'd forged at the house party was stronger than ever.

"I am relieved to share the secret with someone. You appeared just when I needed you," she said with a smile that only deepened the connection he felt with her.

"I'm glad."

Her smile faded, and her eyes darkened. "It's agony to keep the secret from Ellis. I'm actually relieved she's not here with me tonight, for it would be too difficult."

"Is it wrong that I want to embrace you?" he asked softly.

"No." Her eyes found his. "If it were possible, I would eagerly accept it."

"Rest assured, the moment I am able, I will." It could not come too soon.

Another small smile teased her lips. "I'll look forward to it."

How Evan wished she hadn't said that. He was already anticipating it himself, but knowing she was too made the expectation all the sweeter.

She glanced back toward the way they'd come. "I must go to the tearoom. Thank you for your discretion in this matter."

He put his fingers to his lips. "Your secret is safe with me. Rather, Ellis's secret."

"It's the entire family's secret," Min said darkly. "Honestly, it's changed everything for me. I don't quite know how I feel yet. I certainly can't stand being around my mother just now, and I can't even tell her why."

"Do you plan to let her know that you're aware she's Ellis's mother?"

"I must at some point, for I won't be able to keep it inside forever, especially given all the time we will spend together over the next several weeks. But I didn't discuss that with my brother or father today. I will speak with them tomorrow and seek their advice."

"It may be that you'd rather stay with your father and his mistress," Evan said drily.

She let out a hollow laugh. "I considered that, though it would not help my prospects on the Marriage Mart. At this juncture, however, I don't know that I care."

She took her leave then, hurrying away from him. He watched her turn into the corridor toward the tearoom. Her last statement stuck with him. He could understand why she would not be interested in the Marriage Mart after what she'd learned that day, but a part of him wondered if it was more than that.

Another part of him demanded to know why he would think so. Was he hoping she held some sort of tendre for him? He needed to remember that they were friends. He wasn't looking to marry, even if kissing Min had been a thoroughly divine experience. He would remain her steadfast friend and support her as best he could. She would not be interested in anything else anyway.

Evan followed Min's path back to the corridor and turned toward the tearoom. However, before he reached the first doorway, he recognized a familiar figure near the octagon— Harriet Dalton!

His pulse galloped, and he quickly ducked into the tearoom before Mrs. Dalton could see him. The last thing he needed was for his rumored lover, the very reason he had to stay away from London, to see him. Or worse, approach him.

What the devil was she doing in Bath?

~

*M*in had been a coward all morning. She'd taken breakfast in her room to avoid spending time with Ellis because it was too hard knowing the truth and not saying anything. As the noon hour had just passed, Min decided it was safe to venture from her bedchamber.

In a short while, she would invite Ellis to take a walk, and they would go to her father's house, where Min could finally stop hiding what she'd learned yesterday. It felt as though she'd been carrying the weight of the secret for far longer.

As Min passed the drawing room on her way to the staircase, the duchess called for her. Min paused at the threshold and saw her mother sitting near the window, reading correspondence.

"Yes, Mother?" Min worked to keep her voice devoid of emotion. It was difficult when she wanted to rail at her for treating her other daughter so horribly for years and years.

"You've been scarce all morning," the duchess said crossly.

Ellis wasn't the only reason for Min's self-imposed isolation. She had even less desire to spend time with her mother after what she'd learned. Last night had been hard enough, enduring the ball with her. Thankfully, Min had really only needed to tolerate her during the tea. Even then, they'd been fortunate enough to be joined by other ladies and their daughters. Min hadn't even had to sit next to her mother.

As it was, Min had found her attention diverted because Evan had sat just a few tables away with his mother. Min kept looking in his direction, and at one point, their eyes met. She'd felt a rush of heat and blamed it on embarrassment for being caught stealing glances at him. However, she knew it was more than that.

She'd hoped the kiss was entirely behind them, but when

he'd touched her arm in the corridor and then secreted her away to the corner, her heart had raced with anticipation. It wasn't that she'd expected him to kiss her in full sight of everyone at the Upper Rooms. It was only that being in his presence again was exciting.

It had also been soothing, for, as he'd noticed, she'd been very agitated. She probably ought not to have told him about Ellis, but she didn't regret doing so. The moment she'd shared the secret with him, she'd felt better. And he'd been so understanding and wonderful. She was very glad their friendship was intact.

The duchess snapped her fingers, jerking Min from her reverie. "What is wrong with you today?" Her mother's lips were thinner than normal, and her brow was cut into deep furrows. Min could see that she was angry about something, and Min didn't want any part of it.

"I suppose I am tired after the ball last night," Min said flatly. "I danced every set, if you recall."

"I do, and that is as to be expected. You will dance every set at every ball that we attend here in Bath." The duchess smacked her palm on the arm of her chair, making Min flinch. This was unusually angry behavior from her mother. "Did you know that your father is here?"

Min wasn't sure if her mother had posed the question as a trick. Min could reply no, which would be the easiest path, or she could admit that she'd seen him yesterday—along with Sheff and Jo—which would surely enrage the duchess. But if she already knew and Min acted as though she hadn't seen him, that could be worse.

"Yes, I knew he was here," Min replied, keeping her tone even. "I saw him yesterday with Sheff."

"Why didn't you tell me?"

Min arched a brow, for the answer seemed plainly obvious. "Because I knew you wouldn't be pleased."

Her mother sucked in a breath. "Did you see the harlot too?"

Min assumed her mother meant Mrs. Welbeck, her father's mistress. "No, I did not see Mrs. Welbeck," Min said, giving the "harlot" a name. "You mustn't go there again," the duchess said angrily. "You cannot risk even the faintest hint of scandal."

"Is it really a scandal that Papa has a mistress?" Min asked with a light laugh that had no humor. He'd had many mistresses and dalliances, and they were no secret.

"Don't be flippant," her mother snapped. "Your father is a walking scandal. It's bad enough that I have to live *here* now." She stood and paced to the hearth. "Can't I have any peace?"

Min watched her mother warily. "I thought you *wanted* to live here."

Her mother responded with a caustic laugh. "You think I chose to move out of Henlow House? To be banished to the dower house when I'm at Beacon Park? Not that I feel welcome there at all."

Min hadn't realized that her mother hadn't chosen to live here in Bath. But now that she knew, she couldn't say she blamed her father for setting those rules, if, in fact, he had.

"Why does he have to be in Bath?" the duchess went on, pacing angrily, gesturing wildly with her arms as she spoke. "He knew I would be here with you, and yet he came with his strumpet. It's unconscionable. Hasn't he put me through enough over the years?"

Min had to bite her tongue to keep from shouting what she'd learned the day before. The hypocrisy from her mother was staggering.

The duchess stopped abruptly. She took a deep breath and briefly closed her eyes. Then she exhaled and pinned her gaze on Min. "Enough of that. We must focus on you. We're going to Sydney Gardens later today. You must promenade with Spilsby. I have it on good authority that he's serious about courting you. With a promenade today and another dance at the ball on Monday, I should think you could be betrothed by this time next week."

"I'm not going to marry Spilsby!" Min exclaimed. "He was very rude to Lady Somerton, who is a dear friend of mine. He lacks character." He was worse than a rogue, really.

Her mother frowned. "But you danced with him last night. I assumed that meant you were serious about accepting him."

"I have danced with countless gentlemen over the years just to please you. That didn't mean I was interested in courtship."

"You've never had any serious intention of wedding any of them?" the duchess asked incredulously. "That's asinine. You can't really be that stupid."

Min's ire was quickly matching, or perhaps exceeding, that of her mother. "I'm not stupid at all, Mother. I've simply tried to be the daughter you wanted me to be. However, the truth is that I don't want to marry unless I'm absolutely sure I'll be happy. I certainly don't want to be as miserable as you."

The duchess straightened, her hand fluttering to her throat. "Whatever do you mean? I'm a duchess and am well regarded in Society. I've raised two wonderful children, and though one did not marry as well as he could have, the other will marry well enough. I've been a good mother, if not entirely successful."

"Listen to yourself," Min raged. "You gauge your success as a mother on your children's marriages, not whether they are happy or loved. Why did you marry Father? I have to wonder if you ever loved him."

"I've told you before that love isn't necessary to wed. If you're fortunate, it will come in time, and if not…" The duchess shrugged. "If you've married well, that doesn't matter."

Min stared at the woman who'd raised her. How had Min not seen just how cold she was? "It matters to me. Not that you care."

"You are being most disagreeable today," her mother said with a dark glower. "After I've already explained to you how I am being humiliated by your father, I can't believe you would treat me in this manner."

"Just stop!" Min nearly yelled as she finally surrendered to her own fury. "I am weary of your hypocrisy."

"Whatever do you mean?" the duchess asked, her brow knitted with confusion.

"As if you don't know," Min spat. "Well, *I* know everything, Mother. I know you were unfaithful to Father in the past. I know you bore another man's child, and I know he was Jo's father, Rowland Harker. It never made sense to me why you despised Jo so very much." Min shook her head. "It was beyond the fact that her mother owns a gaming hell. There was something far more insidious, and the same can be said about Ellis. You've never tolerated her, let alone liked her. Your extreme aversion to her has never made sense until now."

The duchess's face had turned the color of snow. "Don't say it." Her voice was low, almost a growl.

"Don't say what?" Min purposely kept her voice elevated. She was going to speak the truth loudly and clearly. "That Ellis is your daughter? That she is my half sister? That you have hated her because Papa insisted you let her live in your household? You've had to be reminded of her daily, of the mistake you made. Do I have that right, Mother? I think I understand you now."

The duchess looked as if she might faint. While Min

hadn't wanted to do her mother any harm, she could not muster any sympathy.

"How do you know?" her mother asked tightly.

"Does it matter?" Min didn't mask her bitterness. "I know. Sheff knows, Jo knows, and of course, Papa knows. He's always known. He's the reason Ellis has a family, such as it is."

"What did Ellis say?" the duchess asked warily.

"Nothing yet, because we haven't told her. But we will, and you will not be a part of that. In fact, I would be happy if you were no longer a part of anything to do with us." Min spun on her heel and stalked out of the drawing room.

The momentary elation she'd felt at unburdening herself on her mother evaporated as she saw Ellis dashing up the stairs to the second floor, where her bedchamber was located. Had she overheard? She must have. Min had been speaking very loudly.

Min's stomach dropped to the floor.

Racing after Ellis, Min paused on the landing at the top of the stairs as she saw her hastening toward her bedchamber. "Ellis, wait!" Min took several breaths to try to calm her racing heart.

Ellis turned slowly. She was not quite as pale as their mother, but she was close. For the first time, Min saw traces of the resemblance that they shared with the duchess and with each other. She realized Ellis took more after her father than her mother, a fact that would probably comfort her in the days and years to come. She had his fair hair, and the shape of her face was similar to his. But the blue of her eyes belonged to their mother—except Ellis's were far warmer. Though just now, they looked like a storm.

"You heard what I said downstairs," Min said, aching for how Ellis must feel. She grimaced as she took a small step forward.

Ellis held up her hand. "Please don't come any closer. I want to be alone."

"I understand." Min nodded gently. "I'm so sorry you found out that way. I was going to invite you on a walk to my father's house in Catharine Place. Sheff and Jo are going to be there, and we planned to tell you all together. I only found out yesterday. We could still go."

Ellis just stood there staring at Min.

"Say something. Please." Min felt awful.

"I don't know what to say." Ellis sounded hollow. "I don't want to see her again." There was no need for her to clarify who "her" was. "What am I to do?"

Min's heart cracked. She wanted to embrace her friend. No, her half sister. "You don't have to see her again," she said vehemently. "You don't have to stay here. You can go to my father's house or to Sheff's. I'll take you if you want."

"I want to be alone right now," Ellis said quietly.

"We all support you," Min told her. "Sheff, Jo, Papa—"

"What about Mr. Harker?" Ellis asked, haltingly. "My father."

"He doesn't yet know about you," Min replied. "He doesn't know that he has another child."

Ellis clapped her hand over her mouth. She half turned. "Please, leave me alone now, Min."

Watching Ellis's pain was agony. "You believe me that I didn't know, don't you?" Min asked.

"I do, but forgive me if I can't summon the grace to care what you or anybody else thinks or feels in this moment."

"Of course not," Min said quickly. "Just tell me what I can do, whenever you need me to do it. I will always be here for you."

Ellis turned and fled to her room, closing the door behind her. Min turned and pressed her hand to her mouth to keep a sob from escaping. She walked halfway down the stairs before sinking onto one of the steps.

She sat there for a long time as silent tears tracked down her cheeks, staring into nothing as she tried to imagine what Ellis must be going through. It was always going to be difficult for her to learn the truth, but to find out the way she did was awful.

And it was all Min's fault.

CHAPTER 9

*E*van sat in the small sitting room off the entrance hall at his mother's house and reread the note that had just been delivered for him. It was from Mrs. Dalton, whom he'd glimpsed at the ball last night and had thankfully avoided actually encountering. However, he might not be able to continue to do so as she was asking him to meet her around the corner. Now.

Seeing his mother walk into the entrance hall, Evan tucked the letter under his thigh. He hadn't told her that he'd glimpsed Mrs. Dalton last night. It was possible his mother had seen the woman and chosen not to say anything. In any case, Evan wasn't going to bring her up.

Pulling on her gloves, his mother stepped into the sitting room. "Is everything all right?" she asked.

"Quite," Evan assured her.

Her dark brows drew together. "You seem pensive. I'm sure you're tired of not being able to move around well. I know you would much rather be riding your horse or walking about Sydney Gardens."

"That is certainly true. Where are you off to?"

"To call on a friend over in Queen Square. Mrs. Beckwith, if you recall her." She smiled at him. "It is very nice having you here. You probably wish you were in London, but I'm enjoying our time together."

Actually, he was surprisingly content to be in Bath at the moment, and he credited that to Min's presence, as well as his mother. "I am as well, Mama. Have a nice visit with Mrs. Beckwith."

Once she'd left the house, Evan pulled the note from beneath his thigh. Dammit, he wanted this entire debacle to go away. But now Mrs. Dalton was here in Bath demanding he meet her around the corner as soon as possible.

Evan hoped his mother hadn't seen Mrs. Dalton on her way out. Though he didn't want to meet with the woman, he needed to ensure she stayed away from him or even demand she leave Bath. This was not the way to let a scandal die.

Scowling, Evan rose from the chair with the aid of his walking stick and fetched his hat and gloves from the entrance hall. Outside, he glanced around furtively, as if somebody would be waiting to catch him with the woman with whom he'd supposedly had an affair. He moved as quickly as he could, probably too quickly, for his ankle began to pain him before he even reached Mrs. Dalton.

She stood waiting at the corner of Church Street, her hands clasped. At least, he hoped it was her. He'd only met her one time, and all he remembered was that she was blonde. When relief flashed across the woman's features as he approached, Evan knew it was her.

He took a moment to survey her in the hope that he might recall her better, though he hoped they would never have occasion to meet again. In her midthirties, Mrs. Dalton was very attractive, with dark blonde hair and sparkling blue eyes. She possessed a curvaceous figure that was quite tempting, but Evan had engaged in precisely one affair with a married woman several years ago and had never wanted to repeat the experience. It was perhaps odd that his reputation was far worse than his actual behavior, but he didn't mind, for it kept him from being a primary mark on the Marriage Mart.

"Thank you for meeting me," Mrs. Dalton said anxiously. "I wasn't sure you would."

"I should not." Evan didn't temper his irritation. "I was shocked to see you at the Upper Rooms last night. Why on earth have you come to Bath?"

She blinked, her long lashes sweeping prettily as if it were a practiced effect. "I came to see you. I heard this is where you were spending the autumn with your mother."

"And you thought it would be a good idea for you to intrude on that?" Evan asked with a frown. "The whole point of my leaving London was to allow the fervor around our 'affair' to die down. Honestly, I can't imagine why you would seek me out at all. We have no history together—and no future."

She wrung her hands, and her face paled. "There has been a development, and it is quite terrible. I didn't know who else to turn to. You were so helpful before, going out of your way to save Roger. My husband is still furious about the affair and is considering a divorce."

Evan was glad to have a walking stick to lean on, because he felt as if the wind had been knocked out of him. A divorce would require her husband, Sir Abraham, to prove in court that she had been unfaithful. He would bring a suit against Evan, and there would be a trial for criminal conversation. It would completely ruin her—and Evan.

"You can't let that happen," Evan ground out as anger spiked through him. "I can't be dragged through something like that. I didn't even *do* anything." That wasn't precisely true. He'd taken the blame for something he hadn't done, and he was paying horribly for it.

She continued to worry her hands, her features creased with agitation. "I know. I'm so sorry things have come to this. Perhaps you should have let Roger suffer the consequences."

Evan saw no point in railing at her, or even at Roger. In this moment, he wanted to berate himself for stepping in and taking the blame for Roger's transgression.

But Evan had felt beholden to his friend. One night at Cambridge, Evan had drunk too much and fallen into the river. If he had not been with Roger, he likely would have drowned. However, Roger, who had been quite inebriated himself, had pulled Evan from the river and saved his life.

When presented with the opportunity to return Roger's favor, Evan had grasped it without thinking of the consequences to himself. It hadn't occurred to him that Sir Abraham would go to Evan's father and tell him everything. Evan had hoped the matter would die a quick and painless death.

The opposite had happened. Enduring his father's fury had been bad enough, but now things could become so much worse. Evan could not allow his parents to endure the shame of a criminal conversation trial.

Evan fixed his frustration on Mrs. Dalton. "You must persuade your husband not to do this. Do whatever it takes."

"I have tried," she said in a near whine. "He doesn't seem to care that this will harm me, and I think that's because he wants to. But it will also harm our children. Thankfully, they are not aware of anything at this juncture."

Evan turned his head and looked away from her, his mind churning. "You must simply try again." He returned his gaze to her. "Go back to London, or commit yourself to a convent or something."

She gaped at him. "You can't be serious."

"No, not really." He blew out a frustrated breath. "I don't know what to do. You must not ask to speak with me again, however. We cannot be seen together, and I would very much appreciate if you would leave Bath entirely. I am here to remove myself from the scandal that I'm not even a part of. Your being here only makes things worse. Please say you'll return to London immediately."

She nodded. "I will. But what if Abraham won't listen to me? What if he brings the suit?"

Evan would pray he would not. If he thought it would help, he'd write to the man himself, but he didn't dare. Evan's father had said the man was beyond livid. He'd wanted to challenge Evan to a duel, but Evan's father had convinced him not to, given their difference in age. Never mind that Evan's skill with a blade and a pistol were nearly unmatched.

He met Mrs. Dalton's deep blue gaze. "You must tell me if he's going to file suit. Do you promise?"

She nodded.

Evan was going to have to write to Roger and tell him what was happening. He didn't want to expose his friend to a criminal conversation trial, but there was a limit to what Evan would do for him. He felt badly thinking that after Roger had risked his life to save Evan's. They could very well have both drowned. Furthermore, it had been winter, and the water was frigid. That they'd found their way back to their dormitory without freezing to death or suffering grave illness was a minor miracle.

Evan would hope that Mrs. Dalton could sort things out with her husband. She simply had to. "Please send word with the progress that you've made," Evan said.

"I didn't want to put anything in writing," she replied with a worried look. "That's why I came here in person. I shouldn't be writing to you at all."

"Please don't become overly conscientious now." Evan pressed his lips together. "Just be cryptic, and I'll know what you're talking about, all right?"

She nodded once more. "Thank you for seeing me."

"But never again." Evan turned and stalked back toward Catharine Place. Unfortunately, he ran directly into Sheff after entering the narrow square.

"Afternoon, Evan. With whom were you just speaking?" Sheff asked, his dark blue gaze shifting to look down the street past Evan.

Evan turned his head and was glad to see that Mrs. Dalton was now gone. "Someone I met at the Upper Rooms last night," Evan lied.

"Were you just leaving an assignation?" Sheff asked with a waggle of his brows.

Bloody hell, the last thing he needed was Sheff thinking he'd been meeting Mrs. Dalton for a tryst. He realized Sheff didn't appear to know the woman, but that didn't mean he wouldn't recall her at some point. Evan realized he was worried about a coming disaster—and with good reason.

"Absolutely not," Evan said with perhaps a tad too much vehemence. "I was taking a walk and ran into her. We only exchanged a few words."

Sheff glanced down at Evan's foot. "How's the ankle?"

"Taking forever to entirely heal," Evan replied as he tried to tamp down his agitation. If Sheff detected it, he would hopefully attribute Evan's mood to his injury. Evan sought to divert the conversation from himself. "I'm glad to run into you. I haven't wanted to intrude on you and Jo."

Sheff nodded vaguely, his mouth turning in a slight frown. His brow was creased as if he were worried. Evan could suspect why, after what Min had revealed to him last night, but he didn't say anything, of course. Instead, he asked, "How is Jo?"

"She's quite well." Sheff's features relaxed as he smiled, his eyes taking on an almost lovesick quality.

Evan couldn't help chuckling. "I see marriage still very much agrees with you."

"It does indeed," Sheff replied. "It's the most astonishing thing. No one would ever have predicted I would be married, let alone so blissfully, and with impending fatherhood to boot."

"Yes, though I confess that latter part terrifies me somewhat."

"I'm sure Jo will know what she's doing. She always does." Sheff fixed him with an intent stare. "Do yourself a favor, man, and marry the smartest woman you can find, especially if she makes you feel things you never thought possible."

Evan couldn't help thinking of Min. He missed seeing her on a daily basis. It was shocking how quickly she'd become a regular part of his life, and how much he'd come to depend on her, not for the things she did to help him, but because of her humor and her charm and, yes, her intelligence.

"How is your sister?" Evan asked, hoping he sounded nonchalant.

"She's well enough." The worry had returned to Sheff's features. He was likely concerned about Min and Ellis, which Evan understood and shared. "I heard you and Min spent quite a bit of time together at Longleat, after you injured your ankle."

"Yes, I was fortunate to have her assistance. Though I daresay it was mostly so she could avoid Lady Bath's matchmaking with the other rogues at the party," Evan added with a laugh.

"The 'other' rogues." Sheff arched a brow. "That means you describe yourself as a rogue too."

"Shouldn't I?" Evan asked. "I realize I can't hold a candle

to your roguery before you were wed, but I believe my reputation is that of a flirtatious gentleman."

"From what I hear, you've gone a bit beyond that," Sheff noted with a hint of curiosity.

Evan kept himself from flinching. Did Sheff know about Evan's purported affair with Mrs. Dalton? "What have you heard?"

Sheff lifted a shoulder. "Just a rumor about you and some married woman."

"Well, don't believe everything you hear," Evan said as his earlier frustration roiled once more.

Sheff nodded. "I know how rumors can escalate. Is that why you aren't in London? I confess I did wonder why you've been away so long, but I suppose that's also due to your injury."

"Indeed." That was all Evan cared to reply.

Thankfully, Sheff didn't press. "I do appreciate you letting Min take care of you in order to escape the marchioness's matchmaking. I'm sure Min was grateful. You may have roguish tendencies, but I trust you with my sister."

"Why is that?" Evan asked, trying not to think about how he'd kissed Sheff's sister and that Sheff should not remotely trust him because of it.

"I've known you awhile now, and I don't think that's a line you would cross. Besides, my sister doesn't tolerate that kind of behavior. If she felt safe enough with you to spend time at Longleat caring for you, then who am I to think otherwise? It's good that you're her friend. She needs friends, as life is going to change for her very quickly." Sheff shook his head. "Forgive me for being cryptic. I cannot elaborate."

"It's all right," Evan said, because he knew exactly what Sheff was talking about.

Sheff's gaze moved toward his father's house, which was

situated just a few down from Evan's mother's. "You'll have to excuse me," Sheff said quickly before taking himself off.

Evan looked after him and saw a young woman arriving at the duke's residence. It was Ellis, and she was alone.

What was going on? Were they about to tell Ellis about her parentage? If so, where was Min? Evan couldn't help but worry about her—about all of them—and hoped all would be well.

~

*E*llis was gone.

Not long after she'd retreated to her room yesterday, she'd gone to Min's father's house. Sometime after that, her father's footman had come to deliver a note from Ellis to Min and to collect some of Ellis's things. The note had only said that Ellis was leaving Bath and did not want any company. She apologized for not wanting to see or talk to Min, and hoped she would understand. She'd written that she needed to be alone.

Min had packed up many of Ellis's things and sent them with the footman, along with a note of her own. She'd written that Ellis must take as much time as she needed, and that Min would be there whenever Ellis was ready.

Hopefully, that day wouldn't be too far off, but Min was afraid it might be. There was so much for Ellis to comprehend. Her entire life was not what she thought it was. Min felt much the same, but it was so much worse for Ellis.

And now Min was alone here with her mother. Along with the household retainers, whom she barely knew. Min didn't want to see the duchess, so she hadn't gone downstairs to dinner last night or for breakfast today.

She was tired of being trapped, however, so she put on a walking dress, grabbed her gloves and bonnet, and went downstairs. As she walked into the entrance hall, the butler, Warner, informed her that a delivery had just arrived.

"It's a package from Cardiff," Warner said, gesturing toward the wrapped box on the table.

Min knew precisely what they were and would deliver them as soon as she could—tomorrow, perhaps. Now, she was on her way to the Crescent to call on Pandora. "Would you take those to my sitting room, please?" she asked the butler with a smile.

Warner, a mild-mannered man in his forties, nodded. "Of course, Lady Minerva. And may I say how good it is to see you downstairs? We feared you may be ill."

"'We'?" Min had to assume he meant himself and other members of the household. "I am fine, thank you. I do appreciate your concern. Is my mother here?" She didn't really care, but she thought it best to at least know where she was.

"Yes. She's been keeping to her chamber as well."

Min hoped she stayed there for a good, long while. "I'm taking a walk to the Crescent to call on a friend."

Warner inclined his head. "We'll see you soon, my lady."

Min stepped out into the gray October day. It wasn't cold, but it wasn't warm either. She set a brisk pace on her way to the Crescent, and the walk took less than ten minutes.

At Pandora's aunt's house, Min knocked on the door. The butler answered.

"Good afternoon, Lady Minerva," he said with a smile. "How pleasant to see you."

"Good afternoon, Harding. It's nice to see you too. Is Pandora at home?"

"Yes, do come in." The butler welcomed her inside and closed the door. He took her hat and gloves, then showed her upstairs to the drawing room.

Pandora was seated with her Aunt Lucinda at a table near the windows. As Min entered, Pandora's eyes lit, and she stood, smiling. "Min, I'm so pleased to see you." She strode to meet Min, and they embraced.

"I'm sorry I haven't visited before now," Min said when they separated. "My mother has kept me busy preparing for the Season."

"Your one last chance on the Marriage Mart," Pandora said with a sardonic glint in her eye. It was a shame that she had never had the opportunity to join the husband hunt. With her shining blonde hair and stunning blue-green eyes, she was a true diamond of the first water.

Lucinda rose from the table. Though she was forty, she appeared younger to Min. Her light brown hair didn't show even a hint of gray. "It's lovely to see you, Minerva. I hope you are well."

"Well enough, thank you."

"I will leave you two to catch up." Lucinda looked to Min. "Please give my best to your mother."

Min wanted to say she would not, but she didn't want to explain why—not to Lucinda. She had every intention of telling Pandora everything. It was only right that the other members of the Rogue Rules Club should know. Except, what if Ellis didn't want them to?

Min worried for a moment that she shouldn't say anything, and yet, how else would she explain why Ellis had left?

After Lucinda departed, Pandora moved to a settee and patted the space next to her. "Come, tell me how the first ball went."

Min sat down beside her. "It was fine," she replied somewhat absentmindedly, as her thoughts kept drifting to Ellis.

"That doesn't sound encouraging." Pandora frowned. "Is it that you don't really want to be on the Marriage Mart?"

"I don't know what I want anymore," Min blurted. "Everything is a complete disaster." She was glad there were no tears stinging her eyes. She'd cried so much yesterday. It was no wonder she didn't have any left.

Even so, Pandora could see how upset she was. She took Min's hand. "What's wrong?"

Min told her all about their spectacular family secret and finished with how Ellis had left Bath.

Pandora listened with incredulity. "And you don't know where Ellis is now?"

Min shook her head. "Only my father does, and he won't say because Ellis forbade him. She doesn't want to see or talk to any of us, including her true father."

"Jo's father, you mean?" Pandora asked.

"Yes, but he doesn't know the truth, and we've decided not to tell him until Ellis determines what she wants to do."

Pandora looked at her with sympathy. "What an absolute mess. I'm so sorry for Ellis. I wish I could write to her."

"You can. Give me the letter, and I'll take it to my father to post to her. Or you can have it delivered directly to his house in Catharine Place."

"Do you think she will mind that I know the secret?" Pandora asked.

"I considered that earlier, but I felt I needed to tell you. How else was I to explain why Ellis was gone and why I'm so upset? Even if I'd wanted to hide that from you today, I don't think I would have been able." Min lifted a shoulder. "I suppose I didn't need to call on you, but I wanted to—even if this weren't happening."

"Of course you would. I'm not surprised you aren't interested in the Marriage Mart," Pandora said. "I can't imagine you're in the mood for courtship."

No, she was not. Still, Min couldn't help thinking of Evan and the kiss they'd shared. While that wasn't courtship, Min had to admit she wouldn't mind kissing him again. Instead, she was worried she'd never kiss anyone again. Ever. "I feel alone," she whispered.

"You are not alone." Pandora drew her into her arms, and they embraced for a long moment. "But I know precisely how you feel."

Of course she did. Pandora had felt isolated after she and Bane had been caught together. She hadn't been alone either, but now Min understood.

"Thank you. You are such a dear friend." Min sniffed as they parted. "I don't really want to stay at my mother's house any longer, but neither can I go to my father's. His mistress is with him."

"Yes, Aunt Lucinda had heard that. You could stay here," Pandora invited. "You are always welcome. Although I'm not sure if it would benefit you to take up residence with a pariah like me, particularly if you *are* trying to find a husband."

"You aren't a pariah," Min said firmly. "Your aunt is well-liked and respected here in Bath, and that has helped you over the past couple of years. Hasn't it?"

Min hated to think that Pandora might still be suffering from people treating her poorly. Some had given her the cut direct after Bane had abandoned her, and Pandora had become somewhat of a recluse. She still was. She certainly didn't have a subscription to the Upper Rooms.

"Isn't your brother in town?" Pandora asked. "Could you stay with him and Jo?"

Min had thought of that too. "I'm not sure I want to intrude on them, since they are recently wed. However, that may be my best option, or perhaps I should just go to Beacon Park. I'm not sure there's any point in my staying in Bath."

"Well, besides spending time with me," Pandora said, with a bright smile that made Min laugh softly. "I suppose your mother bought a subscription to the Upper Rooms, not that you need to use it."

"She did. You are correct in that I am not in the mood for courtship, but that won't matter to her. She is determined to see me wed this autumn. Indeed, she's become almost desperate. She wants me to consider Spilsby." She explained Eberforce's new name, and since Pandora knew about Gwen's encounter with him at Almack's, she found it as amusing as Min did.

"You've successfully avoided your mother's machinations in the past," Pandora said. "You will again."

Min slid her a cautious look. "She suggested someone even more outrageous than Spilsby."

"Who is more outrageous than him?" Pandora asked with a chuckle.

Min grimaced. "Bane. My mother thinks he'll be looking for a new wife soon."

Pandora made a sound of disgust in her throat. "I can only imagine how offended you were."

"Quite," Min replied. "And I told her so."

"I do hope Bane would never have the audacity to come to Bath," Pandora said with disdain, "He knows I live here."

Min was surprised to hear that. "How does he know where you live?" Bane had spent the last couple of years in northern England.

"Because he sent me a letter a few weeks ago. I don't know how he knew where I live, but I suspect one of his friends told him, perhaps your brother."

Min gasped. "That is possible. Sheff did visit him several months ago. What did the letter say?"

Pandora shrugged. "I have no idea, because I burned it. Why would I want to read anything he has to say? I don't wish him ill, especially after what he's been through, losing his wife and child, but I've moved on. I don't need to accept his intrusion into my life."

"No, you don't," Min agreed. "You *have* moved on." She hesitated before asking, "Are you ever afraid of being alone?"

"I was at first, but not anymore." Pandora spoke confidently, and Min didn't doubt her. "It helps that I have lived with my aunt these past two years. As a relatively young widow, she has demonstrated how pleasant it is to be independent."

Min could see how that would be appealing. Though, Lucinda's status as a widow was not the same as Pandora's position as a ruined spinster.

"You know I've been writing," Pandora said almost shyly. Min nodded, and Pandora continued. "I've sent a manuscript to a publisher in London, but you mustn't tell anyone. It's a secret. Not even my aunt knows."

Min grimaced. "I'm surprised you would trust me to keep a secret after I told you all about Ellis."

Pandora waved her hand. "There are no secrets among us and our friends. I meant, don't tell anybody outside our group."

"The Rogue Rules Club, you mean?"

"You named us?" Pandora asked, surprised.

"Not me," Min replied. "We have a new member, Miss Iona Shaughnessy. She named the club after Ellis and I told her about it. We met her at Longleat last month before we came to Bath. I invited her to come to Weston with us next August."

"Will we still be going to Weston?" Pandora mused. "What if you're married by then?"

"I've been wondering that for the last several years," Min said wryly. "Yet I remain unwed. Perhaps what we really need is a Spinster Club with you, me, and Ellis. That is, if Ellis stays a spinster. My father has offered to provide her with a dowry if she would like to wed."

"That's very generous of him," Pandora said. "I don't know your father beyond what you have said about him, but I am surprised to hear how supportive he's being with Ellis and this entire situation."

"Well, he did bring her into our household after her adoptive parents died. I think he feels a responsibility to care for her because my mother did not. *Does* not," Min amended with a touch of scorn.

"Precisely," Pandora smiled softly. "I have only ever known of the duke behaving like the worst sort of rogue. But his behavior with Ellis seems different."

"It is somewhat," Min replied with a nod. "He's quite changed in the past few months. He seems to have found love with his new mistress. I hope it lasts."

"So, your own father may have redeemed himself," Pandora noted with a laugh. "And our rules say we can never trust a rogue to change."

Min made a sardonic face. "Given the success of our friends marrying rogues and finding unparalleled happiness, I have begun to wonder if our rules were made to be broken."

Pandora's brow darkened. "Only by the right gentleman. I don't think there are that many of them."

"Unfortunately, I think you're right. That is why I have remained unwed." Min couldn't help thinking of Evan. He was not as bad a rogue as others. Indeed, he seemed redeemable.

"In spite of your mother's desperate efforts," Pandora noted. "How was the party at Longleat?"

"Every single bachelor in attendance was a rogue or nearly one," Min scoffed. "I suppose Mr. Jarvis was the least roguish of the lot. Evan Price was there. He performed one of his tricks on horseback—well, several of them, actually—and fell off the horse."

Pandora's eyes widened. "Is he all right?"

"He sustained a concussion and a badly sprained ankle, but he's here in Bath, hobbling about with a walking stick that makes him look far more dashing than he has a right to be."

"That sounds about right," Pandora said with a chuckle. "I don't know Evan terribly well—just from social interactions in Weston—but he strikes me as someone who doesn't need any help being attractive or popular. Persey has mentioned him a few times in her letters. He seems to be well-liked in London."

Persey was Pandora's older sister Persephone, the Duchess of Wellesbourne, and one of Min's dearest friends. They'd met years ago in Weston, and the Rogue Rules Club only existed because they'd become friends.

Min briefly considered whether she should tell Pandora about kissing Evan but, in the end, decided that she really ought to try to put it behind her. Continuing to think and talk about it would not allow Min to do so.

"Do you know why Evan is here in Bath?" Pandora asked.

"I believe he's just visiting with his mother. She takes a house here in the autumn."

Pandora's brow pleated. "I thought that was to help Gwen find a husband." Gwen was not the most polished of young ladies, and her mother had thought it best for her to attend the Marriage Mart in Bath instead of London. However, after a second autumn in Bath without any marital success, Gwen had convinced her to try a London Season last spring. "And now Gwen is married."

"I think she may be trying to marry Evan off," Min said. "Though, he's said he's not ready for marriage."

"You've discussed that with him?"

Min lifted a shoulder. "I spent a good deal of time with him at Longleat after he was injured. He needed someone to entertain him, and I preferred to stay clear of the rogues as well as Lady Bath's attempts at matchmaking."

Pandora's eyes glinted with humor. "Brilliant. Too bad he doesn't need your assistance now so you could use that as an excuse to avoid your mother's matchmaking."

How wonderful that sounded, and not just as an excuse. Min would much rather be back at Longleat with Evan than here with everything that was happening. "What I really want is to find Ellis and make sure she's all right. But I know she needs time to adjust. We all do, but her most of all. I just wish we could have done it together."

Pandora looked at her with sympathy. "You asked me if I was afraid of being alone. Are you?"

"I think I wasn't before, but I've always had Ellis. And now she's gone…" Min acknowledged the hollow ache that had lodged in her chest since the day before. "Yes, I think I am." Without her, Min felt adrift. Her mother's house was no longer "home."

Pandora took Min's hand again and gave her a squeeze.

Min summoned a smile and pushed her doldrums away. "Will you tell me about this manuscript you wrote?"

"I would be delighted," Pandora replied with a grin.

Min was grateful for the distraction. Because as soon as she went back to her mother's, she would truly be alone.

CHAPTER 10

*A*nother day gone by, and Evan's ankle still pained him from time to time. He didn't need to use his walking stick consistently, but by the end of the day, he was sore and found it was helpful. He'd overdone it yesterday walking too much, so instead of attending church with his mother, he sat in the small study on the ground floor of his mother's house with his foot propped on a stool with a pillow.

He was perusing a newspaper from London when there was a rap on the door, which stood ajar. "Come," he called.

Pushing the door open, the butler stepped just over the threshold. "You've a caller." The butler appeared slightly uncomfortable.

"Is there something amiss?" Evan asked.

The butler grimaced faintly. "It is a young lady by herself —Lady Minerva Halifax."

"Ah, she is a friend of mine. In fact, she is a very good friend of my sister's, and her brother is a close friend to me. We are all friends. It's not unusual at all that she would call. Indeed, she also knows my mother." It occurred to Evan that he was perhaps explaining too much. "Show her in, please."

Evan rose. Despite saying otherwise, he was surprised Min would call on him. It *was* unusual for a young lady to call on a gentleman. "Unusual" was perhaps an understatement. It was unheard of in London, but this was Bath, and Min was going through a rough time.

She appeared in the doorway looking bright and lovely in an apricot-colored gown trimmed with ivory. Her bonnet, which was the opposite, was most fetching. The dark sable of her hair against the ivory was a stunning contrast.

"I know I shouldn't be calling on you," Min said. "However, I have something for you and wanted to deliver it personally."

He realized she was carrying a package. "What is this?"

She went to a small table separate from the seating area where he'd risen and set the package atop the wood.

Evan joined her there. "What is it?"

"Open it and find out," she said with a smile.

He rubbed his hands in anticipation. "This is most exciting." He untied the string and pulled apart the wrapping paper. "Oh," he breathed, recognizing the wooden box immediately. He turned his head to Min, his jaw dropping. "You didn't—"

She gave him a little shrug and smiled with mock innocence.

He opened the box and sucked in his breath at a gorgeous pair of riding boots from his favorite boot maker. "They're beautiful. Exactly like the ones that were ruined by the bonesetter."

"I thought so too," Min said. "That is what I asked for when I wrote to Mr. Davis in Cardiff."

"I can hardly believe you did this," Evan said. "I'm speechless."

He stared at the boots, eager to put them on, but he didn't dare while his ankle was not yet entirely healed. "How I wish I could ride. Is it pathetic that I miss my horse and the exhilaration of the tricks we accomplished together?" He looked toward Min and saw a warm sympathy in her expression.

"Not at all," she replied softly. "I know how much you want to return to your normal life."

That was precisely it. "Alas, I am not yet ready to return to the saddle. The last thing I want is to risk having my boots cut off again." He grimaced, then smiled at her. "This was very thoughtful of you, Min."

"It was the least I could do after what happened at Longleat. You were only trying to entertain people, and look at how you've suffered for it."

"It could have been much worse," he said. "You could have not been at Longleat."

She blushed faintly and looked away. "I wish we were still there."

Was that because of Ellis's situation, or did Min want to recapture the time they'd spent together that had culminated in the best kiss he'd ever experienced? "I've been wondering how you are," Evan said. "I saw Sheff the other day. We were together as Ellis arrived at your father's house. How did she take the news?"

"Quite poorly." Min appeared anguished. "And that is entirely my fault. She overheard me yelling at my mother about what she'd done and how she's behaved toward Ellis all these years. It was the worst way Ellis could have learned the truth."

Evan moved closer to Min but stopped short of taking her hand. "That had to have been awful for her—and for you."

"I don't think she blames me exactly, but she didn't want to talk to me or even see me." Min's eyes were dark, her brow creased with sadness. "She left shortly thereafter, which must have been when you saw her going to my father's. She decided to leave Bath, but I don't know where she's gone. Only my father knows."

"So you're alone with your mother. How is that?" He imagined it wasn't good at all.

Min shuddered. "We're avoiding one another. I don't think either of us is eating in the dining room. I'm certainly not. I've remained in my bedchamber for the most part, except for yesterday when I called on Pandora. That was a nice respite. Though, I can't avoid my mother forever."

"There's a ball tomorrow night," Evan noted. "Will you be going?"

"I don't want to, at least not with her." Min lifted her hand briefly. "I don't see the point anyway. I'm in no mood to dance or laugh gaily or see if I will suit with anyone. The only gentleman I danced with last time who isn't inarguably a rogue was Mr. Jarvis, and well, he doesn't meet my requirements."

"What are your requirements, exactly?" Evan asked, but then he held up his hand. "You don't have to tell me."

"I know I don't, but I will. I think you know I have no desire to wed a rogue."

Evan nodded. "In fact, I understand that you and your friends have rules against rogues."

"We do. However, those rules, apparently, can be broken for the right gentleman." She gave him a wry glance. "Just ask your sister."

"I don't have to," he said. "I didn't care for Somerton showing interest in her, so I can understand your reservations about anyone who displays even a hint of roguishness."

"That includes you," she said pointedly

He grinned but quickly sobered. "I know, but I have

begun to wonder if it isn't time to shed that reputation. I don't think it serves me well."

Surprise flashed in her pale gray gaze. "Does that mean you're ready to wed?"

"Let's not get carried away," he said with a laugh. "We are discussing your requirements for a husband. What else is there beyond not being a rogue?"

She bit the inside of her lip, which prompted Evan to stare at her mouth. And staring at her mouth made him remember their kiss. Recalling their kiss made him want to kiss her again. Thinking of kissing her again ignited his entire body and stirred a pointed response below his waistband. At least this time, he was not wearing a banyan and stood a better chance of her not noticing.

"I don't think I was sure of my other requirements until recently," she said slowly. "I have always wanted love, but I feared that wouldn't be possible. When your parents loathe one another, it's difficult to trust that you can have a marriage with mutual affection, let alone a deep and abiding love. But I do see that it's possible. Persey has that with Wellesbourne. Your sister has that with Somerton. Tamsin has that with Droxford. And now Sheff, unbelievably, has that with Jo. But can lightning really strike more than four times?" she asked with a laugh.

Evan chuckled with her. "That does seem unlikely. There is nothing wrong with wanting love, Min, and there's nothing wrong with holding out for that."

"Thank you for saying so." She pivoted away from him, no longer looking at him as she spoke. "I thought perhaps I could at least settle for passion, if not love. However, I wasn't sure I was capable of passion until you kissed me at Longleat." She darted a nervous glance at him. Her gaze met his just long enough for him to detect a sultry gleam. "Now I fear I will never feel that again. I'm not sure I can accept anything less."

Evan swallowed. She hadn't been sure she could feel passion until they'd kissed? He couldn't think of a more arousing thing someone could say. His cock was now completely hard, and he had to work very hard not to pull her into his arms and make her feel that way again.

"I suppose you'll have to kiss every suitor, then," he said, trying to maintain some lightness, lest he fall headfirst into a dark cavern of desire.

"You know I can't do that," she replied with some exasperation.

"Why not?" he challenged her. "And don't tell me that I'm trying to convert you into a rogue. That's not at all what I'm doing, and you know it. I'm trying to help you find what you want—what you deserve."

She looked back at him, and their eyes locked. "Or you could just kiss me again."

Evan took a steadying breath. "Do you mean that? Because while I would like to reform my reputation, I'm afraid I will not be able to refuse if you ask. And if that makes me an irredeemable rogue, so be it."

Her nostrils flared slightly, and she glanced at the open door. "Is your mother here?"

"No, she's at church." He swallowed, his body thrumming with arousal. "Do you want me to close the door, Min?"

"Yes."

Evan was at the door in two strides, his ankle be damned.

After closing the door, he turned. She stood next to the table by the glorious boots she'd brought him. Her features were serene, but her eyes were dark and chaotic with a myriad of emotions he could not fully define, except one: desire.

He wanted to go slow, to savor the moment. He crossed the room back to her and slid his arm around her waist, pulling her against him. Their eyes connected for the barest moment before he lowered his mouth to hers. He cupped her face with his other hand as he claimed her lips in a searing kiss.

She clasped his shoulder as she leaned into him. Her other hand slipped beneath his coat and pressed against his lower back.

Evan should not allow this, not if he truly wanted to change his behavior and his reputation. But he was powerless to resist Min—a woman he shouldn't even be tempted by. Never mind she was his friend's sister, she was also the daughter of a duke. He had absolutely no hope of a future with her.

Why not?

The voice at the back of his mind was soft but insistent.

Her brother married someone who should have had no chance of wedding the heir to a dukedom.

The voice made a good point.

Evan quieted his mind and poured himself into kissing Min. She tasted like honey biscuits and smelled of violets. He still didn't know what violets bloody smelled like, but he knew Min's scent, and he reveled in it.

She felt divine in his arms, as if she were made to fit perfectly against him. He longed to strip away the clothing between them, to feel the satin of her skin against his own.

Their tongues danced with a rising heat. Evan moved his hand to her nape, holding her tightly as he explored her tantalizing mouth. Her fingers dug into his shoulder as a soft moan drifted from her throat.

Evan kissed along her jaw as her fingers trailed up his neck and she twined them in his hair at his nape. He gently pulled her head back to better expose her neck to his kisses.

She wore a spencer that reached the base of her throat.

He brought his hand up to unfasten the top just as he heard the front door close.

His mother had returned.

Abruptly, he released Min and stepped back. "I believe my mother is home," he said hoarsely.

Min's cheeks were flushed, her lips parted as she breathed quickly. It wasn't quite a pant, but it was close, and the sound was driving Evan to distraction. He needed to rein himself under control before facing his mother.

"I can't see her like this." Min's eyes were wide as she pressed her gloved hands to her flushed cheeks.

"Take deep breaths. I'll tell her you were on your way out and you are in a hurry."

Min nodded. "My apologies for putting us in this position."

"Your apology is declined," he said before he followed his own advice and took a deep breath. "With my utmost respect," he added with a grin.

A smile teased her mouth, but only briefly. "I must go."

Sadly, she must. Evan didn't want to think of what might have happened if his mother hadn't arrived. And yet, he couldn't banish the images from his mind. He saw Min laid out atop the table. He would push the boots aside—or onto the floor for all he cared—and lift her skirts. He would use his hands and mouth to push her to the brink of the passion she so craved. Then he would topple her over the edge until she cried out his name.

And alerted the household.

Perhaps it was best that his mother had arrived.

He moved quickly to open the door. "After you."

She moved past him, and he once again caught her scent. He closed his eyes the barest moment and lost himself in it.

Inwardly cursing at himself to stop being distracted by the very behavior he was trying to change, he followed Min to the entrance hall where his mother was just handing her hat and gloves to Alton, the butler.

"Good afternoon, Lady Minerva," his mother said, her gaze curious. "Alton said you were here."

"Yes, she brought me the boots I asked her to order from my boot maker in Cardiff." He didn't think his mother should know that Min had bought them as a gift. "She wasn't sure of your address here when she wrote to Mr. Davis, so she had them sent to her mother's house."

"That was kind of her," Evan's mother said, sending Min a smile. "Thank you, dear. I'm sure you now realize this is the same house I've had—with Gwen—the past few years."

"Yes," Min replied. What else could she say?

Evan moved to open the front door. "You need to excuse Lady Minerva, as she only dropped the boots off on her way to somewhere else."

"Indeed." Min inclined her head toward Evan's mother. "Always lovely to see you, Mrs. Price."

"And you, Lady Minerva." His mother watched Min depart.

Evan closed the door behind Min, but his hopes to avoid his mother's scrutiny were dashed. She arched a brow at him, and the butler disappeared.

"You must know it's inappropriate for Lady Minerva to call on you," she said.

"Yes, but you live here too. She could just as easily be calling on *you*." He shrugged.

His mother pursed her lips. "You must be careful, Evan. You are already involved in a scandal in London."

Evan gritted his teeth. "It will soon be forgotten." He hoped. He'd written to Roger as soon as he'd arrived home after seeing Mrs. Dalton and then Sheff. He expected Roger's reply in the next few days, as well as word from Mrs. Dalton regarding her efforts to stop her husband from ruining everyone's lives.

"I hope so." His mother didn't sound convinced. She studied him intently. "Is there anything between you and Lady Minerva? You spent a great deal of time together at Longleat and now this. It is curious."

"We're merely friends, Mama. Rather, she is close with Gwen, and her brother is a good friend to me. It is natural that we are friends too, but in the way of brothers and sisters." That blasted description of Min's—*sister-friend*—rose in his mind.

"I suppose that makes sense. She is a lovely young woman," his mother noted. She gave him a small smile. "I would not be opposed to you marrying her."

"I hope you aren't saying that because her father is a duke."

"It doesn't hurt," she replied. "But as I said, she's lovely. Honestly, I would be delighted if you showed interest in marrying *anyone*. I'm going upstairs to the drawing room for tea if you'd care to join me."

"Perhaps in a while." Evan preferred to return to the study where he could look at the boots Min had given him and recall the feel of her lips against his.

As he walked back to the study, he thought of what his mother had asked. He'd lied because there was definitely *something* between him and Min. But what exactly?

She'd said she would wed for passion, and they clearly had that. Would he do the same? He realized he hadn't given extensive thought to what he wanted in a wife or marriage. He'd simply delayed thinking about it.

However, it was now at the forefront of his mind. As was what Min had said about her requirements for marriage. Beyond passion, she didn't want to marry a rogue. Evan could work on not being one. Indeed, he'd already decided he wanted to change his reputation. However, that was going to be very difficult if Sir Abraham filed a suit against him for criminal conversation.

The last thing Min needed was to be associated with another scandal. Evan had truly put himself in a terrible position by trying to protect Roger. Even if he wanted to court Min, he could not. Not until the matter with Mrs. Dalton was settled.

But it was likely moot. Min saw him as a rogue—she'd just said so. And Min would never marry a rogue.

CHAPTER 11

*A*fter delivering Evan's boots yesterday, Min had returned to her mother's and decided she could no longer stay in her household. She and her maid had packed a portion of her wardrobe and all her personal items and gone to Sheff and Jo's house. Min had left a note for her mother.

While Min felt slightly better being at her brother's house, she was still unsettled, mostly because of Ellis, wherever she was. Kissing Evan again hadn't helped matters.

Now that she realized passion could be hers, she wanted more of it. But yesterday had been a near thing with his mother coming home. Min had been mortified.

She shouldn't have called on him in the first place and wondered if his mother had said anything to him. Mrs. Price hadn't seemed to be judging Min, but it was hard to know for certain. Still, Min had known better and had chosen to ignore propriety. The excuse that they were "friends" would not matter.

Min shook herself from thoughts of Evan and whether she'd provoked his mother to think poorly of her. Sheff and Jo would be waiting for her as they were due to leave for the ball at the Upper Rooms. She descended the staircase and met them in the entrance hall.

"You look splendid, Jo," Min said, assessing Jo's vibrant blue gown.

"Thank you. It is the only evening gown I have that fits without making my current state terribly obvious." Jo passed her hand over her rounded belly.

"We could visit the modiste I saw last week," Min offered. She'd accompanied Jo to a dressmaker before—when Jo and Sheff had been engaged in a fake betrothal last spring.

"Brilliant idea, Min." Sheff gave his wife a pointed look. "Please don't argue. I know you don't like to spend an exorbitant amount of money on your wardrobe; however, even you must agree that it's necessary at this point. And for the next few months."

Jo blew out a breath. "You're right." She sent Min a smile. "I would be delighted if you would accompany me to the modiste. It is not my favorite thing to do, and you are much better at selecting items."

"Shall we go?" Sheff nodded at the butler, who opened the door for them to depart.

When they were situated in the coach, Sheff addressed them both. "What is our plan for dealing with the Viper this evening? We will surely run into her."

Min arched a brow. "You're still calling her that?"

Sheff had decided to assign that nickname to their mother the day before. He lifted a shoulder. "Why not? It fits."

"Can't we just give her the cut direct?" Min asked.

"I suppose we could, though, can you do that to your own mother?" Sheff smirked. "There's only one way to know for sure."

Jo pursed her lips. "You can't do that. She's your mother,

and there is likely already gossip about Min leaving her household. You must be cordial, at least."

"Perhaps she won't be there," Min mused, though she doubted that would be the case. Her mother was a master at acting as if nothing were wrong, and would certainly continue to do so, even if the building around her was on fire.

"We will simply try to avoid her," Sheff said.

As the coach neared the Upper Rooms, he frowned as he looked out the window. "There appears to be a bit of a jam. We were running late anyway, but I think you can count on missing the first set and perhaps even the second. Or the start of it anyway." He sent Min an apologetic look. "Sorry, Min."

"No need to apologize," Min replied. "I don't care if I miss all the sets."

Sheff cocked his head. "If you don't wish to dance, and we don't want to see our mother, why are we going?"

"Because we should," Jo responded with exasperation. "Why is it I know more about what's expected than you two? These are your people, not mine."

"They're your people now," Sheff said with a laugh.

"Well, we are dressed and ready and nearly there, so we may as well go," Min said. "But I do think perhaps this will be my last ball for the Season. I see no point in attending them, even though the duchess has bought a subscription for me. I shall spend my time in Bath enjoying your company and visiting with Pandora."

"Oh, I would like to see her," Jo said eagerly.

Min smiled. "You must, for she has your embroidered rogue rules. Perhaps we can call on her tomorrow."

As expected, they arrived in the ballroom in the middle of the first set. Min surveyed the large rectangular room lit with several gorgeous crystal chandeliers.

"She's over there," Sheff said, inclining his head toward the other side of the ballroom.

There was no need for either of them to clarify who "she" was.

Min glanced in that direction and saw the duchess, but quickly looked away before they could make eye contact. Instead, she settled her gaze on a group of young women gathered together. "I wonder what's going on over there."

They gravitated in that direction.

"It's Evan," Sheff said with a chuckle.

Jo arched a brow. "I didn't realize he wanted to inherit your rogue crown."

"I'm not sure he does." Sheff shrugged. "However, his ankle sprain has garnered a great deal of sympathy and interest. I suppose it's rather dashing to have sustained an injury while performing a dangerous feat."

Min snorted. "It wasn't as if he saved an animal or did something heroic." She realized she sounded almost caustic. And why?

Because she didn't like looking at him surrounded by a gaggle of young ladies.

The set ended, and the women around Evan began to disperse. Spilsby approached Min with a smile, though his face appeared pinched. Min hadn't been enthused to dance with him the other night, and she had no intention of dancing with him again, especially since her mother was trying to coordinate a match between them.

"Good evening, Lady Minerva," Spilsby said. He wore a perfectly ghastly waistcoat—a bright pea green with overwrought gold embroidery. "I had not expected to see you this evening." He inclined his head toward Sheff. "Shefford."

"Spilsby, is it?" Sheff asked with a quirk of his brow. "I suppose I must congratulate you on your inheritance, but I shan't."

Min bit back a smile and slid a look at Jo, who was doing the same.

Spilsby blinked, then his eyes darkened with outrage. He turned his attention to Jo. "Good evening, Lady Shefford. I'm pleased to make your acquaintance."

"Good evening, Lord Spilsby." Jo glanced toward Sheff, who appeared as though he were trying not to scowl at the new viscount.

Spilsby shifted his small-eyed gaze to Min. "You must save me a dance later, Lady Minerva."

"Unfortunately, I shan't be dancing this evening," Min replied, wishing she could "accidentally" spill punch on his hideous waistcoat. "But I do thank you."

"Ah, I assumed you were feeling better since you are here, but perhaps not." Spilsby had mentioned his surprise at seeing Min here and now this. What the devil was he talking about?

"I'm feeling fine, thank you," Min said with a hint of annoyance. "Why did you think otherwise?"

Spilsby blinked at her. "I had heard you were ill. The duchess said that was why you were not attending this evening, but here you are."

"What did the duchess tell you?" Sheff asked, his eyes narrowing slightly.

"She said Lady Minerva was ill, and that she had removed herself to your house to keep the duchess from coming down with it." Spilsby smiled at Min once more. "However, I can see you are quite well." He swept his gaze over her as if to punctuate his assessment.

Min did not care for his perusal. "I am. Though not well enough to dance." She would seize on her mother's explanation.

"Next time, then," Spilsby said with a confidence he ought not to have. "You must excuse me as I have a partner for this set." He sauntered off.

"I can't believe our mother wants you to consider him," Sheff muttered, wrinkling his nose.

"I've clearly told her I will not," Min said.

Evan approached them. "Good evening, Sheff, Lady Shefford, Lady Minerva."

"Must you call me Lady Shefford?" Jo asked.

"Here in the Upper Rooms, it's expected," Evan said with a flourish of his gloved hand.

Min tried not to think of it cupping her head as he kissed her. And failed.

"So pompous," Jo murmured as she fanned herself vigorously. "It's very warm in here."

"It was surprisingly warm today," Evan remarked. "I even went for a walk in Sydney Gardens this afternoon. I confess I was hoping I might run into you there." He didn't address anyone in particular, but his gaze met Min's, and she felt certain he was speaking to her.

She, however, could not shake the feeling of irritation that she'd had upon seeing him surrounded by all the young ladies. What was wrong with her? Was it jealousy? She'd never been jealous of anyone, certainly not of a gentleman's attention.

Jo looked to Sheff. "Would you mind taking me outside for a few minutes? I am too overheated."

"Of course not." Sheff's brows drew together with concern. "Min, do you want to come with us?"

"She can stay here with me," Evan offered.

Min sent him a dubious look. What did he have planned? Was he going to steal her away into a shadowed corner again? It wouldn't be private enough for them to kiss. Why was she even thinking about that? Because that was *all* she could think about since yesterday, when she wasn't worried about Ellis or how to deal with her mother.

"Is that acceptable to you?" Sheff asked.

Min ought to go with Sheff and Jo but couldn't seem to decline an opportunity to spend time with Evan. She shook off her earlier irritation. "Yes."

"We won't be gone long," Jo said, madly waving her fan. "I just need a cooling respite for a few minutes."

Sheff escorted her from the ballroom.

Evan turned toward Min. "Do you want to stay here? Or shall we take a promenade through the other rooms?" He offered her his arm.

"Since my mother is in here, I will choose the latter." She took his arm.

They left the ballroom and walked into the octagon.

"Why were all those young ladies swarming you?" Min asked. "Were you regaling them with your brush with death at Longleat?"

Evan laughed. "One of them did, in fact, ask me about that, but I don't think anyone believes I was near death. Do you?"

"Of course not. I was being facetious." She looked over at him as they walked along the corridor toward the entrance hall. "Why are you even here again tonight? You can't dance."

"I'm making my mother happy. She bought a subscription, and I think she misses coming to the balls with Gwen. You're not dancing either. Why are you here?"

"Honestly, I don't know. Sheff and Jo had planned to attend, and we thought it might calm the gossip surrounding our family if we came."

"That's probably not the worst idea. I am sorry about all that," Evan said. "Just ignore them."

"What have you heard?" she asked.

"Just that you are apparently no longer residing at your mother's. And that you may be ill." He shot her a glance as they reached the entrance hall. "I knew that wasn't true, of course."

"But you didn't say so, did you?"

They pivoted to return the way they'd come. "Of course not. Then I'd have to say why I knew, and I'm not going to tell anybody that you called on me yesterday."

Min grimaced. "I've been worried that your mother thinks poorly of me for doing so."

"She does not," Evan said firmly.

A young woman approached them from the octagon. She looked to be a year or two younger than Min and had pale blonde hair and round brown eyes that fixed on Evan. She was petite, but stood with her shoulders thrust back. "Mr. Price."

Evan glanced at Min, then directed his attention to the young woman. He appeared confounded.

"Good evening," Min said to break the awkward silence.

"Yes, good evening," Evan added.

"Do you not remember me?" the young lady asked Evan with considerable disdain.

Evan frowned slightly. "Should I?"

The pretty blonde sucked in a breath, her dark eyes flashing. "You are a horrible scoundrel! I realize we met last spring, but I would think you would remember our encounter."

A grimace passed over Evan's features. "I'm afraid I don't," he said apologetically. "I am terrible with recalling people's names and faces, so please forgive me if I don't remember who you are."

"Or that you kissed me," she hissed.

Min took her hand from Evan's sleeve. The jealousy she'd felt earlier spiked within her, and her heart began to pound.

"This is not an appropriate conversation," Min said to the young woman before narrowing her eyes at Evan.

Evan met Min's gaze with one of mild panic. "Forgive me," he murmured. He turned his attention back to the young lady. "Are you sure it was me?"

He flushed, and Min almost felt sorry for him. She truly believed he did not remember this poor young woman.

The young woman's eyes spat fire. "Of course, I'm certain. I do not have any trouble remembering names or faces or the manner in which you spoke to me, coaxing me into the garden, where you kissed my cheek."

"I do remember now," Evan said grimly. "My apologies, miss."

"Miss Forsythe," the young woman said crisply. "But you needn't remember my name any longer because we shall never speak again. You are a rogue, sir." She looked at Minerva. "If he is courting you, you should run away."

"He is not. And I'm well aware that Mr. Price is a rogue." She slitted her eyes at him.

"I'm not really," Evan protested. "Anymore."

"Don't believe him," Miss Forsythe said, her lip curling. "Rogues never change." She turned and stalked off.

She'd quoted a rogue rule without realizing it. Min gave Evan a sour look. "How many young ladies have you kissed?"

"Not terribly many," he said quickly. "But also not zero."

"How could you not know who she was?" Min wanted to stamp on his injured ankle. Not really, but she was exceedingly perturbed.

"I explained that—I'm terrible with remembering names and faces. I meet someone, and I often don't remember them. I might hear their name, but I won't be able to see their face, nor would I recognize them if I met them again. Or sometimes I see someone and think they look vaguely familiar, but I couldn't recall their name if my life depended on it."

Min arched a brow at him. "You never seem to have a problem with remembering me or my name."

"*You* are different." His voice was deep and husky and elicited a response Min did not want to have right now.

"And yet I am just another young woman you have kissed," Min said derisively. "If you truly want to change and not be known as a rogue, perhaps you should stop kissing women you don't intend to wed."

She turned on her heel and stalked away down the corridor. She didn't know why she was so angry. Why did she care whom he kissed or that he didn't remember them? None of that had anything to do with her.

But just as he'd called her different, she knew he was too. He was the only bachelor she called friend and the only man who'd ever stirred her desire. Whatever was between them was singular—at least for her.

As she reached the entrance hall, she stopped short. Her mother stood there.

"I didn't expect to see you here, Minerva," she said coolly.

Min didn't bother reining in her temper, which Evan had already pricked. "I gathered that, since you've been telling people I am ill."

The duchess narrowed her eyes. "What else was I supposed to say? That you threw a tantrum and moved to your brother's house?"

"A *tantrum*? That's what you think this is?" Min's ire was already boiling, but now she felt as though she might explode. "You must excuse me, Mama. I wish to leave before I say something I will regret."

"Yes, please do. We can't have a scene. Things are bad enough as it is. I do expect you to return home tomorrow."

"Why?" Min asked, flabbergasted. "I don't want to spend time with you, and I'm certainly not going along with your marriage demands."

"You must," her mother insisted. "I've sent a note to your father this afternoon, telling him that your opportunity to find a husband is nearly gone. He responded promptly that he agreed."

Min clenched her jaw. What did that mean? Was her father going to insist she wed too?

"Neither of you can force me to marry," Min said, gritting her teeth.

"Perhaps not, but if you don't, you will be our responsibility." She looked down her nose at Min, which took skill since she was probably an inch shorter. "I don't think any of us wants that. You've made it clear you don't wish to live with me anymore, and I can't imagine you'd want to reside with your father and his strumpet.

"While it might be fine with you to stay with Sheff and his wife for a short time, they will soon be parents, and they won't want you around either," she said haughtily. "The time has come for you to forge your own path, and the only way you can do that is with a husband. I have allowed you too much independence for far too long. You will return home tomorrow, and you will attend the ball on Thursday, where you will dance every set, and we will make it known that you are eagerly awaiting a proposal."

The entire time she'd spoken, Min's body had tensed until she felt as though she were made of knots. "You may as well slap a sign on me Thursday evening inviting suitors to offer their bids."

"If it would not be terribly gauche, I would." With a final, supercilious glower, she walked past Min on her way back to the ballroom.

Min had to work to keep her jaw from dropping. It was as if her mother had dropped all artifice now that her secret about Ellis was out in the open. Looking back, however, Min now realized that her mother's expectations had long been antagonizing. Min had simply accepted it, thinking it was her duty to marry well and suffer her mother's demands toward doing so. The truth was that the duchess was driven by her own wants and needs. She did not care for anyone else, and that included both of her daughters.

Fuming, Min started toward the door. If Jo and Sheff were not outside, she would simply walk to their house. However, they appeared in the doorway just as she reached it.

"I need to go home," Min blurted.

"Oh, good," Sheff replied. "Jo still isn't feeling well, and I need to take her home. You're certain you don't mind leaving?"

"Not at all," Min assured him. "I've just run into the Viper. That should tell you how ready I am to go."

"I see." Sheff frowned. "You can tell me all about it in the coach."

Except Min didn't. She didn't want to tell him everything their mother had said, or how horrible she'd made Min feel, because she was right. Min didn't have a place anymore. There was nowhere for her to go except the altar.

❧

*E*van had spent the day following the ball in poor spirits. He'd tried to see Min, calling on her at Sheff's house, but he'd informed Evan that she'd returned to their mother's house. Then he'd asked why Evan was calling, to which Evan had blithely said, "No reason." Sheff had not seemed entirely satisfied with that answer, but Evan had beat a hasty retreat.

Then, in the evening, Barswell had invited him to a public house along with several other gentlemen. Evan had heartily accepted—and proceeded to drink far too much. Thankfully, Barswell had helped Evan home, because walking on a healing sprained ankle while inebriated turned out to be nearly impossible, even with the aid of a stick.

Today, he was still in poor humor because of what had happened with Miss Forsythe—her name would be emblazoned on his brain now—and Min. He wanted to apologize to Min again, but he didn't want to bother her at her mother's house.

Or perhaps Evan was just a coward. He feared their friendship was damaged.

He could only hope it wasn't irreparably so.

Evan was also frustrated that he hadn't yet received a letter from Mrs. Dalton. He wasn't sure if that was good news or bad. As he sat at the desk in the study, he contemplated writing to her to inquire about the situation with her husband.

His mother came into the study and interrupted his thoughts, which was most welcome. "I missed you at breakfast this morning," she said. "I heard you arrived rather late last night. Is all well?"

"Oh, yes. Just an evening out with some friends. Are you going out?" He noted she was wearing a bonnet.

"Yes." She smiled placidly. "I'm glad to hear you are fine. You seemed out of sorts yesterday, and I wondered if something was amiss."

"I'm weary of being injured," he said with a frown.

"I know." She looked at him with a mother's sympathy. "Perhaps you should consult with a physician again."

"I'd planned to call on him later this week," Evan said. "I hope he will say I can return to my regular pursuits, particularly riding."

"Well, I hope that if you do, you will not be attempting any more daring acts." Now she looked at him with a mother's consternation.

"I won't promise that," he said with a smile. Indeed, he

could hardly wait to return to, as Min had called it, his normal life. And that included his "daring acts."

"Delay them for a while, then. At least until you are well and truly healed." She pursed her lips at him. "Can you promise your poor mother that?"

"There's nothing poor about you, Mama. But yes, I will make you happy."

She exhaled and smoothed her hands against her skirt. "I'm going to the gardens. Would you like to come along? I'm going with Mrs. Bainton from next door. In fact, I should hurry. I think she's waiting for me."

"I'll come." Evan followed her into the entrance hall and saw that the post had been delivered. Perhaps Mrs. Dalton had written.

"Actually, I'll catch up with you," Evan said. "I want to read the post first."

"All right, dear," she replied as she drew on her gloves.

After she departed, Evan looked through the missives. Nothing from Mrs. Dalton, but there was a letter from Roger.

Evan opened the letter and scanned the contents. Roger was incredibly distressed at the prospect of a criminal conversation case. As he should be, for it would ruin his career. Roger wrote that he deeply regretted his actions with Mrs. Dalton and lamented the fact that it had been an incredibly short affair. They had met on only two occasions. It hardly seemed fair.

Evan glowered at the letter. It was even less fair to him. He hadn't met Mrs. Dalton for a tryst *at all*. If she wasn't able to persuade her husband not to file suit, Evan needed a plan. He would likely need to consult his father for advice. He would not be happy that Evan had lied and taken the blame for something he didn't do, but Evan suspected he would also understand. His father was a man of high principle and integrity, and Evan had tried very much to be like him.

Then why are you kissing young ladies in gardens without remembering who they are, and drinking too much in public houses with known rogues, when what you really want is to sort out how you feel about Min?

The voice in his head was becoming a major distraction, particularly since the ball the other night.

As if conjured from his thoughts, he saw Min through the window. She appeared to be on her way to her father's house. Without thinking, Evan plucked up his hat and dashed outside. As he raced to intercept her, he stepped on his foot wrong, and pain shot through his ankle.

Muttering a curse, he worked to ignore it as he caught up to her. "Good afternoon, Min."

She turned as he limped a final step and glanced down at his ankle. "Have you hurt yourself again?"

"I'm fine." He didn't want to talk about his injury or how he'd stupidly caused himself more pain in his eagerness to reach her. "I'm glad to see you. I called on you yesterday at your brother's, but he said you'd returned to your mother's house. I'm surprised you went back."

"I don't have anything to say to you." She continued toward her father's house.

Evan touched her arm briefly. "Wait, please."

She stopped and turned toward him. "Whatever you have to say, make it quick, because I'm on my way to my father's house."

"I can see that," Evan said. "I want to apologize for the other night."

"You've nothing to apologize to me for. You should be apologizing to Miss Forsythe for your cavalier treatment of her."

"It was a flirtation," Evan said with a grimace, thinking

how terrible that sounded. "I recall our encounter now. She had asked if we could promenade into the garden, and she actually asked me to kiss her and—"

"I find that hard to believe," Min said.

"Why? You asked me to kiss you." He wished he hadn't said it as soon as the words left his mouth. It might be true, but it did not seem the right thing to say at this particular time.

Min narrowed her eyes at him. "I suppose that's true. Are you telling me you don't make a habit of kissing young women in gardens?"

"Not generally, no." He shrugged. "I like to flirt, Min. I enjoy making women smile and feel good about themselves, so I flatter them. I make them feel special."

"Is that what you did with me?" she asked quietly.

"Yes." Though it had come far more naturally. Making Min smile was as easy—and vital—to him as breathing. "But there's more to it than that. We have a connection—a friendship, at least." He stopped short of telling her he'd begun to wonder if there was something more.

She pivoted toward her father's house. "I really must be going."

"I can't bear it if you're angry with me, Min. I have decided to change. I won't flirt anymore, and I won't steal kisses."

"Not even from me?" She didn't look at him.

"Not even from you."

She slid him a glance that held a tinge of skepticism. "Do you really think you can do that?"

Her gaze had softened a bit, making him think he was perhaps breaking through her anger. "I'm going to try," he said. "Though, you make it difficult. You can't want to kiss me either. It's not helpful."

She looked toward her father's house. "Perhaps we should

just stop spending time together. It seems we are too tempted."

He could not argue with her, and yet he didn't want to contemplate not seeing her anymore. "I miss our habit of being together every day when we were at Longleat. I thought you enjoyed that too."

"I did." She glanced at him once more. "But we weren't able to resist temptation then, either."

"I promise we can maintain our friendship and nothing more." At least Evan would try for that. "Perhaps I'll see you at the gardens later. I'm going there shortly to join my mother."

"Not today," she said. "My father has something to discuss with us. Perhaps tomorrow."

Evan felt a surge of anticipation in his chest. "I shall hope so."

Their gazes caught and held. She looked away first and continued on her way to her father's house.

Evan watched until he could no longer see her, then he turned and went back to his mother's. His ankle hurt too much to join his mother at Sydney Gardens.

Reflecting on his conversation with Min, he wasn't quite sure what had just happened or what he'd agreed to, but he hoped he would see her tomorrow.

And if his ankle still pained him, he'd suffer through it. Min was worth the agony.

CHAPTER 12

$\mathcal{M}$ in was torn between still being annoyed with Evan and being incredibly flattered by everything that he said. He was either a consummate rogue or incredibly charming. She would give him the benefit of the doubt for now.

Shaking off her encounter with him, she walked into her father's house as Jurgens held the door. The butler welcomed her with a smile. "His Grace, his lordship, and her ladyship are upstairs in the drawing room."

"Thank you, Jurgens." Min gave her hat and gloves to him before going upstairs.

Sheff and Jo sat together on the settee, while their father stood near the hearth. He looked a bit agitated, with lines fanning his mouth. His jaw was clenched.

"Afternoon, Min," Sheff said. "How are things with Mother?"

"As strained as you might imagine." Min sat in a chair angled near the settee. She looked over at their father. "Papa, are you going to sit?"

"In a moment." He waved his hand. "Sheff, you go first."

Why did Min feel as though she'd walked into a tense situation in which everyone else knew far more than she did? She'd come here thinking it would be a haven from her mother, but now felt as though she needed to be on guard. Jo gave her a sympathetic look, which didn't help matters.

"This doesn't appear to be good news," Min said. "Just tell me what it is."

"We're returning to London," Sheff said. "Jo would rather be at home. Well, not the home she used to live in, but in London." Sheff blew out an exasperated breath. "You know what I mean."

Min nodded. "I do." She understood why Jo would want to go home. She'd never been far from London before. And she was newly married and expecting a child. She was also a countess and would be a duchess someday. It was a great deal of change all at once.

"My father is also keen to return, as he finds Bath too sedate," Jo said with a grimace. "You are more than welcome to come with us."

Min was surprised she didn't leap at the chance, but what her mother had said about Jo and Sheff not wanting her around screamed in her mind. Even if Min didn't fully believe that, neither did she want to insert herself in their new married life together. And that would be required since they would be living at Henlow House, which was Min's home in London. Although, without Ellis there, it would not feel like home.

Min still didn't know where that was anymore.

"I think I'll stay here in Bath," Min replied

Both Sheff and Jo blinked, appearing surprised.

Min shrugged. "I know it's shocking, but Mother and I stay out of one another's way. I can suffer her presence awhile longer. However, I may yet decide to return to London sooner rather than later," she added.

"Whenever you want to come, you are more than welcome," Sheff said. "Not that you need our invitation. Henlow House is as much your home as it is ours. In fact, it's more your home since I've been residing at the Albany the last few years."

"Yes, but your future lies there, whereas mine does not." Min had no idea where her future would be, which only increased her unrest. She looked to her father. "Is that why you summoned me here today?"

"Not entirely." Her father finally moved to sit down, taking the chair nearest Min. He looked from her to Sheff, then back again as he spoke. "My news is far more disruptive, I'm afraid. I have thought for a long time about this, and I've never wanted to do it because it seems hypocritical. And yet, I've come to the conclusion that it is the only way forward in which we can all find peace." He took a deep breath. "I'm going to seek a divorce from your mother."

"What?" Sheff blurted, leaning forward. His brows pitched over his eyes as he stared at their father. "As bad as things are with you and Mother, you can't do that."

"I *can* do that," the duke said calmly. "I realize it will be difficult and cause a furor. But I cannot continue as I have these many years. I have you to thank for that, Sheff."

"Don't blame me for this," Sheff said sharply.

Jo reached over and took his hand, clutching him tightly. Min wished she had that kind of support, or any support, really. How she missed Ellis.

"Think of Min." Sheff sent her a furious glance, but she knew his anger was not directed at her. "This will ruin her chances for marriage. It doesn't matter that you're a duke. This will be a horrendous scandal."

"I realize that." Their father gave Min an apologetic smile. "I won't do anything until after you're wed. That said, I would very much appreciate it if you would marry soon."

This must have been why he'd agreed with her mother's insistence that Min marry. He wanted her to hurry up and wed so he could cause a scandal. If he did that before she married, her value on the Marriage Mart would completely evaporate. That her father would put her in such a position reminded her of where she ranked in this family, which was at the very bottom.

"You presume I can snap my fingers and have a husband?" Min said coolly.

His mouth twisted into an almost smile that ended up looking more like a smirk. "There was a time, my dear, when you could have had your pick of any gentleman."

Was. That time had passed, apparently. How she hated being reminded. As if she'd failed because she hadn't wanted to settle for anything less than what she wanted. "I found all of them lacking. You must forgive me if I choose not to shackle myself to someone without being completely certain I could suffer them for a lifetime. I would expect you, of all people, to understand that."

The duke flinched, which gave Min a small amount of satisfaction. "Of course, I do," he said quietly.

Min felt as if she'd been cast adrift in the ocean. She was bobbing about in the waves, her hands flailing, her body sinking as she struggled to stay afloat. Her heart beat faster, as if she were actually having difficulty breathing.

"Have you really thought this through, Papa?" she asked.

"An excellent question," Sheff said. "You would file a suit against Jo's father?"

Jo paled. "Please don't do that," she said to the duke, her brow furrowed with grave concern, as she seemed to grip Sheff more tightly.

Their father gave her a sad look. "I don't really want to involve your father at all, Jo, but I can easily prove that the duchess was unfaithful with him."

The ensuing scandal enveloping Jo, her father, and Ellis, along with their own family spread out in Min's mind. It would be horrible at a time when Jo and Sheff had never been happier. And Ellis was still likely trying to comprehend the truth of her parentage, only to have all of Society hanging on every salacious detail.

Min pressed her hand to her cheek. "You can't involve Ellis, Papa. You *can't*."

"I don't want to do this at all." The duke stood and paced to the hearth and back again. "I have no choice. Don't you understand? Your mother has made my life hell for nearly thirty years. I have put up with it, but no more."

Sheff scowled at him. "You 'put up with it' by indulging yourself in every way possible. You are not blameless, and yes, it is *incredibly* hypocritical of you to file a criminal conversation suit against your wife's lover. What of all your lovers?"

"It's the height of hypocrisy," Min said, crossing her arms over her chest. She looked over at Jo, whose gaze was fixed on her lap as she took deep breaths.

Sheff let go of her hand and put his arm around her, holding her against his side. He glared at the duke. "You've upset Jo."

"I know." Their father at least appeared anguished. "I've upset you all, and I'm deeply sorry. I have tried to endure this marriage and your mother's hatred of me, but I have finally found a love that is reciprocated. It pains me greatly not to be able to claim that publicly."

"So you would inflict pain on us all," Sheff said, his voice low and angry. "Your plan, then, is to divorce Mother, plunge the entire family into an irredeemable scandal, and then marry Mrs. Welbeck? You think you're going to be allowed to parade her about Society as if you hadn't ruined us all. It's incredibly selfish of you."

That was exactly right, Min thought, and she was glad Sheff had said it. Once again, she felt an overwhelming pressure to wed. She had no other choices. She understood that her father felt trapped. Min felt the same. However, her father could continue with Mrs. Welbeck just as they were right now. That would be more acceptable than if he divorced their mother and married her. It made no sense, but nothing did to Min. Not anymore.

She abruptly stood. "I agree that you're selfish, Papa, but I don't know how we will dissuade you from this plan. I have long blamed you for the strife in our family, and I now realize it was largely Mother's fault. However, this will be entirely on you, not that it matters where I'm concerned. My duty is to marry. Then I will no longer be a part of this family, for I will become the property of my husband. I hate that you would do this to Ellis and her real father, whom she hasn't even had a chance to know."

And with that, Min stalked from the drawing room and hastened down the stairs. As she donned her hat and gloves, Jo caught up to her.

"Come back to London with us," Jo pleaded. "You don't have to stay here."

Min tied the ribbon of her bonnet. "I know I don't, but I need to marry. Since there are eligible bachelors here, I may as well try." She didn't have any other choice. If she didn't marry now, she wouldn't have another chance. Not after what her father was going to do. So much for wanting to marry for love. She would likely be trapped in an unhappy marriage.

Jo looked stricken. "I'm so sorry, Min. It doesn't seem fair that I'm the one married when I had never planned to be."

Min gave her a slight smile. "I am exceedingly glad that you and my brother found each other. I would never begrudge you your happiness." *Someone may as well have that,* she thought, because right now, she doubted that it would ever be her.

"I'll see you before you leave for London." Min gave her sister-in-law a quick hug, then left the house.

Emotion overwhelmed Min as she walked along the pavement. Nearing Evan's house, she slowed. Despite her previous irritation with him, she yearned to stop and speak with him, to tell him what had just happened. He would console her, and she would feel better. But she couldn't call on him a second time, no matter how much she wanted to. Hurrying past the house, she bit her lip to keep it from trembling.

She wanted Ellis more than anything. Her absence had left a gaping hole.

Min couldn't face her mother. She would go to Pandora's instead.

Thank goodness she had Pandora. Min only hoped she wouldn't start crying before she got there.

❧

The moment Pandora greeted Min, she could see straightaway that Min needed consolation. Pandora asked for tea and cakes to be delivered to the cozy sitting room next to her bedchamber, then took Min under her arm—literally—while escorting her upstairs. They kicked off their shoes and curled up in a pair of chairs. Min told her everything that was happening with her family and barely stopped to take a breath. Pandora had embraced her, after which they'd sipped tea and eaten too many cakes.

"Do you really think he'll go through with the divorce?" Pandora asked.

"He seems committed." Min recalled the set of her father's

mouth and the determination in his gaze. "I don't think he understands how terrible an ordeal it will be for everyone."

"How can he and go through with his plans?" Pandora murmured sympathetically.

Min was angry with him, but a part of her understood. "It's not hard to comprehend or even sympathize with his sentiments. It's just wholly unfair that this is the way to end a union that probably never should have happened in the first place."

Pandora shook her head. "It's horrible that people, especially women, must suffer through unhappy marriages."

As a young woman, Min felt completely trapped. "Now more than ever, I am afraid of being stuck in a marriage I don't want. And yet, if I don't marry before my father files suit, my chances to do so will be greatly diminished."

Pandora looked horrified. "He wouldn't do that, would he?"

"He says he won't, but I feel as if nothing is certain, especially with Ellis gone." Min's life had completely changed in the last week, and she didn't know when things would settle.

"Perhaps not marrying won't be the worst thing," Pandora said. "But I do understand why it would upset you. I was devastated after Bane ruined my chances for marriage." She pursed her lips briefly. "However, I can't blame Bane alone. I should have known better than to let my emotions drive my actions. It wasn't as if Bane forced me to kiss him."

"Mrs. Lawler is the one who's really to blame." Min referred to the extremely officious woman in Weston who had witnessed Bane and Pandora's embrace and then told everyone about it.

Mrs. Lawler had done the same thing to Tamsin and Droxford. The difference was that Droxford had married Tamsin. Thankfully, their compromising situation had led to a love match. They were lucky. Min worried she would not be.

"Mrs. Lawler *is* to blame," Pandora agreed. "But we should not have given her any fuel for her gossip. I will say that being a spinster is not terrible. In fact, there is much to recommend the state."

Min laughed softly. "That's easy for you to say. You have your aunt, who has supported you."

Pandora's parents, Lord and Lady Radstock, had nurtured high hopes for her marriageability. With her beauty and charm, they'd expected her to marry extremely well, and had written off her older sister. But it was Persey who had married a duke, much to their parents' shock.

Neither Persey nor Pandora had anything to do with their parents any longer, for they'd never truly cared what happened with their daughters, provided their marriages bolstered their father's coffers. Lord and Lady Radstock were spendthrifts, and the baron was in debt. Persey's husband, Wellesbourne, had made them solvent but refused to continue to support them. They'd had to drastically change their lifestyle.

"She's also loved you and been as much a mother to you these past two years as your actual mother." Min had no such person.

Pandora smiled softly. "I know I'm fortunate. Just as I know you don't have an Aunt Lucinda. However, you do have places you can go. Your father has many properties. You could even live at the Grove in Weston."

Min tried to imagine a life as a spinster in the sleepy village near the sea. While she always looked forward to the time she spent there every summer, she couldn't imagine not living in London at least part of the year. She loved the bustle of the city and would miss too many things about it.

She also realized that while she was fortunate to be the

daughter of a duke, she did not have the luxury of continuing as she had. She would not be invited to house parties like the one at Longleat if she were not a potential bride or married. And she would be completely cut from Society after her father filed suit against Jo's father. Min still couldn't believe he would do that to Jo. And to Ellis.

Min smacked her hand on the arm of the chair. "I'm so angry with my father."

"I know." Pandora reached over and patted Min's hand briefly. "If you decide to go to the Grove, I'll accompany you, if you like."

"I'm sure Mrs. Ogilvie can come to chaperone."

Pandora laughed. "You think spinsters need chaperones? Why would we bother? Indeed, we can become companions and chaperones ourselves at some point." She waggled her brows at Min as if she'd just imparted delightful news.

Min didn't particularly want to be a companion or a chaperone. She realized she *had* expected to marry. She'd assumed the right gentleman would cross her path. But now she had to accept that it might not happen. She was well and truly out of time.

"You could stay here with us for a while too," Pandora offered with an encouraging smile. "Just know that if you choose spinsterhood, you have a fellow spinster awaiting you."

"I must say, you make spinsterhood look appealing. But don't you miss—" Min broke off as heat flushed her cheeks.

Pandora's pale brows drew together. "Don't I miss what?"

"That you won't ever experience the passion part of marriage. I think I would miss that."

Her blue-green eyes gleaming, Pandora leaned slightly toward Min. "I'll confess something to you. I *have* been worried about missing that. And I shall also blame Bane for that, because if he'd never kissed me, I wouldn't know what I was missing. However, it was rather wonderful, damn him, and so I *do* know. I've spent the last two years lamenting that I wouldn't experience what happens next." She squared her shoulders and looked Min in the eye. "I am pleased to report that I have resolved that issue."

Min sucked in a breath. "What did you do?"

"Obviously, you can't tell anyone, and that includes our Rogue Rules Club. I haven't even told Persey. I don't think she would judge me poorly, but it's not something I want to write to her about in a letter." Pandora's lips curled into a small, secret-filled smile. "Recently, I spent the night with a footman from a neighboring household."

"How? Where?" Min goggled at her. "Tell me everything. Well, maybe not everything, but as much as you'd like to."

Pandora laughed. "He arranged for us to spend the night in a room over his household's mews. It wasn't the most romantic setting, but I can't say that detracted from the event."

"It was an event?" Min asked.

"Well, you know what I mean," Pandora said with a giggle.

"And was it what you'd hoped?"

Pandora smiled. "Oh, yes. You should try it—not necessarily with a footman, though obviously, I take no issue with that—but if you find the opportunity to have a passionate encounter with someone, you should seize it. Just be careful to avoid getting with child. There are ways around that."

Min's brain was already spinning with thoughts. "How did you know you wanted to do that with the footman?"

Pandora lifted a shoulder. "I found him very attractive. Starting last spring, when I would go out for a stroll, I ran into him from time to time as he walked the neighbor's dog. We would walk together sometimes. I found him charming and amusing."

"You were attracted to him, then. You wanted him to kiss you…and other things."

"Yes." Pandora's brow creased. "Do you find it strange that I would be attracted to a footman?"

Min worried that her friend thought she was judging her. "Not at all," Min hurried to say. "I think it's wonderful that you felt that pull toward someone. I have never felt that way toward anyone." Until recently.

Pandora's eyes rounded briefly. "No one? You don't see a man across the ballroom and think, 'Oh, he's attractive. I wonder what it might be like to promenade with him or even kiss him'?"

"I suppose I have *thought* those things," Min said slowly. "But I never felt an overwhelming urge for physical contact. Until recently." This time, she said the last part out loud.

Pandora's brows shot up. "What changed?"

"I spent time with a certain gentleman, and it turns out I *am* attracted to him. I did actually kiss him, and it was nice." Min shook her head. "No, nice is a vastly inferior word for what it was."

Pandora grinned. "Is it Evan Price?"

Min gasped. "How did you know?"

"It was purely a guess, because I haven't seen you together. But I do know you spent time with him at Longleat, so I assumed it was likely him, especially since he's here in Bath." Pandora studied her a moment. "Are you still attracted to him?"

Min nodded.

"And is he attracted to you?"

"I believe so. We kissed at Longleat, and things turned very awkward. Then we kissed again the other day. Things were somewhat awkward again, but that was due, in part, to a young woman at the Upper Rooms the other night who said Evan had kissed her last spring. Evan didn't remember doing so. He didn't remember her at all, actually."

"Well, that is certainly roguish behavior." Pandora clucked her tongue. "I gather he's not marriage material, then."

"He's trying to change, actually," Min said, feeling surprisingly defensive of him.

Pandora laughed. "Well, we have a rogue rule about that, don't we? Never trust a rogue to change."

Min exhaled. "I can't stop thinking of that rule. I also can't ignore the rogues we know who *have* changed when they married our friends. Beyond reason, my own brother has reformed. If he can do it, anyone can."

Pandora made a sound in her throat. "I do not agree with that. I don't think there is any hope for someone as debauched as Bane."

"You are probably right about that," Min acknowledged. "Though Evan is not as bad as Bane, at least from what I've seen."

"Has Evan indicated any interest in marriage?" Pandora asked.

"No."

"So, when he talks of changing, he isn't doing so for any particular reason."

Min shrugged. "He just wants to change, I suppose. And doesn't that make his motivation seem more genuine? He's not doing it to win me or someone else."

"I am not one to advise you on such matters." Pandora shifted in her chair. "I don't trust any of the opposite sex. What is it you want from Evan, if anything?"

Min sat back and took a deep breath. "I don't know what I want. Just because I enjoy kissing him doesn't mean I want to marry him. I have no guarantee we would be happy."

"Nobody can have that," Pandora said darkly. "At some point, you have to decide to take the risk or not."

"Would you ever do it if the opportunity presented itself?" Min asked.

"Absolutely not." Pandora's response came fast and vehement. "But I went through a terrible situation and suffered the consequences. I was given the cut direct. I have been mocked."

"You have survived," Min said.

"Yes, but I'm a spinster with no hope of marriage, which is what I was raised to expect. It has been a transformation of what I thought my life would be." Pandora spoke matter-of-factly, but Min's heart still ached for her friend. "Still, in spite of everything and everyone, I *have* survived and am almost flourishing. You will too." Pandora smiled. "Survive your father's divorce, I mean. You just need to decide how you want to weather it. Will you rush to take a husband, or will you forge ahead on your own? Regardless of what you choose, I will be at your side and support you."

"Thank you," Min said. "I don't know what I want to do, but it helps to talk about it."

Pandora arched her brow and gave Min a suggestive look. "If nothing else, you might consider another passionate encounter with Evan."

Min laughed. "I'm not sure I could dare."

"Kissing him made you feel good, didn't it? It seems to me you're going through a terrible time with what's happened to Ellis and having to live with your mother, and now this business with your father. I don't think it's wrong to want to create a wonderful memory that's entirely for yourself."

Min hadn't thought of it like that. "Is that what you did with the footman?"

"Absolutely," Pandora said without regret. "And I would do it again. Not that I have plans to," she added with a laugh.

She'd given Min a great deal to think about. But Min didn't have much time. Her window was closing, and she needed to decide which path to take before the choice was taken from her.

CHAPTER 13

All morning, Evan had looked forward to hopefully seeing Min at Sydney Gardens that afternoon. However, his hopes were dashed when he received a note from her saying she would not be going. She would, however, be at the ball at the Upper Rooms that night.

Evan wouldn't miss it.

Before he could go upstairs and inform his mother of his plans, which would delight her, Alton delivered the post to the study. At last, there was a letter from Mrs. Dalton. Evan tore it open and scanned the contents with growing frustration.

Her husband had refused to listen to her pleas regarding the divorce. He'd banished her from his household—which was how she was writing a frank letter about the matter—and she was now staying with her sister. Evan felt badly for the poor woman. While she had made a mistake, this punishment was surely excessive.

Evan set the letter aside and stared off into nothing, his mind and gut churning. He ought to go to London at once to deal with this matter. He needed to speak to his father. Perhaps he could talk sense into Sir Abraham.

Except Evan didn't want to leave Min and whatever was happening between them. At the same time, he couldn't pursue anything with her with this horrible business hanging over his head.

He wasn't sure how long he sat there considering his options, but the butler returned to inform him that Sheff had arrived.

Shaking himself from his stupor, Evan rose. "Send him in."

Sheff came into the study, and right away, Evan could see there was a dark cloud over him.

"Afternoon, Sheff," Evan said. "You don't look like the happily married man and father-to-be that I've seen recently."

"I am still those things," Sheff said gruffly. "However, I am also a thoroughly angry son."

Evan was familiar with the Duke of Henlow's penchant for indulging in activities that generated gossip. Setting up house in Bath during the Season with his mistress was a prime example. However, as it was expected from him, the gossip wasn't that his behavior was shocking, but merely interesting. Could the duke even provoke outrage anymore?

"Blast, what has your father done now?" Evan asked. He gestured to the seating area and returned to his chair.

Sheff sat across from him and ran his hand through his hair. "He's completely lost his mind. As awful as his behavior has been for years now, what he wants to do next makes everything pale in comparison."

Perhaps there was room for shock after all. "That sounds ominous." Evan immediately thought of Min and how this might affect her.

"He's planning to divorce our mother," Sheff announced with a faint curl of his lip.

Evan's breath caught. "That *is* terrible."

"It's abominable!" Sheff's voice rose. "Do you know how damaging it will be to everyone? He will file suit against Jo's father. I'm absolutely livid. I can't believe he would do that to my *wife*."

"That is indeed beyond the pale. And what of your sister?" Evan knew it would damage Min's reputation. He worked to hide his rising anger lest Sheff question it.

"It will ruin her chances of marriage." Sheff threw his hands up. "I cannot countenance why my father would do that to Min. It's unconscionable. He's endured marriage to my mother for nearly thirty years. Why seek to dissolve it now? Because he's found love again and finally has love in return."

Evan was glad for the duke in spite of what he was prepared to do. "Neither of your parents is happy. It's a shame they can't go their separate ways."

"I agree, but they *can* live apart and completely avoid one another." Sheff blew out a breath. "I do feel for my father and understand his desire to publicly acknowledge his love for Mrs. Welbeck. I can't imagine if I were not allowed to marry Jo, if I had to hide our relationship in the shadows."

Evan felt bad for all of them, especially for Min. He could, of course, not help thinking of his own situation with Mrs. Dalton and how damaging it would be to his family. He thought of how upset his parents would be, but had he really considered how it would affect his mother? She was a popular hostess, and the life she knew would be destroyed. His sister might fare better, since she was now married to the Viscount Somerton, but it could taint them, at least for a while. Evan needed to put a stop to this.

In fact, he never should have stepped in to take the blame

in the first place. But he'd wanted to help his friend and had thought the risk to his reputation would be minimal. He'd been a fool to think the affair would be regarded as a rakish exploit. He also hadn't expected that he wouldn't want to be seen as rakish.

He was tempted to talk to Sheff about it, but he didn't want to burden his friend. Not now. He was also, he realized, embarrassed.

"I'm sorry to saddle you with all this," Sheff said. "I just needed to talk to someone who wasn't Jo. She's very upset, as you can imagine, and I don't wish to cause her further distress, especially with the babe. We've decided to return to London tomorrow."

"Have you? Is Min going with you?"

Sheff's eyes narrowed slightly. "We invited her, but she declined. My father made it clear to her that she needs to marry as soon as possible. Though, he said he won't initiate the divorce until she is wed."

Evan imagined the enormous pressure Min must feel. She had to be terribly upset. Perhaps that was why she wasn't going to the gardens today. Except she *was* going to the ball.

What better place for her to find a husband?

It occurred to Evan that *he* could be that husband.

He considered telling Sheff that he had a solution for Min. Evan wouldn't care that his father-in-law would plunge the family into scandal. Though Evan's very proper father *would* care, even if the man was a duke.

However, Evan would not say anything at all until he spoke with Min. He frowned at Sheff. "Is there no way of talking your father out of it?"

"There doesn't seem to be." Sheff scowled. "Things had finally improved between my father and me."

"And now he's gone and decided to upend everything for love," Evan said.

Sheff's scowl deepened. "Are you arguing there's something romantic about this?"

"No, I only feel sorry for him and his position."

"I do too," Sheff said with a sigh, his features relaxing. "I will always feel bad that he is trapped in a hate-filled marriage, but he can be happy with Mrs. Welbeck—even somewhat publicly. It's not as if he hasn't had mistresses before. But he doesn't want Mrs. Welbeck to be another one of his many mistresses. She is different in his eyes, and I understand that too."

"What a bloody mess." Evan paused before asking, "Do you ever think love is not worth the turmoil?"

"Having experienced it for myself, no." Sheff met Evan's gaze. "It is worth every agony. I suppose I can understand my father's motivations, but just as he will fight for his love, I must fight for mine."

Evan could see how fiercely Sheff cared for Jo. "Your love for your wife is inspiring. If a rogue like you can reform so completely, I think there's hope for the rest of us."

"Does that mean you are hoping to shed your reputation?" Sheff asked.

"I have been considering that," Evan said evenly.

"I encourage you to do so before it gets worse, not that it will. But speaking as someone who was a consummate rake, I regret my behavior." Sheff grimaced briefly before fixing intently on Evan. "Is there another reason you're looking for redemption? I notice you keep asking about my sister, and you did spend an inordinate amount of time with her at that house party. Should I be concerned?"

"Concerned about what?" *Perhaps things such as me kissing your sister?* "I hold your sister in the highest esteem. I consider her a good friend." *And I would like her to be more than that, truth be told.*

"It's nothing more than that?" Sheff asked.

"It is not." Not yet anyway. "Would it be bad if it were?"

Sheff's brows shot up. "Not *bad*, but surprising. Really, it isn't my business. I will not direct my sister on whom she should wed, as our parents have done. However, if you *are* interested in my sister in that way, you must be committed to being the love of her life. That is what she needs and what she deserves. If you can't do that, don't waste her time."

Evan understood. He nodded.

"Are you seriously considering a courtship?" Sheff blinked at him.

"I'll keep that between your sister and me, if you don't mind." The truth was Evan didn't know. He certainly had a deep affection for her and was wildly attracted to her.

"Smart man." Sheff gave him a nod of approval. "She could do far worse than you."

Evan laughed. "Thank you?"

They spoke for a few more minutes before Sheff stood to take his leave. Evan wished him a safe trip to London and bade him give Jo his very best.

After Sheff was gone, Evan's thoughts turned completely to Min—she hadn't been far from his mind—and how she must be feeling. He was anxious to see her tonight. To talk with her about marriage.

But should he? He hadn't yet resolved the matter with Mrs. Dalton, and he really should before he could consider the future with Min. He would not allow scandal to touch her, not after all she'd been through.

If he were smart, he would travel to London tomorrow too.

∾

*S*ince her conversation with Pandora yesterday, Min had thought of little else but the choices facing her. She'd been so consumed by what to do next that she'd decided not to go to the gardens to meet Evan. There was simply too much weighing on her mind. Furthermore, spending time with him would likely encourage her to do what Pandora had suggested. Indeed, many of Min's thoughts had centered on spending a night with Evan, particularly as she'd tried to sleep last night. Desire had flushed through her as she recalled his kisses and his touch—and imagined what else he would make her feel.

"I think that may be my favorite gown," Min's mother said as they rode the short distance from her house to the Upper Rooms for tonight's ball.

Min glanced down at her pink ball gown, which was the one she would have chosen to wear a week ago. She didn't point that out to her mother. She'd avoided speaking to the duchess since yesterday's stunning revelation from her father. In truth, Min now generally avoided speaking to her at all—since the prior stunning revelation regarding Ellis.

This was far too much turmoil for one family to endure.

Min had written to Ellis last night for the third time and had a footman deliver the letter to her father's house so he could post it. She'd wanted to lament to Ellis about the divorce, but hadn't. Ellis had her own problems and didn't need to hear about Min's.

Instead, Min had told Ellis how much she missed her, that she was well, and that she hoped to see her soon. She also wrote that she was closer than she'd ever been to accepting a proposal of marriage—not that there was anyone specific.

Because she had to before her father plunged the family into scandal.

Min squared her shoulders against the squab. "Mother, I

have decided to wed with due haste. However, the choice of groom will be mine and mine alone," she said firmly. If she could not have love or passion, she would at least choose someone she could respect.

"I'm pleased to hear it," her mother said. She even smiled, which made Min want to roll her eyes. "I do expect him to hail from a noble family. After your brother's marriage, it's very important that you make a good connection."

Important to whom? Min clenched her jaw.

The duchess continued, "I know you had mentioned Mr. Jarvis, and while he does seem pleasant enough, he is not nobility. You deserve someone better, and you know that, Minerva. You are the daughter of the Duke of Henlow. You should be marrying the heir to another dukedom, or a marquessate, at the very least, an earldom. But I will settle for a viscount." Her exhalation was tinged with disappointment.

"*You* will settle?" Min asked with a look of disgust. "My marriage has nothing to do with you, and given your rather poor history with marriage, forgive me if I don't want your input at all."

Her mother bristled. "You must also not consider Evan Price," she said, as if she hadn't heard what Min had just told her.

Min had to keep from glowering at her. "Why would you even bring him up?"

"Because I've seen you speaking with him, and I know you spent time with him—too much time—at Longleat." The duchess sniffed as if she smelled something unpleasant. "His family is fine, I suppose, but again, there is no title. Furthermore, his reputation isn't…pristine. On that front, Mr. Jarvis would be a better choice. But again, you shouldn't choose either of them."

"Mother, *stop*. I will wed whomever I want. That includes

Mr. Jarvis or Mr. Price or a blacksmith." The coach came to a halt, and Min was grateful she could leave the coach.

As they made their way inside, Min wondered if she'd made a mistake in coming tonight. Was she actually hoping a new gentleman would appear? Someone with whom she would fall instantly and madly in love? Or at least with whom she could share the same passion she did with Evan?

The thought of enduring another series of dances tonight without Ellis by her side or any of the other members of the Rogue Rules Club was both depressing and frustrating. At least she'd had Pandora to talk to, even if she wasn't here at the ball.

They entered the ballroom, and for the first time, Min felt uncomfortable. She thought of never having to attend another event like this and didn't think she would mind one bit. There were two ways to achieve that end. As a spinster, she would no longer attend balls, just as Pandora didn't. While as a wife, she might very well continue going to balls, but she would do so with entirely different expectations.

She suddenly glimpsed years into the future and wondered how it might feel to attend a ball like this with her own daughter. Her breath halted in her lungs as she contemplated that never happening if she became a spinster. For a moment, she couldn't breathe.

"Here comes Lord Spilsby," her mother said eagerly. "I know he is not your first choice, but I do believe he has changed since inheriting his title. I think you should give him a chance."

Spilsby, once again wearing a horrid waistcoat—this time in the hue of brownish-purple that made one think of decay —arrived before Min could state that she had no intention of doing so. He bowed. "Will you do me the honor of dancing the next set with me, Lady Minerva?"

Min could not say no, especially since she'd somewhat

broken a rule when she'd refused him the other night. However, her mother had inadvertently given her an excuse to do so when she'd made up that story about Min being ill and having to stay at Sheff's house. Was Min to blame for seizing on that?

"Certainly," Min replied with a forced smile. She took his arm and glanced at the profile of his long face. He had wispy brown sideburns that arced along his jawbone. Some men sported facial hair to compensate for a feature that was lacking. In Spilsby's case, Min didn't think there was enough hair in the world to make him look anything other than disagreeable.

As they took their places on the dance floor, he gave her an earnest look. "I owe you an apology, Lady Minerva. I understand you may hold some disdain for me based on an unfortunate event that happened at Almack's last spring. I'm afraid I reacted poorly to something that happened involving a friend of yours, and it was not well done of me."

Min narrowed her eyes at him. She suspected her mother had put him up to this in order to bolster his chances. Except he had no chance with Min whatsoever.

"I'm not the one you should apologize to," Min said. "That would be Lady Somerton, though I daresay she wouldn't want to speak with you. Even if you tried, her husband would probably call you out."

She laughed as if she were telling a jest, but she was not. And given the shadow that passed over Spilsby's eyes, she thought he knew it too.

"Furthermore," Min continued, "one might excuse what happened at Almack's because perhaps you were simply having a bad night. However, there is no excusing the rumor you spread later in an attempt to ruin Lady Somerton. That, I am afraid, is unforgivable."

He opened his mouth to speak, his brows knitting, but

Min held up a hand. "I don't think there's anything for us to discuss."

"Still, I would like to explain," Spilsby said, his face flushed. "Might I call on you tomorrow to do so?"

She did not want him calling on her, for that would only encourage him. "No, that is not acceptable to me. In fact, this will be the last time we dance together. You must not ask me again, because I have no interest in marrying you. There will be no courtship. You must turn your interest elsewhere."

Spilsby's eyes rounded, and his nostrils flared. His jaw clenched, and little lines formed around his mouth. He didn't glower, exactly, but he did not look pleased. The music started, and they made their way through the dance rather awkwardly.

Halfway through, Min spied Evan near the wall. He looked magnificent, with his dark hair styled so a few waves moved across his forehead. He did not have his walking stick, and Min found she missed the accessory. It added something to his appearance that was undeniably attractive. Though, Min found him handsome at every turn—whether he'd just fallen from a horse or was suffering after having a bonesetter prod his injured ankle.

Each time she saw him, her heart beat a little faster and her desire to be close to him increased. She wished she could dance with him. Perhaps the absence of a walking stick meant that he could.

"Careful," Spilsby said crossly, interrupting Min's mooning.

Min realized she'd lost track of where she was supposed to be moving. She did not respond, except to send Spilsby a faint glower.

She found Evan once more, and this time, he was looking in her direction. Their eyes met, and Min knew in that moment that she wanted what Pandora had suggested. She wanted that one night for herself. And she wanted it with Evan Price.

CHAPTER 14

*E*van was sorry he'd left his walking stick in the cloakroom, because he found himself wanting to clutch the horse's head at the top and wield it like a sword as he watched Min dance with that scoundrel Spilsby. He should have called him out when he'd insulted Evan's sister—first by blaming her for the accidental ruin of his hideous waistcoat and then again when he'd started a rumor meant to ruin her. To see him with Min made Evan's stomach churn.

The fact that Min kept looking in his direction soothed him, however. In fact, it did more than soothe him—it stirred him. The moment the dance ended, Evan moved to intercept them as they left the floor.

"Spilsby," Evan muttered from between his clenched teeth. That was the most he could manage when he really just wanted to plant a facer on the man. He happily turned his focus to Min. "I believe the next set is mine, Lady Minerva."

"It is indeed," Min said with a brilliant smile that made Evan's chest expand.

"No walking stick tonight?" Spilsby asked, glancing at Evan's leg.

"No," Evan replied crisply. He met Spilsby's gaze. "And you should be grateful." He offered his arm to Min, who appeared to be hiding a smile.

"Farewell, Spilsby," she said as Evan escorted her away. Since the next set wouldn't start for a few minutes, he would at least take her to the opposite side of the room away from Spilsby.

When they were out of his range of hearing, Min said, "Did you just vaguely threaten violence against the viscount?"

Evan lifted a shoulder. "I may have. It's no less than he deserves after the way he treated Gwen."

"I agree completely. I'm glad I won't have to suffer his presence any longer."

"Yes, I heard you say, 'Farewell.'" Evan glanced at her and momentarily lost himself in the beauty of her profile. Her jawline was exquisite. "What did you mean by that?"

"He wanted to call on me tomorrow," she replied in a tone that implied such an idea was ludicrous. "However, I made it clear that I will not be dancing with him anymore, and there will be no courtship as I have no interest whatsoever in marriage to him."

Evan grinned. "Bravo."

"You should have heard him on the dance floor." Min rolled her eyes. "He tried to apologize for his behavior after Gwen tripped and spilled her drink on him at Almack's."

Evan felt a fresh spike of fury. He turned his head to look back at wherever Spilsby might be. "Tell me he didn't try to blame it on my sister again."

"I think he was only trying to slither into my good graces, but he's no chance of managing that. I told him he didn't need to apologize to me, but to her."

"I should make him," Evan seethed.

"Then I explained that even if Gwen could excuse his

rotten behavior that night at Almack's, there would be no excusing the rumor he started about Gwen and Somerton."

"The man is an absolute bounder. Should I call him out now?" Evan escorted her toward the center of the ballroom as the next set was about to begin.

"For what? Being an annoyance?" Min brought her free hand up to touch his forearm. "You must do what you think is best, but I wouldn't want you to get hurt."

Evan laughed. "Not to sound arrogant, but are you aware of how well I shoot? And fence?"

She slid him a tantalizing look as they moved to take their places for the dance. "I have heard you are an excellent shot and quite graceful with a sword. Perhaps you'll demonstrate your prowess for me sometime when your ankle is fully healed."

She was flirting with him, by God, and Evan was bloody thrilled. "I shall do so at the earliest opportunity," he said, even while knowing his time with her was short, at least for now. He had to get to London and take care of this situation with Sir Abraham. When he returned to Bath, he could completely focus on Min and consider wooing her to be his wife.

"Perhaps you could teach me to shoot as well." Min took her hand from his arm, which was supremely disappointing but also necessary for them to position themselves across from one another for the dance. "I imagine that might be diverting," she added.

Her eyes met his, and he couldn't tell if she was just saying so to flirt with him or if she actually wanted him to teach her. He decided it didn't matter. He would do anything he could to spend time with her, whatever the reason.

It was their turn to dance between the lines, but halfway down, he turned his ankle. Pain shot up his leg, and he bit his cheek to keep from cursing. Min moved closer and clutched him, supporting him as he put his weight on his right leg.

Lines furrowed her brow as she gazed at him with warm concern. "Oh dear, your ankle again."

"It just won't bloody heal completely," he growled. He ought to consult the physician tomorrow before he left town, but he wouldn't have time. He wanted to get to London right away to take care of matters so he could return to Bath—and Min—as quickly as possible.

"You need to sit," she said. The other dancers paused as Min helped Evan move out of the way.

He limped alongside Min as she guided him out of the ballroom into the corridor. While he hadn't at all meant to trigger his injury, he couldn't say he minded the current situation in which he found himself.

"Let's sit in the tearoom," she said. "There won't be many people in there, so it will be quiet, and you can prop your foot up on another chair if you need to." She led him to a corner and pulled a chair from a table so he could sit. "Where's your walking stick?"

"In the cloakroom, which isn't terribly helpful."

She smiled at him. "I'll fetch it."

"Later. Just sit with me for now, if you don't mind." Evan sat and gently moved his foot, rotating the ankle slightly to gauge how badly he'd hurt himself.

"I can see you wincing." She angled the chair beside him to face him and sat down. "Have you been doing too much? The doctor cautioned you about rushing your recuperation."

"Yes, and he lectured me about it a second time when he returned after the house party at Longleat concluded. I confess that when my ankle feels good in the morning, I probably do too much. I must give it more time to heal."

She arched a brow at him. "Will you promise to use the

walking stick at all times? You can't very well teach me to fence if you aren't fully healed."

"That is certainly excellent motivation." He gave her a sly smile. "However, I don't need a fully functional ankle to teach you to shoot."

"No more dancing either," she said in a rather commanding tone that Evan found more than mildly arousing.

"Yes, your ladyship. I do not regret dancing with you tonight, though." Their time on the dance floor, though abbreviated, had been glorious. He'd reveled in the heat of her gaze and the seductive set of her lips. Had she any idea how badly he wanted her?

Of course not. Because he hadn't said. He wasn't much of a rogue after all, apparently.

"I'm glad you did—dance with me, I mean." Her lips curved into a brief but heart-wrenching smile. "It was the brightest spot I've had for a few days now."

"I heard what happened with your father. Sheff came to see me yesterday. I'm so sorry you are facing that in addition to everything else."

"Thank you," Min said quietly. "Father said he will wait to file his suit until I am betrothed, but he would like me to make that happen soon. As if I can cast a spell and conjure the man I want to marry—and that he would want to marry me too."

"Any man should want to marry you," he said softly.

There were a few people at the other end of the long, rectangular room, but Evan and Min were alone in this corner. Evan realized he could broach the subject of marriage with her now.

"I have something to talk to you about," he said at the same moment she said, "I'd like to speak with you about something." They both laughed.

"You first," Evan said, still smiling.

She clasped her hands in her lap, appearing suddenly nervous. Pink flagged her cheeks, and she didn't quite meet his eyes. "Since I've yet to find anyone I would want to wed and my family is shortly to be plunged into scandal, I've been considering whether I want to marry at all. Pandora has helpfully pointed out that spinsterhood is an option. She may not have chosen it, but she's not completely unhappy, and I confess she has a measure of freedom that is appealing."

"You're considering spinsterhood?"

"I'm considering a future in which I don't marry. Which is what I wanted to talk to you about."

Evan's curiosity spiked. "How can I help?"

Flattening her palms against her lap, she took a deep breath. "If I don't marry, the thing I know I will miss out on is the passionate side of marriage. I would not have realized that if we hadn't kissed, so thank you." She locked her gaze with his, and Evan wanted nothing more than to immerse himself in the emotions blazing in her eyes. "I know now that I want to fully experience passion, and I would like to do that with you."

Evan dearly wished they were not in the middle of the bloody tearoom. For then he would show her every way he could make her feel passion.

He launched himself from the chair, heedless of his ankle and the lack of a walking stick, and clasped Min's hand. Pulling her up, he led her into an alcove in the corner, tucked behind a pillar. It wasn't completely private, but for now it shielded them, particularly since there was no one at this end of the room.

"Evan, you shouldn't be standing on your ankle."

"The hell with my ankle," he muttered before cupping her face and kissing her.

Her lips molded to his, and the passion she said she

wanted flared between them. Her tongue met his in a dazzling, erotic battle, enflaming him. He moved one hand to her back and pressed her body to his. He splayed his other hand against the bare flesh over her collarbone and the base of her throat. He cursed his gloves and every other item of clothing they wore.

"Is this what you want?" he whispered between kisses.

"Yes." She couldn't say more because he devoured her mouth as need coursed through him.

He tore his lips from hers long enough to say, "Good, because I want you more than I can say. More than I have ever wanted anyone."

She tugged at the back of his head and brought his mouth to hers once more. She dug her fingers into his nape and pressed against him.

Evan slid his hand down over her breast, cupping her through the fabric of her too many garments. He closed his teeth gently over her lower lip, pulling on it before he moved his mouth down her jaw and neck.

"No."

The single word made him freeze. "You want me to stop?"

"No," she said hoarsely. "I mean, this isn't what I want. Not exactly. I want more. I want everything, Evan. Show me. Please."

He groaned against her neck and managed to stop himself before he closed his mouth over her flesh and suckled her until he left his mark. He wanted the world to know that Min belonged to him.

Evan squeezed her breast, prompting her to gasp. "How I wish I could strip every garment from your body, Min." He kissed her again, long and deep, claiming her with every stroke of his tongue and sweep of his lips.

When he pulled back, he was breathless, as was she. "Marry me," he rasped.

She opened her eyes and stared at him, a shaft of light from the tearoom illuminating her features. "What? No, I'm not asking you for that."

A sound nearby drove them apart. Evan pivoted and looked out of the alcove. A footman was doing something at a table.

When Evan turned back to Min, she was smoothing her skirt. "We should return to the table. Actually, you should go home to rest your ankle."

Evan had all but forgotten the pain, but now it sliced back, and he adjusted his weight to his right side. He pressed back against the wall and let Min pass by him to step out of the alcove.

She did not sit back down at the table.

Evan limped to his chair and sat.

"Let me fetch your walking stick now," she said.

"Wait a moment," he said quietly. "I meant what I asked you."

She arched a brow at him. "I don't recall you asking me a question."

He hadn't. Overcome with desire, he'd issued a command. "No, I did not. But I will, and not in a dark alcove at the Upper Rooms." He looked into her eyes. "I *will* ask you. What will you say?"

"Until you do, I can't give you an answer." Her cheeks were still slightly flushed from their encounter.

Evan longed to see her entire body in a state of arousal—and he would.

"I have to go to London tomorrow." He hated the surprise followed by disappointment in her gaze. "I won't be gone long, but it's imperative." He ought to explain why, but he didn't want to soil this moment by discussing his mistakes. He would tell her everything when he returned.

"How long will you be?"

"Two days to travel there, a day to conduct this necessary business, and two days back." Weather permitting. It bloody well better not rain.

"So, I'll see you Tuesday, probably?"

Too damn long. And perhaps longer depending on how things went with Sir Abraham. Evan was particularly frustrated that he couldn't ride, which would make the trip much faster. "Yes. Tuesday. If I can return sooner, be assured that I will. Then we will talk."

"But I would rather do other things." Her gaze swept over him, and his cock, which had finally started to relax, hardened once more.

"Min, do not look at me like that unless you are prepared for me to throw you over my shoulder and take you home, where I will thoroughly ravish you. Hell, we may not make it that far, for I will not be able to keep my hands off you in the coach."

"If you don't stop talking, I won't be able to walk to fetch your stick," she said, again sounding breathless.

"My apologies. I didn't mean to detain you." He couldn't help himself.

"It isn't that. What you say… It turns my knees to jelly. I might need your walking stick to support myself—since you can't throw me over your shoulder," she added with a wicked smile that made Evan groan softly.

"Away, woman. You torment me."

She gave him a saucy smile. "Good."

As he watched her saunter through the tearoom, Evan grinned to himself. He would move heaven and earth to return to her as quickly as possible.

*E*van left the ball shortly after their encounter in the alcove, and the rest of the evening passed at an interminably slow rate for Min. Between the lingering intoxication of Evan's kisses and the shock of him bringing up marriage, Min could barely concentrate on dancing. She'd considered asking her mother to leave early, but she hadn't seen the duchess since supper. And though they'd sat at the same table, Min's mother had been engrossed in conversation with a pair of other ladies, including the horrible busybody, Mrs. Lawler.

Min had been glad to not to have to speak with her mother, for she was too overcome with thoughts of Evan. She kept thinking of his hands on her and the delirious way his tongue invaded her mouth. Her body hadn't yet recovered. She quivered in dark, secret places and yearned for the moment when she could be alone with him again. There was no question that she wanted him.

But then his talk of marriage had jolted her. He hadn't even asked her. Instead, he'd commanded that she marry him. Something about the way he'd said it had sent shivers through her. It was as if he'd been unable to control himself, and that his lack of control was because of her. There was something darkly erotic about that.

She had to think he'd been just as caught up as she was and that was why he'd mentioned marriage. They'd been flirting and then taken it to a dizzyingly dangerous degree with talk of more in the future. She'd asked him to give her the passion she desired. Of course he would assume they should marry.

Perhaps he'd forgotten her requirements—that she needed love and would not marry for less. Passion alone, which they had in surplus, apparently, was not enough. She would remind him of those facts when he returned. If he refused to give her what she wanted without marriage, she would be disappointed, but she would respect that. She would not, however, surrender what she wanted in a marriage.

She hated that he was leaving. First Ellis, then Sheff and Jo, and now Evan. She realized she'd included him in a group of people who were dearly important to her. People she loved. Her pulse sped. Could she possibly love Evan? The question lingered in her mind the rest of the evening.

Finally, the ball concluded, and Min could go home. Her feet ached a bit as she climbed into the coach with her mother.

The duchess fixed her gaze on Min as the coach began moving. "I wish you hadn't danced with Mr. Price. Even more, I wish you hadn't disappeared into the tearoom with him after he apparently hurt himself." Her frown was clearly visible in the dim light of the coach.

Min looked out the window into the darkness. "What's done is done, Mother. Those things *did* happen, and I went on to dance every set afterward. Clearly, there was no harm done."

"Well, you mustn't have anything more to do with him, because there *will* be harm done now that news of his exploits have reached Bath."

"Exploits?" Min shot her gaze back to her mother.

The duchess gave Min a superior look. "I told you I'd heard he might be involved in a scandal, and it turns out he has been carrying on an affair with a married woman called Mrs. Dalton in London."

That didn't make sense. "How is he carrying on an affair with someone from London when he's in Bath?" Min tried very hard not to roll her eyes. Her mother was likely just trying to stir up trouble.

"Mrs. Dalton was here in Bath only last week," the

duchess replied. "Their affair started last summer, and the rumor is that her husband, Sir Abraham, is going to seek a divorce. You can see why you mustn't have anything to do with him."

Conflicting emotions shot through Min. On the one hand, she wanted to laugh at the irony of her mother lecturing her about the risk of association with divorce ruining her. But of course, the duchess had no idea what her husband was planning, and Min wasn't going to tell her.

Secondly, Min didn't want to believe that Evan had lied to her by omission. Why wouldn't he have told her about Mrs. Dalton? She wanted to think this was simply an untrue rumor. But while Mrs. Lawler was a horrible gossip and a terrible person, everything she repeated was verifiable. She hadn't ever fabricated the rumors she spread, as far as Min knew.

Furthermore, Evan was returning to London tomorrow to take care of something. Was he going to address this issue in the hope of curtailing the scandal? She needed to find out.

Dread settled along Min's neck and in her chest. She didn't want to believe that Evan had behaved badly, or that he'd failed to tell her. Yet, he *was* a rogue, and as the rules stated, one could never expect a rogue to change.

"I think you must reconsider Spilsby," her mother said. She wrinkled her nose. "Or you may have to end up settling for that fortune hunter Claxton. At least he has a title."

"Mother, I've told you that *I* will choose my husband. I do not require your input."

The duchess's brows pitched into a V. "It seems you do, because you have gravitated toward someone who is wholly inappropriate, even after I told you not to bother with him. Will you listen to me now?"

The coach stopped in front of her mother's house in the Circus.

"Enough, Mother." Min didn't bother disguising her agitation. "I don't wish to discuss this with you anymore. In fact, I'm going to Father's house. I will sleep there tonight."

The coachman opened the door, and her mother hesitated. She fixed her haughty stare on Min. "Why is it you are doing everything possible to ensure you will never wed?"

Min met her gaze coolly. "As I've explained to you before, you've ensured that marriage is almost completely unappealing to me. That you keep trying to shove me into it is perplexing and disappointing. Do you really want me to live a life like yours?"

"I don't regret my life," her mother said. "I'm quite happy as a duchess with a respected place in Society."

"That is not enough for me," Min said, notching up her chin. "I want a happy home with a husband I love and children I adore and who hopefully love me in return."

The duchess sucked in a breath. "I don't know why you've decided to be so cruel to me of late, Minerva."

Min gaped at her. "You accuse *me* of being cruel. After everything you've done to Ellis, you expect that things would not have changed? You must realize that I would see you in a different light now that I know the truth."

"Enough of that." The duchess glanced toward the coachman, whose face was impassive. She waved her hand at Min. "Go on to your father's, then, but don't expect me to send your maid."

The duchess climbed out of the coach with the coachman's assistance.

"That's fine," Min muttered. "It's not as if my father's house doesn't have someone who can help me out of my gown if I need it, and I can brush my own bloody hair."

After Min's mother had gone into the house, the coachman looked into the interior at Min. "You're going to His Grace's house in Catharine Place, then?"

"Yes, please. And when we get there, I will need you to wait for a few minutes. I have an errand for you to run." She sent him a direct stare. "And you must keep it between us."

The coachman gave her an understanding look. "Rest assured, my lady, no one in the household goes out of their way to share anything with Her Grace."

Min smiled. "Well, that is interesting to know. Thank you."

He closed the door, and they were shortly on their way to Catharine Place. When they arrived, Min told the coachman she would return presently with a note for him to deliver to Mr. Evan Price, just two doors down. She gestured toward Evan's mother's house.

"Very good, my lady," the coachman replied with a nod.

Min dashed into her father's house. It was late, and the butler was no longer at his post, so a footman welcomed her inside. She informed him that she would be spending the night. He left to tell a maid to prepare a bedchamber on the second floor.

Meanwhile, Min went into the study to find parchment. The space smelled like her father's cologne and reminded her of times she would visit him in his study at Henlow House. She'd climb onto his lap, where he would tell her a story, usually about mermaids that frolicked near the shore in Weston not far from the Grove. Min had looked for those mermaids every summer when they were at the Grove until she'd grown old enough to realize they weren't real.

Shaking the memory away, she wrote a quick note to Evan, asking him to meet her on the green in the center of the narrow square. It wasn't terribly private, but it was dark, so Min didn't think it mattered. She simply couldn't wait to learn the truth.

She assumed he was leaving first thing in the morning, so she wouldn't have time to speak with him then. It had to be tonight. She went back outside and handed the note to the coachman, then watched as he delivered it to Evan's mother's house.

When the coachman returned to the coach, he saw that Min was still standing there. "You must go inside, my lady."

"I will in a moment. It's a nice night, and we won't have many more of them before winter." She gave him a smile and hoped he would not ask to stay with her while she remained outside.

Thankfully, he wished her a good evening and departed. Min hastened to the green and positioned herself beneath a tree. A few minutes later, Evan appeared outside his mother's house and looked about. Min knew the exact moment he saw her, for he launched forward, limping slightly as he came toward her. Why didn't he have his walking stick?

As he drew close, she could see his brow was furrowed. "Min, what on earth are you doing outside at this hour?"

"I needed to speak with you." She glanced down at his ankle. "Where is your walking stick?"

"In the house. I only took enough time to throw on a coat. I thought it imperative that I join you with alacrity," he added drily. "What's wrong?"

Min clasped her hands in front of her. "Why are you going to London tomorrow? Please don't lie."

She could see immediately that he'd been hiding something. Guilt shadowed his eyes, and his jaw tightened. "I have been involved in a scandal there. I didn't want to tell you about it until I'd resolved the matter."

"Of course not," she said, feeling utterly dejected. "You're a rogue, and rogues never change."

CHAPTER 15

"*R*ogues *can* change," Evan insisted. The distress in Min's eyes and in her voice tore through him more painfully than his ankle sprain ever had. "You've seen it. Your brother has changed. Wellesbourne has changed. Somerton has changed."

Min did not appear moved. "You've been having an affair with this Mrs. Dalton, and she was here last week. Now you are returning to London. It doesn't look to me as if you've changed."

Evan blew out a breath and ran his hand through his hair. "Let us not have this conversation out here. We run the risk of creating our own scandal if anyone sees us standing alone in the dark at this hour. Can we go into the duke's house?"

Min pursed her lips at him, then stalked toward her father's house. Evan hurried to keep up with her and ignored the protest of his ankle. Min led him down the stairs at the front of the house to the lower level. She opened the door and walked inside, leaving him to close it.

They stood in a corridor that almost certainly led to the kitchen, but she didn't take him there. Instead, she slipped into a narrow alcove with wine stored along one side. She folded her arms over her chest and glowered at him expectantly.

He joined her in the alcove. It was small enough that they could not face one another without almost touching, especially with her arms crossed. The wine was behind Evan. "I haven't lied to you, Min. I just didn't want to tell you what was happening, because...I'm embarrassed. I've made a terrible mistake, and it isn't that I was having an affair with Mrs. Dalton. I barely know the woman. I was helping a friend."

Min's eyes narrowed. "Explain."

Evan told her about Roger and why he'd wanted to help him. "You see, I could not ignore the opportunity to return his kindness."

Her features softened a bit, but her brow remained furrowed. "So, you confessed that you were the one having the affair with Mrs. Dalton?"

"Yes, to protect Roger. I didn't think it would amount to anything, and stupidly, I didn't think people would care since some had started calling me a rake anyway."

"And why is that?" Min asked. "I know you kissed Miss Forsyth in a garden and that you like to flirt. That's not *terribly* rakish."

"It is when you're also known for daring pursuits," he said with a faint grimace. "I've also done nothing to discourage that reputation from growing. I keep company with rakes and rogues, and the truth is that I like feeling as though I belong." He suddenly realized he was always seeking connection with others. It was why he flirted with women and why he hated missing things. He liked to feel...included. "I suppose I enjoyed being part of a set, like with your brother and his friends in Weston."

"So you've pretended to be a rake to make friends?"

"That's rather simplifying things. I've fit in and found a place."

"As a rogue." She scowled at him briefly. "Why are you going to London?"

"To fix this mess." He brushed his hand down the side of his face. "Mrs. Dalton came to Bath to tell me that Sir Abraham planned to file suit against me for criminal conversation in order to divorce her. I sent her back to London to try to persuade him not to do so. However, her efforts failed. Now I must reveal the truth to Sir Abraham."

"As you should. A divorce would ruin you," she said quietly. "I can't believe you listened to me and Sheff talk about our father bringing the same sort of suit, and you didn't say anything."

"That is a terrible enough problem for both of you." Evan looked at her with sympathy. "I wasn't going to compound it by sharing my own troubles."

"What about your friend?" Min asked. "The suit will ruin him, especially since he's a barrister, I should think."

"I plan to speak with my father and hope he can talk some sense into Sir Abraham. There's no guarantee that the divorce would even be granted, so why drag everyone through the mud?"

Min cocked her head. "Are you saying Sir Abraham should just forgive his wife who betrayed him and act as if everything is fine?"

"Something like that," Evan said. "I don't know the specifics of their marriage, but Roger told me she is very unhappy. Sir Abraham is considerably older than she is. I imagine there are…areas where that could be challenging."

"I'm inclined to be as outraged as Sir Abraham." Min made a sound in her throat. "But then I am also sympathetic to someone who says they are unhappy. Now do you see why marriage terrifies me?"

He had known why she was inclined to dislike it, but he hadn't seen that she was genuinely afraid. "I do."

"I can't believe you would even bring it up, as you did earlier when you were in the midst of all this...roguery. It doesn't matter that you didn't have the affair. You weren't honest about it. Furthermore, you know what I want in a marriage, and you are not offering me that."

He edged toward her so that his chest nearly met hers. "I know I handled this poorly, but I intended to tell you when I returned, when all this was behind me. Then I could look to the future—a future that I hoped to spend with you. I would be free to declare my love for you."

Her nostrils flared slightly, but she did not soften. Indeed, her eyes were bright with outrage. "You've created a scandal, and you've lied to me. By your own admission, you didn't want to complicate my life. *You* made that decision for me. How can we build a future on deception and selfishness? I've had far too much of that in my life."

Evan felt as though he'd fallen from his horse again. The wind was completely knocked out of him, and he experienced a rush of something akin to panic. "I was trying to protect you. But I can see why you are upset. I should have been honest with you and let you decide whether we could remain friends." He could not believe how badly he'd bungled this. "I don't want to lose you, Min. That feeling of belonging I seek—it's never been stronger than with you."

"*Evan.*"

He braced his hand on the wall behind her. "I'll go if you tell me to. But I don't want to. I will prove to you that nothing and no one is more important to me than you."

They stared into each other's eyes for a long moment. He held his breath, praying she wouldn't send him away.

"I have never been drawn to any man the way I am to

you," she whispered. "It scares me, I think. I don't know what I will do if I lose you too."

"You won't lose me," he vowed. "Not ever."

"What about tonight? Will you stay?"

He lowered his head next to hers, putting his mouth near her ear. "What are you asking me for, Min?" His lips were tantalizingly close to her flesh. He could feel the rapid rise and fall of her chest and practically hear the beat of her heart in her neck.

"What I asked you for earlier." She gripped his waist beneath his coat with both hands and pulled him against her.

Evan nipped at her ear then kissed her neck, careful not to mark her though he wanted to. She lifted her chin, lengthening her neck so he had more area to taste.

She curled her fingers into his lower back just at the top of his backside. Evan moaned before he took her mouth in a blistering kiss. He pressed into her, rotating his hips. She arched against him, tugging at his shirt.

Desperate to feel her, Evan reached down to pull up her skirts. Her hand joined his, raising the layers of fabric to expose her leg. She held the gown and undergarments while he found the top of her garter. He skimmed his hand along her bare flesh, moving up her thigh and around to the back, where he gripped her and lifted her leg. He caressed her, his fingertips molding into her bare backside.

Her skirts were now bunched between them, frustrating him because he wanted to feel her against his cock. She seemed to understand and feel the same, for she gathered them at her waist. They were still too cumbersome for him to press as close as he wanted to be, but she was open to him now.

"Put your foot against the shelf behind me," he instructed softly, his voice as ragged and tortured as he felt.

She did as he instructed, bracing herself so Evan could

release her leg and move his hand between her thighs where he found the soft nest of her curls. He stroked his fingers along her crease, then kissed her again, long and thoroughly. She whimpered, clutching at his shoulder as her hips moved with his touch.

He increased his pressure and speed. Her thighs quivered. As he drove his tongue deep into her mouth, he slipped his finger into her sex. She twitched, and he slowed his movements.

"More," she demanded between kisses.

"Not here." He removed his hand from between her legs and guided her leg down so she could stand. "Where is your room?"

She stared up at him, her lips parted, her eyes dark with her pupils enlarged. "Second floor. We can take the servants' stairs. But I don't know if I can walk just yet."

He smiled at her. "Then I will carry you."

"You can't. Not with your ankle."

"You will find, my dearest Min, that there is nothing I won't do for you." He swept her into his arms and carried her from the alcove.

～

Somehow, Min had directed Evan to the right staircase. However, after the first flight, she'd demanded he set her down. "I will not be responsible for further injury," she told him.

"If it means you at my bedside caring for me, I will have no quarrel." He grinned at her with seductive promise, and she was unable to resist kissing him.

Evan swept her against him with a groan, and it was several minutes before they continued their ascent.

On the second floor, she opened the door and led him from the servants' staircase, then froze.

"What is it?" he whispered.

She turned to face him. "I'm not entirely sure which room is mine. The footman said he would have a maid prepare it, but then I went outside to meet you."

"Are we in danger of encountering someone?"

"I suppose we may run into a servant, but my father and Mrs. Welbeck are on the first floor."

"We'll be careful," Evan said before waggling his brows. "What an adventure."

He moved in front of her and went to the first door. It was a bedchamber, but did not appear to have been prepared —there was no fire, and the bed was not fully dressed.

"Not this one," she whispered before moving on to the next.

The second chamber was the one—it had a freshly stoked fire. And there were bedclothes. They were pink and floral.

She walked in, and Evan chuckled as he closed the door.

"Your favorite decorating scheme," she said with a smile as she removed her gloves and tossed them on a chair near the hearth. Turning to face him once more, she moved so that her skirt swirled about her ankles. "And it matches my gown, which you surely loathe."

"I don't dislike pink at all when you're wearing it." He moved toward her. "Indeed, your lips are a delectable shade of pink, as are your cheeks, particularly after I kiss you or say something naughty."

"I don't recall anything you've said that's particularly improper."

"I've definitely *thought* plenty of inappropriate things, and I am doing so right now. I do wonder what else about you is pink." He pulled her into his arms. "I look forward to finding out. Pink may very well become my favorite color."

He kissed her and cupped her nape, his fingers tangling in her hair. She reached up and began to pull at the pins, holding them in her hand as she loosened the locks. He grabbed a length of her freed hair and tugged gently.

Then he lifted his head and stared down at her while she finished taking the rest of the pins out. "You are so beautiful," he murmured.

Min deposited the pins on a dressing table with a mirror and kicked her slippers from her feet. She slipped her earrings off and set them next to the pins.

Evan came up behind her, and she could see him in the mirror, his head bent toward hers as he nuzzled her hair.

"Will you unfasten my necklace?" She lifted her hand and swept her hair to the side.

He did as she asked and dropped the necklace on the table, his arm grazing hers. His gaze met hers in the mirror. "Is there anything else I can unfasten?"

"The hooks on the back of my gown. There aren't very many." Because the bodice was very short, with the waistline coming nearly to the underside of her breasts.

Evan's arm was still lightly touching hers. He skimmed his fingertips along her flesh, up past her elbow, until he met the sleeve of her gown.

She shivered where he'd touched her and recalled the way he'd used his fingers in the wine cupboard. Her sex tingled as she anticipated him continuing what he'd started.

He unfastened the hooks of her gown, and Min brought the garment forward so she could pull her arms from the sleeves. She pushed it down to the floor and stepped out of the circle it formed as it pooled.

Before she could retrieve the gown, Evan swept it up and took it to the chair, where he gently laid it over the back.

"You could be a lady's maid," she said as she untied her petticoat.

"Only for you." His eyes glinted seductively as he removed his coat and laid it atop her gown.

"Then come help me." Min wriggled out of her petticoat, and he rushed to take it from her. Then she presented her back to him so he could loosen the laces of her corset.

Again, she moved her hair, sweeping it over her left shoulder. He tugged at the laces, but then she felt his lips against the back of her neck. She closed her eyes as he kissed from her nape to the top of her chemise, his mouth tracing along her spine. He slipped the straps from her shoulders, then pushed the corset down her body before taking it away.

Min turned to face him as he returned. Without his cravat, an alluring triangle of his near-olive skin was exposed to her gaze. She longed to touch his flesh and feel him against her.

"Should we get into the bed now?" she asked.

"If you like." His voice was husky, his expression hungry.

She held his gaze as she moved around to the side of the bed and climbed onto the mattress. Unsure of what to do, she knelt there as he followed her path and stood beside the bed. Min pivoted to face him.

"Sit." He clasped her waist as she moved her legs toward him and sat flat on the coverlet. "Closer," he whispered, tugging her toward him. "And part your legs around me."

She opened her legs so that he stood between them. He thrust his hands in her hair and held her head as he kissed her. His thumbs stroked her cheeks while he plundered her mouth.

Min placed her hands against his chest. He was warm even though his shirt separated her flesh from his. Eager to touch him directly, she moved her hand up and slid it into the open collar of his shirt. He released her momentarily so he could remove his shirt. This time, he did not carefully retrieve the garment and take it to the chair with the rest of their things. He cast it aside and reached for her once more.

He kissed her, then looked into her eyes. "You must tell me if you want me to stop. Or if you don't like something."

"What if I do like it? What if I want more or... something?"

His lips spread into a heart-stopping smile. "You must tell me that too. I would say loudly, but I suppose we don't want to alert the household to my presence."

"No, we don't want that," she murmured. "I should like you to continue what you were doing in the wine cupboard, please."

Evan moved one hand to her thigh. He gripped the chemise that still covered her there and pushed it up to her waist. "I will. But first, if you will humor me, I have long wanted to see your breasts."

"I hadn't realized." Min found the drawstring at the neckline of her chemise and loosened it. With her finger, she pulled it down to reveal one breast. "Is that better?"

His gaze fixed on her naked breast, and his lips parted. "Lovely." He lifted his hand to her and cupped her flesh.

Sensation shot through her. It was a simple touch, but she felt the electricity of it everywhere. His fingertips stroked her nipple, and she felt that directly in her sex. The pulse that had started there when he'd kissed her at the Upper Rooms intensified. She gasped.

He closed his fingers around her then, lightly pinching. There was no pain, just a more insistent ache that needed satisfying.

"More," she rasped.

He lowered his head and kissed her where his hand had been. His lips feathered her skin as he held her. Then his mouth closed over the nipple, and he suckled her.

Min grasped his head as her world tilted. She closed her

eyes and gave herself over to the dizzying sensations. She cast her head back and was soon leaning backward. A moment later, she was flat against the mattress with Evan bent over her. He brought her hips closer to the edge of the bed, and she felt him press against her bare sex.

Her eyes flew open, and she looked up at him. His eyes were slitted as he rotated his hips against hers. As much as she'd loved him touching her breast, this was even better.

He pushed her chemise up, and together, they took it over her head. As with his shirt, he simply threw it to the side. Then he untied her garters and slipped her stockings off, letting them fall to the floor. He thrust his hips into hers, and she met him, realizing that was his sex, hard and long, beneath his fall.

As he rubbed against her, she closed her eyes again and moaned softly. Then his mouth was on her other breast, drawing on her nipple so that she arched up from the bed. She clutched at his head and whimpered as the passion she'd sought ravaged through her.

He stroked her sex again, his fingers sliding along her folds as he'd done earlier. When he touched that spot at the top, her body shuddered with need. She could feel something building and knew it was the release Persey had told her about. But Persey hadn't told her everything, and Min hadn't expected she would feel the same. Why would she when no man had ever aroused her in the slightest?

Evan, however, was making up for that. Min began to quiver, her body pulsing with overwhelming sensation. He moved his mouth to her other breast and continued to tease her sex. At last, he slid his finger inside her as he'd done earlier—that was what she craved, what she needed. She bent her legs, opening herself to him completely.

His mouth left her breast as he kissed down her abdomen. He kept descending, and she couldn't imagine he meant to keep going. But he did, until his mouth met his hand. He licked at her sex as he pumped his finger into her. Pleasure pulsed through her, and she surrendered to her body, letting it move as it would. She thrust her hips and cast her head back.

Evan gripped her hip, his fingers curled around her backside and digging into her flesh. He held her steady as his lips and tongue drove her to the brink of control. She writhed on the bed, unable to stop herself from careening wildly into an unknown release. He stroked her hard and fast until her muscles tightened, and she broke apart.

Min cried his name, then clapped her hand over her mouth as she recalled what he'd said about alerting the household. She whimpered into her hand as wave after wave of ecstasy washed over her. Evan did not cease his attention until she began to float down from the impossible heights she'd reached.

Working to catch her breath, she opened her eyes. He stood next to the bed, his gaze fixed on her. His lips curled into a devastating smile. "I should let you sleep now."

He started to turn. Min scrambled to sit up and grasped his arm. "Wait. You can't leave."

"I can't spend the night," he said with a chuckle.

"But that isn't everything." She frowned at him rather exaggeratedly. "I told you I wanted everything."

His features tightened as he appeared to be in pain. "We should not."

Min slid from the bed and stood in front of him. She put her hands on his bare chest, her fingertips grazing the dark hair in the center. "I won't let you leave."

She recalled what he'd said to her earlier, about her telling him if she wanted him to stop. Perhaps Evan *wanted* to leave. Taking her hands from him, she dropped her hands to her side. "Unless you want to."

"I don't." His answer was low and hoarse.

She met his gaze. "What do you want to do?"

"Wicked, sinful things."

"Show me." Min took his hand as she returned to the bed.

"You're sure?"

"Never more." She narrowed her eyes at him. "You're wearing too many clothes, I think."

"Definitely." He tore off his remaining garments and joined her on the bed.

She couldn't help staring at his sex. "May I touch you?"

"Please." He stretched out beside her on his side with his head propped on his hand, and she rolled to face him.

Tentatively, she wrapped her fingers around his length. His flesh was softer than she would have imagined, which was silly. It wasn't as if he went around with it exposed to the elements. "What you did to me with your mouth... Is that something I should do to you?"

"You could," he said slowly. "But perhaps for now, we should start with something...simpler."

Min stroked his shaft. "Can it be that complicated to put my mouth on you? Is there some special technique?"

"Er, no. I suppose it is rather easy." He closed his eyes and moaned as she continued to move her hand along his length.

"You seem to like this," she said, enjoying the pleasure written in the lines of his face.

"Immensely. You could move your hand even faster if you like."

Min complied, stroking him from the base to the tip with increasing speed.

"Or not," he said through gritted teeth. "I don't want to spend myself in your hand. But perhaps I should."

Spending himself meant going through what she had. But he would also spill his seed. "Yes, I imagine it's preferable if you do not come—is that the right word, I think it is—inside me. However, you can start that way, can't you?" She tried to remember what Persey had told her.

He opened his eyes and looked into hers. "Is that what you want?" He ended the question by sucking in his breath as she moved her hand to the soft sacs underneath his shaft.

She cupped them gently, massaging him before returning to his cock. "Yes."

Evan came over her, pushing her to her back and settling himself between her legs. "I can't wait another moment." He stroked her sex, his fingertips gliding through her folds. "You're wet again," he murmured.

"That's good?"

"It makes things much easier. Though, I've ways to make you wet." He gave her a wicked smile.

"It seems as though there is a great deal to this. How many variations to sexual intercourse are there?"

"Endless," he hissed as he positioned himself at her opening. "Ready?"

Min wrapped her legs around his hips. "More than."

He thrust into her, moving slowly, methodically, as he buried himself within her body. When he was fully seated, she felt uncomfortable, but not painfully so.

"All right?" he asked, brushing a kiss against her temple.

"I think so. Is that it?"

He laughed. "No. I was giving you a chance to get used to this feeling before I start to move. I'm going to pull out." He did so, removing himself from her sheath. "Then slide back in." He slid forward, filling her once more.

"Like you did with your finger. And your tongue. But this is different. Perhaps even better."

He withdrew and thrust again. Then again. He began to move faster, his body crashing against hers.

"Definitely better." She dug her heels into his backside, eager for every thrust. She clutched at his back and shoulders as pleasure built within her once more. They moved together, and she was reminded of a horse and rider who were perfectly trained to ride as one.

"Min, I have to—" He groaned loudly as her muscles clenched around him.

Then he was gone from her, his sex replaced by his hand as he worked her flesh. Somehow, she realized he would need the same assistance, and she reached for his cock. She wrapped her hand around him and stroked him as she'd done before.

"Faster, Min," he begged, and the ecstasy roiling through her shot even higher.

At last, he cried out, and she felt warmth on her hip.

Their breath came hard and fast as their movements slowed. Evan collapsed beside her and gathered her into his arms. He kissed her as long as their breathlessness would allow.

Min laid her head against his chest and listened to his heart slow. It lulled her into a drowsy state, and she closed her eyes. She'd no idea how long they lay together entwined.

"Min?" Evan whispered.

"Mmm." She was too sleepy to form words.

"I meant what I said earlier tonight—at the Upper Rooms. I do want to marry you, and when I return from London, I will ask you properly."

His words brought her awake, but she didn't move. She opened her eyes and tried to keep her pulse steady. She didn't know what to say.

Earlier, when they'd been in the wine cupboard, he'd mentioned declaring his love. But he hadn't done so. Much like he hadn't *asked* her to marry him. She wasn't sure what he was about, but she also didn't want to discuss it right now. After the most amazing experience of her life—and with all the turmoil surrounding both of them—she just wanted to relish this moment. She didn't want to think of the past or the future. There would be plenty of time for that.

Min allowed her eyes to close once more.

Evan stroked her back, his fingertips gliding along her spine. He pressed a kiss to the top of her head. "Good night, Min."

She ought to make sure he would leave without being seen, but she trusted him to escape undetected. So, she surrendered to sleep and vowed she wouldn't dream. Tonight, at least, her dreams had already come true.

CHAPTER 16

*E*van departed for London early Friday morning. He'd been tired after being up late with Min. He'd stayed longer than he'd intended, watching her sleep and not wanting to disturb her by leaving. He was careful not to fall asleep himself, lest he not wake up early enough.

But he'd had to go, so he'd carefully extricated himself from her limbs. She'd sighed and burrowed into the bedclothes. He realized he could gladly watch her do that every night.

After dressing, he'd stolen from the house without being detected, then limped home because he hadn't brought his walking stick. He would do it all again, or even walk across the city of Bath multiple times without his stick, to have another night with Min.

He hoped it would be the first of many—for a lifetime—but first, he needed to deal with the Mrs. Dalton issue. After spending last night at a coaching inn, Evan had continued on to London and arrived this evening. Rain had slowed him down a bit, so he'd gone directly to his parents' house and caught his father just after he'd dressed to go to dinner at one of his clubs.

Llewellyn Price was not a large man, but he possessed a bearing that commanded attention and respect. Perhaps it was the flecks of gray in his dark hair that made him appear wise, or the way he carried himself—with immense confidence and little fear. Those traits had served him well, as he had elevated himself to Lord Commissioner of the Treasury. But he had always been a formidable man of great integrity, which was why, Evan suspected, people were drawn to him, including his mother.

Catriona Price had married beneath her station as the daughter of a viscount, but Evan's grandfather had never found her choice of husband lacking. Indeed, his grandfather, Lord Coleford, had been Evan's father's staunchest supporter.

Evan was quite grateful for the warmth of his family, especially after what he'd seen of Min and Sheff and their family's troubles. That sentiment made Evan's visit to his father even more difficult.

Evan had behaved poorly. He'd leapt to his friend's defense without considering the effect on his family. All because Evan thought to weather a scandal to protect a friend. It had been unfair of him to expect his family to do the same, and he understood that now.

His father came into the study where Evan was waiting for him. "I'm surprised to see you here." His gaze flicked to the walking stick Evan held, and his brow creased with concern. "The ankle is still troubling you?"

"A bit," Evan replied. "Though spending the better part of the past two days riding in a coach has forced me to rest. I am hopeful it will be fully healed soon."

His father assessed him with a narrowed eye. "I take that to mean you have not been resting it as much as you should."

Evan lifted a shoulder. "You know me too well, Papa. I have done my best." He flashed a smile.

His father grunted, then went to pour a brandy. "Do you want a drink?"

"Yes, I think I do," Evan said evenly. Perhaps it would help the coming discussion.

His father poured two small tumblers and came to hand one to Evan. Then he sat in his favorite chair near the hearth. "How is your mother?"

Evan took the other chair across from him and rested his walking stick against the arm. "Very well." He sipped his brandy as his father did the same.

"What did she say about you returning to London?" his father asked, holding his glass on the arm of his chair. He gave Evan a pointed look. "We'd agreed you would stay away until I summoned you."

"I know, but it became imperative that I return." Evan took another fortifying drink of brandy. "I told Mama I needed to return to take care of a matter."

"And is that why you're here? You have a matter that requires your attention?"

"Unfortunately, yes. It involves the Mrs. Dalton situation." Evan tried to relax the tension bunched in his shoulders.

His father leaned forward, his eyes blazing. "Do not tell me you came here to see her. You are not to spend time with her at all."

Evan blew out a breath. "The truth is, I have *never* spent time alone with her. Except when she came to see me in Bath last week."

His father's eyes widened. "What the devil are you saying?"

"I hope you won't be too angry. I did not have an affair with Mrs. Dalton. I only said I did."

"You *lied* about it?" His father blinked, and he shook his head in bewilderment. "Why would you do such a thing?"

"To protect my friend, Roger Martin. *He* was having an affair with Mrs. Dalton." Evan went on to explain why he'd protected Roger and why Mrs. Dalton had come to see him.

His father listened, his jaw clenching through the part about Roger and his face paling as Evan explained about Sir Abraham intending to file suit for divorce.

When Evan finished, his father leapt out of his chair and paced across the study. "This is an unmitigated disaster."

"It has turned into one, yes." Evan hated that he was causing his father such distress.

He swung around and glowered at Evan. "You must fix this."

Evan shifted in his chair. "I know. That is why I've returned to London. The time has come for me to tell the truth."

His father marched toward him, his features etched in disgust. "The time has come and gone, my boy." His father sat back down. He turned his attention to the fire, his expression fixed in an angry, contemplative mask.

"I'm sorry," Evan said quietly. "I never meant to cause so much trouble. I should have been more thoughtful."

"Indeed, you should have. What you did was embarrassing to our family—and it wasn't even *true*." His father slammed his hand on his knee as he shifted his angry gaze back to Evan. "You are smarter than this, Evan. What possessed you?"

"I explained why I wanted to help Roger," Evan said. "However, if I had it to do over again, I would not have taken the blame. I thought I could weather the scandal. I did not think how it would affect all of you." Or how it would affect Evan and any plans he might have had for his own future. Because he hadn't remotely considered that he might want to court or marry someone. He'd never expected to fall in love, which was precisely what had happened. The acknowledgment filled him with a radiant joy in the midst of this tumult.

His father harrumphed. "Hopefully, once the truth is known, the damage will be undone."

To Evan, but what of how this would hurt Roger? "I do feel badly for how this will ruin Roger and his career."

"He made a mistake," his father said crisply. "He must own it and do his best to survive the consequences."

"He doesn't have a father like you to guide or advocate for him," Evan said with regret. Roger had lost his father when he was quite young and had attended Cambridge due to the kindness of a gentleman in the district where he'd grown up. The man had seen Roger's intelligence and promise and arranged for him to be educated.

Evan continued, "I also feel bad for Mrs. Dalton. I barely know her, but she seems truly distraught. Sir Abraham has banished her from the household and forbidden her from seeing her children. Roger told me that Sir Abraham was often cruel to her, that she was very unhappy. And the man is old enough to be her father."

His father exhaled. "I know all that."

"All of it?" Evan asked. "Even the part about how Sir Abraham treats her?"

"Yes." His father drummed his fingers on his knee. "Sadly, there are many unfortunate marriages with one or both parties enduring a miserable existence. I'm afraid that is the way of things."

"It shouldn't be," Evan said with more vitriol than he'd planned. "There's no reason people should have to remain in a union where they are both unhappy."

"That may be true, but people manage. What choice do they have?"

"That's easy for you to say." Evan found his father's cavalier attitude irritating. "You and Mother are incredibly happy. Have you any idea how fortunate you are?"

His father gave him a direct stare. "Yes, we do. We say that to one another all the time. But don't think for a moment that marriage is one extreme or the other. It is for a lifetime, and over that course, there are good and bad times. Some people are simply better suited to one another than others." He eyed Evan intently. "For a young man who has eschewed marriage—or even talk of it until now—you seem quite interested in the estate. What has roused your passion on this topic, or are you simply advocating for Mrs. Dalton? I've always credited you with a caring heart, my boy, which is why I was doubly disappointed in your behavior with her. I confess I'm relieved it's not true."

"Thank you for saying that," Evan said. "As it happens, I *am* interested in marriage."

"Are you?" His father's brows shot up. "Is there someone in particular?"

"Yes," Evan replied. An image of Min filled his mind and heated his body. He felt a surge of love just thinking of her and in anticipation of when he would return to her. "I'm particularly eager to put this matter with Mrs. Dalton behind me because I plan to propose marriage."

He prayed Min would say yes. Despite their shared intimacy the night before he left, he couldn't stop thinking of the conversation that had preceded it. She'd been right to call him out for not being honest. Even worse, he'd found himself in a mess—of his own bloody making—that was far too similar to the sort of turmoil Min's father had subjected her to. It was imperative that he fix things before he could even ask her to spend forever with him.

His father's entire demeanor changed as a grin swept over his features. He lifted his brandy toward Evan. "This deserves a toast."

Evan picked up his glass and tapped it to his father's. They each drank.

"Do I know this young lady?" his father asked.

"In fact, you do—Lady Minerva Halifax."

His father blinked in surprise. "Henlow's daughter? It's no wonder you had quite the commentary about marriage, given the family you plan to marry into. Are you sure you want to step into that fray?"

"I would leap into a pit of snarling lions to marry Min."

His father's features softened. "You're in love," he said gruffly.

"Yes, I am." Evan's chest expanded as he confirmed that out loud.

His father smiled warmly, which was a rather rare occasion. "Then we must fix this situation with Sir Abraham with due haste."

"Yes," Evan agreed. "I am hoping you can talk him out of the divorce."

His father's brows drew together. "You want *me* to speak to Sir Abraham."

"After your impassioned speech about the trials of marriage, I think you're the best candidate," Evan said wryly. "Mostly, I didn't think it wise for me to call on him alone."

"You are probably right about that. We'll speak to him together, then. He'll be at the club tonight. He has avoided speaking with me—for obvious reasons—but we will impress upon him the need for a discreet conversation. The man can't want to put himself and his children through such an ordeal as divorce."

Evan found it impossible to have this conversation and not think of Min and what she would be facing when her father did the same thing to her and, by extension, to Evan and his family once they were wed. That assumed she accepted his proposal. He could not take for granted that she would. Aside from this scandalous problem he'd created, he had no idea if she loved him in return. And that was of vital importance, for if she didn't love him, she wouldn't marry him.

Nor should she.

Evan looked at his father and shifted in his chair once more. "I should tell you something else."

His father's expression turned guarded. "I'm not sure I like the sound of your tone."

"Since we are speaking of divorce, I should tell you that the Duke of Henlow is planning to file a divorce suit against his wife and her one-time paramour."

"That's rich coming from him," his father said with a hint of derision. "I never would have believed Her Grace was unfaithful. She's always appeared above reproach—a veritable saint next to His Grace and his well-known affairs."

"Yes," Evan replied. "His Grace doesn't dispute his own transgressions. However, as you know, the law doesn't seem to care what men do. Women, on the other hand, can be held to account if they have been unfaithful and if their husband cares to take them to court to prove it."

"Can he prove it?"

Evan nodded. "But I would rather not say how." That would mean bringing Ellis into the conversation, and he would not do that. He wished he could protect her—and Min—from this. What he ought to do was fight to ensure that Min's father didn't go through with his plan. If Evan could expect to convince Sir Abraham, why not try to persuade Min's father to do the same?

"I confess I was thrilled to hear you will marry the daughter of a duke," his father said somewhat ominously. "But now that I know what's in store, I cannot support it." He gave Evan a sad look. "I'm sorry, son. It will be a terrible ordeal for all of us. You can't put your mother through that

—or your sister. She has her own family to think about now."

He wouldn't support Evan's marriage? Evan hadn't expected that. He felt as if the floor were caving out from under him. "I will convince His Grace not to file the suit."

"You think you can?" His father sounded skeptical.

"I think after we are successful persuading Sir Abraham, I will have both the motivation and experience to do so, yes."

"Your confidence has always been an attribute," his father said with a chuckle.

Evan smirked. "I wonder where I got it from."

"Your mother would say it's arrogance, but between us, she *likes* that." His father studied him a moment. "What is your motivation exactly?"

"Marrying Min," Evan said quickly. Eagerly. "I love her, and I *will* marry her." He prayed she loved him in return.

"Very well. First things first." His father swallowed the rest of his brandy and stood. He looked at Evan and frowned. "You'll need to change your dress before we go to the club. Be quick about it," he added before going to pour more brandy.

Evan rose with the aid of his walking stick. "Thank you, Papa."

His father turned to face him. "I'm glad you finally told me the truth. I just wish you had done so earlier. Actually, I wish you'd never had a reason to."

"Surely you can see why I wanted to help my friend?" Evan asked.

"I do. As I said, you have a kind heart, and I cannot fault you for that. We will set this matter right, but I make no guarantees about your friend."

"I know. We can only do our best." Evan fervently prayed he would have good news to share with Roger by the end of the evening. And then he could leave for Bath first thing in the morning.

Min would be in his arms by Monday night.

～

*B*y the time Min strolled in Sydney Gardens with Pandora on Monday afternoon, the rumors about Evan and Mrs. Dalton were being openly discussed. Overhearing a third such conversation, Min paused on the path.

Pandora arched a brow at her but said nothing.

Min turned and went to the pair of women discussing Evan and Mrs. Dalton. "Pardon me, but I couldn't help hearing what you are loudly saying. I felt beholden to tell you that the matter between Mr. Price and Mrs. Dalton is a grave misunderstanding."

"How do you know that?" one of the women asked, her eyes bright with curiosity. She and the other women were about ten years older than Min.

"I have it on good authority." Min used her haughtiest daughter-of-a-duke tone. "The Price family are friends of ours. Mr. Price is not the rogue he is purported to be. You should not believe every rumor you hear."

Min spun on her heel and rejoined Pandora on the path.

As they walked away from the encounter, Pandora slid her a smile. "That was quite a passionate defense of Evan. Is all that true?"

Min hadn't seen Pandora since she'd learned of the rumor —and the truth of it from Evan. "Yes. It's a horrible mistake of Evan's own doing, and it's why he's in London right now. He is putting things to rights." She went on to explain how Evan had confessed to an affair with Mrs. Dalton to protect a friend.

"I would say that's rather gallant of him," Pandora noted. "Though, perhaps ill-advised."

"I was quite cross with him because he didn't tell me about any of it. I had to hear the rumor from the Viper—my mother—after which, I confronted him."

"I can see why that would be upsetting," Pandora said with a frown. "He didn't lie, exactly, but he wasn't honest either."

"Exactly. He explained why he didn't tell me—he wanted to fix the mess he created so that I was not embroiled in another vexing, scandalous situation. He thought my problems with my family were troubling enough, and he was right. Still, I wish he'd told me, and it gives me pause that he didn't. Creating chaos and scandal is my father's forte, and I would rather not invite that into my life."

Pandora looked at her with sympathy. "Have you forgiven him? It seems you may have, since you are defending him today."

Min lifted a shoulder. "I don't know that 'forgiven' is the right word. I'm not angry with him. In fact, he spent the night—or part of it anyway—with me after we discussed the matter."

Pandora gasped. "And you're just now telling me?"

"I probably ought to have called on you straightaway on Friday, but I confess I was rather tired," she said somewhat sheepishly.

"I'm sure you were," Pandora said with a smirk. "Was it everything you hoped it would be?"

"And more," Min said, unable to keep from smiling.

"So things are good between you, then?" Pandora asked.

"I suppose so," Min replied with hesitation. "I can't stop thinking about the encounter we had in one of the alcoves in the tearoom on Thursday night. We kissed, and he said, 'Marry me.' He didn't ask me. He *demanded*."

"That's more than I've ever been...asked," Pandora said wryly.

Min grimaced. "I'm sorry. I didn't think about that. When I pointed out he hadn't asked me, he said he would do so properly, and that he would declare his love."

Pandora stopped and turned toward Min. "He said he loved you?"

"Not exactly. He said that he *would* declare his love. It was like a plan he'd laid out. I don't know how to describe it, but it wasn't the sweeping emotional moment that one would hope for after hearing that someone loves them. "

"I understand your hesitation. At least you *seem* hesitant." Min nodded, and Pandora continued. "You aren't yet certain you can trust him to be the man you need."

"Yes." Min was so relieved that Pandora understood. "I want to trust him, but I do need to be sure that he will be committed to me and our family—if we marry—and that he will be wholly honest."

"Perhaps he is waiting to give you a sweeping, emotional moment until he's resolved this matter in London," Pandora said gently. "I can understand him wanting to do that. He is not the sort of rogue who would promise those things and then abandon you like Bane did to me."

"No, I don't think he is," Min admitted. "I think part of me also wonders if he only wants to marry me because of the passion we share. But that may be because, to me, it's a singular connection. He's experienced this before, while I have not."

They started walking once more, and Pandora's brow creased. "Has he? It sounds as though you need a frank discussion about both love and passion. I think, for you, they are completely intertwined."

"I agree. I keep thinking about how Evan and I started as friends, and everything has built from there. I've never had that with a gentleman before, and I can't help wondering if that is at the heart of why he's the first man I've known who's actually stirred me to consider marriage. Not because I have to wed, but because I want to." She realized that was true. She *did* want to marry Evan. Because she loved him. "I think I'm in love with him," she whispered before she could censor herself.

Pandora gave her a wide smile. "I think you are too. But I wasn't going to say so. I knew you'd puzzle it out."

Min laughed. "You are a dear friend."

"What are you going to do?"

"Wait for him to return, hopefully tomorrow." Unless he'd found some way to shorten his trip. The prospect gave Min a flash of anticipation. She was eager to tell him that she loved him. But could she until she knew for certain that he was the man she thought he might be? "What would you do in my situation?"

Pandora shook her head. "I don't have any advice beyond what I've already shared. I've made my peace with being a spinster, and I frankly can't imagine anything else."

Min hated to think that her friend would not ever have a lasting relationship. "You really have resigned yourself to that?"

Pandora nodded and did not seem sad about it. "Soon enough, I should leave my aunt's house. She is a proper widow, and I am a spinster who writes novels and wants the freedom to have an occasional liaison. I shall take a cottage somewhere, perhaps in Weston."

"Well, that would be lovely," Min said. "Because we will always be there together in August."

Pandora sent her a sideways glance. "I know that is your intent, but I don't see that happening. More than half of us are married now, and you will probably be next."

"I have not committed to anything, nor have I been asked," Min reminded her.

Pandora smiled. "Yes, I know, but it's likely you will, and then it will be just me and Ellis in the Rogue Rules Club."

"Plus our new member, Iona," Min said. "You will like her."

"Has she a reason not to marry like Ellis and I do?" Pandora asked.

"Not that I am aware of."

"So as I said, it will be Ellis and me together at my cottage every August in Weston. Don't feel sorry for us."

"I shan't, because I may be there with you. As I said, I have not committed to anything," Min assured her. "Are you going to write to Ellis about your cottage plans?"

"I may mention it in my next letter," Pandora replied.

"Your *next* letter? You've already written to her?"

Pandora nodded. "The other day. I had a footman deliver the letter to your father with a request that he forward it to Ellis. He sent word back that he had done so."

"Will you tell me if she replies to you? She has not responded to any of my letters." Min hadn't told anyone that. It hurt that Ellis didn't even want to write to her when Min missed her terribly. Ellis was like a sister, even before Min had discovered she truly was one. Now, Min was trying to decide the course of her life without her dearest friend and sister. "I would give anything to talk to her right now."

"I know you would," Pandora said softly.

They'd reached the area where carriages were parked.

Pandora stopped and faced Min. "This is where I leave you. My aunt's coach is just over there, and I'll wait for her inside."

Min knew Pandora didn't care to linger when the park was teeming with gossiping busybodies. Pandora wasn't a prime topic of gossip anymore, but some women still occasionally cast her a censorious look.

"Do you want company?" Min preferred to delay returning to her mother, who was not too far distant with a few of her friends.

"That isn't necessary. Aunt Lucinda sees me and will join me shortly." Pandora looked her in the eye. "However, I want to hear what Evan has to say as soon as possible. No more waiting a few days to tell me what's happening," she added in a mock scolding tone.

Min put her hand on her heart. "I promise."

They bid farewell, and Min started, begrudgingly, toward her mother. If she wasn't ready to depart, Min could wait in their coach as Pandora was doing.

As Min neared a large oak tree, Lord Spilsby stepped from behind it. He blocked her progress along the path. "Good afternoon, Lady Minerva." He gave her a bright but thoroughly irritating smile. Today's waistcoat was a violent orange.

"Good afternoon, Lord Spilsby." Min did not bother smiling in return.

"May I escort you to your mother?" He offered her his arm before she could respond.

Min frowned. "I have been clear about not wanting to spend time with you. That includes promenading. You must excuse me."

As she tried to move past him, he snaked his arm around her waist and pulled her toward the tree. "Come now, Lady Minerva, I think you will find we have much in common."

Min couldn't believe he would grab her like that. She pushed at his chest as he hauled her against the tree trunk on the side away from the path. "I can't imagine what you would think we share. It certainly isn't fashion sense. Or how to behave in public. I demand you release me at once!"

He gripped her more tightly and moved close so that his chest touched hers. He lifted his left hand to stroke her cheek. "You are very lovely." He bent his head as if he meant to kiss her.

Min shrieked as she pulled her head back, knocking it against the trunk. She shoved at him and squirmed to escape.

"What is going on here?" a voice cried out.

Ducking under his arm, Min managed to wriggle free. She stepped away from the tree and pivoted to see who had spoken. Mrs. Lawler stood not ten feet away.

Of all the people to see what had just happened! The irony was too much.

"Did you see what Spilsby did?" Min said to Mrs. Lawler.

Mrs. Lawler pursed her lips tightly in a wholly judgmental fashion. "I saw the two of you embracing." Her tone was accusatory.

"That was not *embracing*!" Min cried. "That was him accosting me!"

"It didn't look like that to me," Mrs. Lawler said with a shrug.

Min saw what was going to happen. Mrs. Lawler would repeat what she thought she'd seen, that Min and Spilsby had been caught in compromising position. All the busybody had to do was walk along the path and share that news with everyone she encountered. There were enough people milling about this fine afternoon that the rumor would spread like an unchecked fire.

It was too perfect. Min would be forced to marry Spilsby. The coincidence of this happening with Mrs. Lawler, the notorious gossip on hand to witness it, was too much.

Min turned on Spilsby. "You planned this," she hissed.

He didn't deny it. "I only wanted a moment alone with you, Lady Minerva. It is my deepest desire that we should wed, and I know you will agree it is a good match. I would like to speak with your father immediately."

"You will do no such thing," Min said firmly. "You are a scoundrel and a rogue. No, I won't even call you a rogue. That's too kind a word for you. You're an absolute black-guard." Unable to control her ire, she slapped him across the face. It wasn't truly a slap because she was wearing her glove. The crack of her bare flesh against his would have been much more satisfying.

She turned to face Mrs. Lawler once more and saw that her mother was approaching.

"What's happened here?" the duchess said.

Min froze. Something about her expression was wrong. She did not appear concerned, aghast, or anything other than mildly curious. And she had to have seen what Min had just done. At the very least, she would be outraged by Min's attack on Spilsby's person.

"You are behind this, aren't you, Mother?" Min whispered.

The duchess appeared nonplussed, but Min saw the glint of victory in her gaze. "Behind what?"

Min glanced toward Mrs. Lawler and caught the flash of guilt in hers. Yes, they'd all planned this.

"I'm going home, Mother," Min said. "And then I'm going to Pandora's. Permanently."

Min stalked to their coach and instructed the coachman to take her home. Her mother could bloody well walk.

CHAPTER 17

*E*van arrived in Bath late Monday afternoon. He'd wanted to go directly to Min, but decided it was preferable to wash the grime of the road away first. He wanted to look and smell his best when he properly asked her to marry him. But first he needed to speak with his mother. He found her in the drawing room.

She stood as he entered and smiled. "I'd heard you'd returned. I'm pleased to see you."

Using his walking stick, Evan made his way to her and bussed her cheek. "I'm pleased to see you as well and happy to be back."

"Are you?" she asked in surprise. "I wondered if you might stay in London."

"I have a specific reason for returning, which I will tell you about shortly." First, Evan wanted to explain about the Mrs. Dalton situation.

His mother's eyes lit with interest. "That sounds intriguing. Will you attend the ball with me this evening?"

"I'm afraid not, Mama. I hope you're not disappointed."

She waved her hand. "Not at all. I wasn't expecting you until tomorrow."

"I wanted to tell you why I went to London," Evan said. "I needed to deal with the situation regarding Mrs. Dalton."

His mother's brows drew down, and her eyes narrowed slightly.

Before she could speak, he said, "I did *not* have an affair with her. I only said I did to protect a friend to whom I felt I owed a favor. I have since realized it was selfish of me to taint the family with my decision to help him."

Evan was not going to tell her about Sir Abraham's plans to divorce his wife, because he and his father had successfully changed Sir Abraham's mind. After tracking him down at the club, they'd spent a considerable amount of time persuading him, and he'd ultimately agreed—for a price. He'd demanded the name of his wife's true lover and then insisted Roger leave London and never return.

Later that evening, Evan had told Roger what had happened while also conveying his regret that Roger would have to leave London as well as his promising career. Roger had been devastated but understood that things could have turned out worse if Sir Abraham had proceeded with a divorce. He was most grateful to Evan for his assistance.

Evan's father had also talked Sir Abraham into making it clear that Evan had *not* carried on a liaison with his wife. Sir Abraham had agreed to clarify the matter, but would not promise that he wouldn't name Roger instead. It was the best they could manage. And Evan's father was pleased, which relieved Evan.

His mother gazed at him with sympathy and keen understanding. "My dearest boy, I don't know that I agree your behavior was selfish. Ill-considered, perhaps." Her lips curled into a fleeting smile. "I'm glad you sorted the matter. The gossip has been moving about Bath the last few days," she added with a grimace. "I will do my best to refute the gossip tonight. Interestingly, I heard Lady Minerva did that earlier in the gardens."

Had she? Evan couldn't help smiling. That she would defend him was surely a positive sign.

"You're grinning like a fool," his mother said with a laugh.

"Yes. That is due to the reason I hastened back to Bath. I am very much hoping that by the end of this evening, I will be betrothed."

She gasped and briefly lifted her hand to her mouth, her eyes lit with joy.

Evan couldn't help laughing. "This may be the happiest I've ever seen you. And you were exceptionally thrilled on Gwen's wedding day."

His mother embraced him tightly. "I'm so happy for you."

"She hasn't said yes yet." And he couldn't assume she would. He ought to have confided in her about the "scandal" with Mrs. Dalton, especially after she'd come to Bath and a true scandal was imminent.

His mother stepped back. "Who is it, or do you not want to say until she's accepted?"

"I've already told Papa. It's Lady Minerva."

"Of course. Her defense of you today and your reaction when I mentioned it revealed all." She smiled broadly.

Evan very much wanted his parents' approval. Since his father hadn't been entirely enthusiastic about the match, particularly after learning about the Duke of Henlow's intent to divorce his wife, Evan worried his mother wouldn't be supportive. "You like her, don't you?" Evan asked tentatively.

"Of course, I do. Why would you ask?"

Evan did not plan to tell her about the duke's plans for divorce. He fervently hoped he would be able to talk the duke out of them. "His Grace often attracts gossip regarding his behavior. I wasn't sure if that would upset you."

"Everyone knows and accepts he and Her Grace are estranged. While it is not ideal, at least they aren't divorced."

Quashing an ironic grimace, Evan nodded.

She cocked her head. "Since you are proposing, you must have a ring. Did you purchase one when you were in London?"

"I did not," Evan replied. "Papa said you had a ring that you hoped I would use."

"Indeed, I do. It belonged to my grandmother and has always been intended for your betrothed. I haven't ever mentioned it because you've been very clear about not wanting to marry yet."

"It was good of you to be patient," Evan said with a chuckle.

"Let me fetch the ring, and then you can decide if you want to give it to Lady Minerva."

Evan was anxious to be on his way, so he hoped she would be quick. Thankfully, she was, returning just a few minutes later with a small box. "If you don't care for it, you can choose something else."

He accepted the box and opened it. "I'm sure it's perfect." Looking down, a pang of joy and a sense of absolute rightness filled him. The ring was a rose-cut sapphire and almost exactly the color of the forget-me-nots Min had given him at Longleat. "It is indeed," he murmured.

"I'm so glad," his mother said.

Evan hugged her again and tucked the ring into his pocket. "Wish me luck."

"You don't need it. Lady Minerva defended you today. She clearly feels the same way you do."

Until Evan heard Min say so, he wouldn't know for sure. He left and made his way by coach to the Duchess of Henlow's house in the Circus.

As he knocked on the door, he took a deep breath and

prayed for the outcome he desired. He was most nervous to tell Min how he felt, for if she did not love him in return, he didn't know what he would do.

Unfortunately, she was not at home. The butler said she had left the household and was now staying at Pandora's aunt's in the Royal Crescent.

But she wasn't there either. Confounded, Evan asked to speak with Pandora or her aunt. The butler welcomed him into the entrance hall and went to fetch them.

"It's good to see you, Evan," Pandora said as she entered with her aunt. "Harding says you came here to see Min, that you think she is staying here."

Evan's heart began to pound. Something was wrong. He told himself not to worry. Perhaps the butler at Min's mother's house had been mistaken, and Min had gone to her father's house. Except Evan doubted the butler was wrong. Mayhap Min had changed her mind.

"Her mother's butler told me I could find Min here," Evan said to Pandora. "He said that she'd left her mother's household and was staying with you."

Pandora's brow gathered. She appeared very concerned. "She's not here, nor am I expecting her. I saw her in the park this afternoon, and she didn't mention anything about coming to stay with me. I didn't think you were returning until tomorrow—that's what Min said, anyway."

"I shortened my trip," he said. "I'm most eager to see her." Evan wondered if Pandora knew why, but he wasn't going to ask about that now. He needed to find Min. He couldn't shake the feeling that something was amiss.

Pandora's aunt wore a dark expression.

"Do you know something, Mrs. Barclay-Fiennes?" Evan asked.

"I was just thinking about what happened in the gardens earlier."

Pandora looked to her aunt. "You mean the scene with Lord Spilsby?"

"What the hell happened with Spilsby?" Evan asked, his alarm merging with rage at the mention of the loathsome man.

"I didn't see what happened," Mrs. Barclay-Fiennes said, her green eyes narrowing slightly. "But as I walked toward the coach to join Pandora, I heard someone talking about Lord Spilsby and Lady Minerva embracing. They were seen by Mrs. Lawler."

Pandora's lip curled. "That meddlesome hag is spreading rumors about Min now."

Mrs. Barclay-Fiennes's light-brown brows climbed. "Apparently, Min defended herself and hit him before she stalked away."

Evan felt a rush of pride.

"Good for her," Pandora said smugly before looking to Evan. "Do you think it's possible Min went to her father's house?"

"I suppose. However, the butler was clear about telling me she'd come here. I don't think he would have got that wrong."

"Perhaps she changed her mind," Mrs. Barclay-Fiennes suggested, echoing Evan's earlier thoughts.

"That is possible." But Evan doubted it. "I must go back to Her Grace's house and determine what's happened."

"Will you let us know what you find out?" Pandora asked. "I'm afraid I won't be able to rest until I know she's safe, given what happened with that idiot Spilsby."

Evan didn't think Spilsby was capable of violence. The bounder was an annoying prig, but surely not dangerous.

"You must excuse me," Evan said with a nod before beating a hasty retreat to the coach. He instructed the coachman to return to the Circus with haste.

The coach had barely stopped before Evan leapt out

without bothering with his walking stick—much to his ankle's distress. He ran to the duchess's door, where he hammered upon the wood with his fist.

The butler answered quickly, his brow forming deep furrows. "Mr. Price, whatever is wrong?"

"Lady Minerva is not at Mrs. Barclay-Fiennes's house," Evan said darkly. "No one there has seen her, nor do they expect her. Where is Her Grace?"

"She is preparing for the ball." The butler appeared distressed. "Is Lady Minerva missing?"

"She is not where she is supposed to be. Her Grace must know where she is."

The butler nodded. "I'll fetch her at once."

Evan paced, and his ankle protested. After his jumping from the carriage, it did not appreciate being further abused. Not that walking should have been abuse, but his ankle thought otherwise.

It was several minutes before Her Grace finally appeared. She was fully dressed, with her hair artfully arranged for tonight's ball. She gave Evan a supremely haughty look. "Mr. Price, Warner said you were most anxious and needed to see me. I understand you are looking for Minerva."

"She is not where she is supposed to be."

"And where is that?" Her Grace asked with an irritating coolness.

"You don't know?" Evan asked crossly. "What kind of mother are you? She left your household and has gone to stay with a friend. Except she's not there."

Her Grace frowned deeply, her entire face creasing, and Evan almost believed she was concerned. "I don't know where she is. This is most upsetting. Perhaps she's gone to her father's. Have you looked for her there?"

"No, but I will." Evan wasn't sure he believed her, but

what if she didn't really know? "I heard Lord Spilsby accosted Min in the gardens today, and that she struck him."

"Regrettably, yes," Her Grace replied stiffly.

What did she regret? Spilsby's behavior or her daughter's? Evan didn't ask. "Do you think it's possible Spilsby has anything to do with Min's disappearance?"

Her Grace frowned at him. "You are too familiar with my daughter, referring to her as 'Min.' It's highly inappropriate."

Evan barely kept himself from yelling at the woman. "What about Spilsby?"

"Spilsby has nothing to do with wherever Minerva has gone. The viscount is an affable young man. Indeed, I looked forward to him and Minerva becoming betrothed."

Fury sparked anew in Evan. "You must know that is never happening." Even if Min didn't consent to marry Evan, he knew she would never marry Spilsby.

Warner had come back to the entrance hall, and Evan looked to him for answers. "How did Lady Minerva leave?"

"In Her Grace's coach," the butler replied. His eyes rounded, and he looked to Min's mother. "You are not taking your coach to the ball tonight. You said you would be riding with Mrs. Lawler."

Evan's patience snapped. He turned on the duchess without bothering to check his anger. "You know your coach is gone—with Min in it. Where is she?"

Her Grace's nostrils flared. For the first time, discomfort flickered in her eyes. "A friend needed to borrow my coach."

"Wrong answer," Evan snapped. "Where is your daughter? Answer me before I lose every remaining shred of politeness I possess."

The duchess flinched. She pressed her lips together and looked away. "I did loan it to someone—Lord Spilsby."

Evan began to shake with rage. "Why in the hell would

you do that? Did he not just accost Min at the gardens today?"

"He did no such thing," Her Grace replied crisply. "They were caught sharing an embrace. They are to be married."

"That's absolute horseshit." Evan abandoned all semblance of propriety. There was no time for it, and the duchess didn't deserve it. "He's taken Min, hasn't he?"

"I believe they have eloped," she said. Was that approval in her tone? She definitely looked pleased with herself, and Evan fought to keep a rein on his temper.

"Min would not agree to that," Evan growled. "She detested Spilsby. Where did he take her?"

When Her Grace did not respond, the butler stepped toward her. He looked nearly as angry as Evan felt. "Tell him." Warner regarded his employer with contempt, and Evan decided he would hire the man to run his household when he and Min were wed. "What have you done to your own daughter?"

Min's mother still didn't respond. She lifted her chin and stared at them both as if they were vermin.

Evan somehow managed to keep his voice even, but he did not stop his lip from curling. "I'm sure Warner will be happy to fetch His Grace. Perhaps you'll tell him where Min has been taken." Kidnapped, more like. Evan clenched his fists as a fresh storm of fury thundered through him.

Her Grace's eyes rounded the barest amount. "Lord Spilsby has taken her to Bristol."

"That is not a place where people elope," Evan said with derision. They would still need a special license or to have the banns read. "Why would he take her there?"

"Spilsby planned for them to be seen together, so that she would have to marry him," Her Grace replied. "Because you are correct. She did not want to wed Spilsby, despite him being the best match she could make at this juncture. She said she would have been happier with someone like you or Jarvis. Was I supposed to let my only other child marry beneath her station? It's bad enough my son wed the most common trollop."

Evan had to bite his tongue to keep from unleashing his fury. However, he couldn't ignore what Her Grace had said about her "only other child."

"But Min isn't your only other child, is she?" Evan pointed out softly.

Min's mother gasped. "Why would you know anything else?"

"Because your daughter trusts me and cares for me and, God willing, will be my wife." Evan turned to Warner. "Please send word to His Grace about what has happened and that I am on my way to Bristol on horseback and will intercept Lady Minerva and Spilsby."

"I will, Mr. Price, and thank you." The butler regarded him with appreciation. "Godspeed."

Evan dashed from the house. He was tempted to run up to the mews near Catharine Place, but he instructed the coachman to drive him there. His ankle was already paining him, and he was about to put it through much worse, including stuffing it into his new riding boot.

When he arrived at the mews, he sent a groom to fetch his boots—and his pistol—from the house while he saddled Merlin himself. The horse seemed quite pleased that Evan was finally going to ride him. Evan murmured words of affection and encouragement. "We must ride faster than we ever have, my boy."

Evan's ankle protested when he donned the boot and again as he climbed into the saddle and put his foot into the stirrup. The pain faded as he focused on rescuing Min.

He rode out of the mews and kicked into a high gallop toward Bristol.

CHAPTER 18

*M*in had been in the coach with Spilsby for at least an hour. She did not know where they were going because he wouldn't tell her, but she believed they were traveling west. She still couldn't believe what was happening and that her mother had facilitated her kidnapping by this horrible blackguard.

After returning home from the gardens, she'd asked the coachman to wait while she packed her things to go to Pandora's. Her maid had told her to go and that she would gather everything and follow.

Grateful, Min had gone back to the coach and was shocked to find Spilsby inside. Before she could climb out, the coach had begun moving.

The events that had followed had repeated in Min's mind several times as she tried to think of a way that she could have escaped her current predicament. But such thoughts were pointless. She was here now.

Still, she couldn't help recalling what happened yet again. She'd demanded to know what Spilsby was doing in her mother's coach. Then, when they'd started moving, she'd insisted he let her out. She'd even pounded on the roof, because surely the coachman would hear her and stop.

However, Spilsby had merely given her a malevolent smile and told her she could pound all she wanted while the coach would continue on its way.

Min had said her mother's coachman wouldn't do that. To which Spilsby had replied, "It's not your coachman, he's mine."

"But this isn't your coach," Min had cried. "Where are we going?"

Spilsby had given her a superior look. "You don't need to know that right now. Just settle back and enjoy our journey."

"I'm to enjoy you *kidnapping* me? I think I'd rather jump from the moving coach." That was when Min had reached for the door.

But Spilsby had leapt upon her, the brute. He'd pulled something from the other seat, which she hadn't noticed earlier. It was a length of rope that he used to bind her wrists. Then, he used a second to bind her feet. That was how she found herself trussed in her current position as they traveled to God-knew-where.

Min's attempts to persuade him to explain what he was doing had been met with grunts and taunting. He would only repeat that they were to be married and that she should feel lucky.

The farther they traveled from Bath, the more Min wondered where Evan might be. He was likely far from Bath still and wouldn't arrive until tomorrow. Her chest constricted, and not just because he likely couldn't rescue her before she was forced to spend the night with Spilsby.

She also knew, without question, that not only was she in love with Evan—she was ready to take the risk to marry him. *If* he loved her in return.

She would give anything to see Evan now.

He would be furious that Spilsby had dared to kidnap her. It occurred to Min that she could taunt her captor with Evan's rage. She could remind Spilsby that Evan was particularly skilled with weaponry.

First, she would try to be sweet. As sweet as she could muster, anyway. "You could at least tell me *where* we are to be married," she said with a cajoling lilt and what was probably a feeble smile. "It seems like we're going west. Is it Bristol? Why Bristol?"

He scowled. "It isn't Bristol. Can you just stop talking?" So much for charming him.

His reaction made her think it was definitely Bristol.

"What do you think is going to happen when we get there?" Min asked. "I'm not going to agree to marry you."

"You will be ruined." He gave her a taunting smile. "What choice do you have?"

Min laughed. "I think you forget that one of my closest friends was ruined, and she's not married." Indeed, the irony was that Min had considered just such a life. Furthermore, her father meant to sue her mother for divorce, which would surely devastate their entire family. If Spilsby meant to traumatize her with his threats of ruination, he would be wholly unsuccessful. "You can't force me to wed you. In fact, you should be worried about going to prison, because I will ensure you are held accountable for kidnapping me."

Now he laughed. "I think *you're* forgetting how difficult it is to prosecute a peer."

"Do not think you will be immune," Min said with a glower. "You may be a peer, but my father is a duke."

Spilsby crossed his arms over his chest with a mocking expression. "You seem to think your father does not support what I've done."

"Of course he doesn't." Min spoke without hesitation, but she realized she couldn't be entirely certain. Her father wanted her to marry as soon as possible so that he could go forward with his divorce. Would he have agreed to Spilsby's scheme? It seemed her mother was definitely in support of Min's kidnapping, unless she was unaware that Spilsby had taken her coach. What had happened to her coachman?

"You didn't hurt my mother's coachman, did you?" Min asked.

"Not at all. He went back to the mews."

"My mother had to have helped you," she said.

Spilsby blew out a frustrated breath as he unfolded his arms. "Minerva, if you cannot be quiet for a while, I'm going to have to gag you."

Her jaw dropped. "You wouldn't dare."

He glanced at her bindings. "I think you know that I would, and as your husband, I am perfectly within my rights to do so."

"You are *not* my husband, nor will you ever be," she spat.

"Have it your way." Spilsby pulled a length of cloth from his pocket and moved to push it into Min's mouth.

She jerked away from him, squirming from his touch to the best of her ability.

"Hold still, damn it," he barked as he tried to shove the fabric into her mouth. When his fingers were close, she bit him as hard as she could. It was too bad he was wearing gloves.

"*Bloody hell, you termagant!*" He fell back against his seat, glaring at her. "I have no wish to commit violence, but you leave me no choice." He raised his hand.

Min fought the urge to flinch. She would not give him the satisfaction.

Something moving outside the window drew her attention. Was there another coach? Perhaps she could cry for help!

No, it was a horse with a rider.

She gasped. It was Evan.

"What are you looking at?" Spilsby demanded.

"Your doom," Min replied with a smile. "You may hit me if you like, though I daresay it will only further enrage Evan."

"Price? What the devil does he have to do with this?"

"I believe he wants to marry me, and he's on a horse outside the window." She glanced toward Evan, who was now very close. He rode Merlin, and Min held her breath as Evan pulled his feet from the stirrups and moved to stand atop the saddle.

"The hell he is." Spilsby moved close to the window and swore.

Min scooted toward the window, her focus glued to Evan. He wobbled, and she worried about his ankle. She prayed he wouldn't fall again.

Then he leapt toward the coach, and Min squeezed her eyes shut.

⁓

*E*van glimpsed Min through the window of the coach, and his heart leapt to see her safe. He bent low over Merlin.

"Here we go," Evan said softly, praying his ankle would hold up.

He took his feet from the stirrups and pulled his legs up to stand on the saddle, as he'd done dozens of times before. But this was not like any other time. His ankle hurt and was not quite secure.

Evan refused to fall. He had to get to Min.

The distance between Merlin and the coach was not great, but due to Evan's sprain, the jump was risky. It was also necessary.

Clenching his jaw, he released Merlin's reins and leapt at

the moving vehicle. He landed on his stomach on top of the coach, which had been his intent.

Evan glanced toward the coachman, who whipped his head around to look at Evan.

"Stop the coach!" Evan commanded. "I have a pistol. You're helping Spilsby kidnap the daughter of a duke."

Evan didn't wait to see or hear the coachman's reaction. He spun around on his stomach and inched over the side. He eased himself down, just enough so he could reach the handle of the door.

He pulled it open as the coach began to slow. Relief that the coachman had listened flooded through him. Evan considered whether to climb down the side and jump into the coach or wait until it stopped.

Spilsby stuck his head out through the open door. Looking up, he met Evan's gaze. Spilsby's eyes widened. He gripped the inside handle of the door and tried to pull it closed.

"Let go!" That was Min's voice.

Spilsby jerked and disappeared into the coach with a howl. What had happened?

They were moving quite slowly now, and Evan took his chance. He released the door handle and gripped the side of the coach as he swung his legs down and into the interior. This movement required him to land on his feet.

His ankle buckled, and he teetered to the side, which was fine because he decided it was perfectly acceptable to fall on top of Spilsby. They crashed onto the forward-facing seat.

Min was on the opposite seat, and if Evan's eyes had not deceived him, she was bound at the wrists. This knowledge fed his rage. He brought his hand back and planted his fist into Spilsby's face. The bounder tried to squirm away, but Evan clutched his coat tightly. The coach stopped, and they rolled to the floor. Evan worked to gain the advantage, rising up over Spilsby.

"Are you all right, Min?" Evan yelled.

"I'm well. Do be careful!"

Spilsby tried to land a punch, but Evan pulled himself out of the way. This allowed Spilsby to scramble, and he ended up near the open door. Evan launched himself forward and tackled him out of the coach onto the ground. He landed on top of Spilsby, who grunted again.

"You bloody blackguard," Evan snarled. He pulled himself up and sat atop Spilsby, then lifted his fist in a threatening manner. "I can hit you again, or you can stop moving. And I shall tell you what I told your coachman—I have a pistol."

Spilsby went completely limp.

"Good decision." Evan glowered at him before standing. He hobbled as he stood, putting the bulk of his weight on his right side. He desperately wanted to get back into the coach to untie Min, but he also needed to fetch Merlin and tie him to the coach for the return trip to Bath.

"What are you going to do?" Spilsby asked, his eyes narrowed with uncertainty.

"I'm taking Lady Minerva back to Bath. What *you* do is up to you, but know that wherever you go, you will be found, and you will be held to account for what you've done."

"You're just going to leave me here?" Spilsby sputtered as he sat up and brushed dirt from his garments.

"You're lucky that's all I do," Evan growled.

"I had no idea he was kidnapping her," the coachman called from the seat. "I swear."

Evan turned his head toward the coachman. "I'm glad to hear it. Now, please fetch my horse."

"Right away, sir." The coachman climbed down from the seat and hastened to Merlin, who was nearby.

"You can't leave me here," Spilsby protested. "I'll ride on the seat with my coachman."

"You'll do no such thing," Evan scoffed. "On your way." He glowered at the cretin before he turned and started to climb into the coach.

Min sat on the rear-facing seat, her wrists bound with rope. Her gaze was fixed past him, and her eyes rounded. "Evan, look out!"

Evan really hadn't thought Spilsby would be foolish enough to try anything further. Pulling the pistol from the inside of his coat, Evan turned and pointed it at the man. "Come any closer and I will shoot you."

Spilsby had lifted his foot but wobbled to keep from moving forward.

"Back up," Evan ordered.

Spilsby took several steps backward.

"Not far enough," Evan snapped. "See that tree?" It was some thirty yards distant. "Go over there. *Quickly.*" He cocked the pistol.

Spilsby turned and ran to the tree.

The coachman had returned with Merlin. "Shall I tie him to the coach?"

"Yes, thank you." Evan went to soothe Merlin for a moment while the coachman completed his task. He nuzzled the horse's nose. "You've done very well today."

Evan looked over at Spilsby to make sure he was still standing by the tree. Satisfied the bounder would not trouble them any longer, Evan put the pistol back in his coat and at last climbed into the coach.

The coachman appeared at the door. "To Bath, then?"

"Yes," Evan replied, then pulled the door closed.

He perched on the edge of the forward-facing seat and reached over to untie the rope around Min's wrists. He was glad the rough binding had not been against her flesh. "I'm so sorry, Min."

"I'm fine, Evan. Will you untie my ankles too, please?" She stuck her feet out from the hem of her skirt.

The blackguard had tied them too? Evan wanted to go back and hit Spilsby again. Evan bent down to untie the rope around her ankles. Then he sat back on the seat, his heart still pounding from the entire encounter.

Min leapt on him instantly, covering his lap as she cupped his face with her hands.

"Are you all right?" She searched his features with grave concern.

"Yes." His heart was now racing for an altogether different reason.

"Including your ankle? Tell me the truth."

"It hurts a bit." Evan clasped her waist. "I do hereby vow that I will rest until my bloody ankle is fully healed."

She narrowed her eyes at him. "You will indeed, because I will make certain of it."

"You aren't angry with me, are you?" Evan had been surprised that she jumped on him. And thrilled.

"Of course not! I am grateful. But I knew you would find me—well, I *hoped* you would find me. I knew you'd be furious."

"Furious doesn't begin to describe what I felt." He stroked her cheek and gazed into the silvery beauty of her eyes. "I'm very glad you're all right."

"How *did* you find me?" she asked. Then she shook her head quickly. "Never mind. Tell me later. I'm just so happy to see you."

She pressed her mouth to his before Evan could reply, not that he was able to form words at the moment. He could scarcely believe what she'd said. And now she was kissing him.

He pulled away. "Can I trouble you to remove my left boot? My ankle did not appreciate being forced into it, and it's protesting quite vociferously."

She scrambled to the floor and frowned. "I don't want to hurt you."

"It hurts now. Removing the boot will be a relief. Just be as quick as you can."

"I will say, these are very smart-looking boots." She gave him a charming smile that lit her eyes in a thoroughly provocative way.

"Take off the damned boot so you can come back here and keep kissing me."

"Since you phrased it so nicely." She grinned, then sobered with an expression of determination. It took her a few tugs, and his ankle complained, but she removed the boot. She looked up at him pensively. "Are you sure I should return to your lap? Perhaps you should rest."

Evan reached for her and hauled her up. "Temptress," he murmured before he kissed her.

He clasped her nape and massaged her hip and backside. She adjusted her position so that she straddled him. He moaned softly, his body vaulting into keen arousal.

Then she ground down against him, and Evan's cock twitched in response. He pulled his mouth from hers. "On second thought, you should probably return to the other seat or sit beside me."

"But I love you, Evan." She kissed his neck.

"If you don't, I'm going to lift your skirts and—" He cut himself off. "Did you say you love me?"

"Yes." She continued kissing his neck, pushing his cravat and collar away to expose his flesh.

He put both hands on her head and tilted her face up to his. "I love you too."

Surprise flashed in her eyes, followed by a heady warmth. "You do?"

"You can't be surprised. I told you I was going to declare my love for you when I proposed. Which I had a plan to do, but then that idiot Spilsby ruined—"

She kissed him again, and he could feel the joy radiating from her. It matched his own.

He reached up and tugged at the knot of his cravat until it loosened. She separated the fabric of the garments at his throat, baring his flesh to her mouth so she could continue her seduction.

Evan gripped her skirts and shifted them upward so he could slip his hand beneath them. He stroked her thigh and squeezed her backside. She moved against him in response, then adjusted her garments that were twisted between them so that her bare sex pressed against his fall.

There was so much Evan wanted to say—including offering his marriage proposal—but the primal need surging within him would not be denied. He unbuttoned his breeches, no easy feat with one hand and the woman he loved moving against him. As soon as he finished, he transferred his attention to her sex, sliding his fingers along her slick folds.

She lifted her head from his throat with a gasp. He teased her clitoris, drawing sultry groans from her as she rotated her hips against his hand.

"Please, Evan," she whimpered.

"What do you want, my love?" He kissed her neck above the edge of her spencer. He wished she was wearing far less, but he couldn't wait to divest her of her clothing. She was wet and ready, and he was desperate to claim her.

"You," she rasped. "I want you. Now. Inside me."

He thrust two fingers inside her, curling them gently as

he pressed deep. She gasped again, over and over, as he pumped into her. "Is that what you want?"

"Yes. *No.* I want you. Your sex."

"My cock, Min. You want my cock."

"*Yes.*" She clasped his head and looked into his eyes. "Now, please."

Evan pulled his cock from his fall and guided it to her entrance. "You will ride me, do you understand?" At her nod, he held her gaze. "Don't look away from me. Lower yourself onto my cock. Do you feel it?"

She nodded again and did not look away or close her eyes. They narrowed as she impaled herself on him, moving slowly. She was tight as a new glove and wet as a downpour. Evan fought to keep his own eyes open. This connection between them was too wondrous to break. He felt such an overwhelming surge of emotion and a desire so strong, he feared he could weep.

"God, I love you, Min."

With a twitch of her hips, she was fully seated on him, her heat surrounding him. "I love you," she whispered, her mouth curling into the sweetest smile he'd ever seen. "What do I do now?"

"What do you want to do?" He squeezed her hip as he brought his other hand under her skirts to grip her other side.

"Move."

"Then move."

She lifted her hips slowly, then came back down over him, moving over and over with a gradually increasing speed. The friction was a delicious torment. Evan held her hips and guided her as he lifted from the seat to thrust into her.

"Faster now, Min," he urged, his fingers digging into her.

She quickened her pace, her muscles tightening. Every

time she ground down, he speared into her. Her moans and whimpers said she was close, as did the clenching of her sex. Evan slid his hand over to stroke her clitoris. She came hard, crying out as she quivered around him.

Evan kept up his pace as ecstasy built inside him. He thrust deep and hard into her, then clumsily tried to withdraw before he spilled himself.

But she would have none of that. Her legs gripped his and she pushed down, taking him and keeping him inside her.

"Don't leave me," she growled in a dark, seductive tone that sent Evan completely over the edge into oblivion.

The strength of his orgasm made him cry out her name and grip her fiercely to him. He pumped into her again and again until he was spent.

When their breathing had slowed a bit, she eased away from him and collapsed onto the seat beside him. Evan used his cravat to tidy as best as he could, then tucked himself away and rebuttoned his fall. He turned toward Min, whose eyes were closed, her head leaning back against the squab.

"Can I tidy you up?" he asked softly.

She opened her eyes to slits and regarded him. "I managed all right, but thank you." She smiled softly. "You're very thoughtful. Now tell me how you found me."

He relayed the story of going to her mother's house, then to see Pandora, then back to her mother's, where he forced the truth from her.

Min sat up, her eyes blazing. "My mother is despicable. I refuse to return to her house. Ever."

"You don't have to. It is my fondest hope that your home will be with me." Evan slid from the seat and turned to kneel in front of her. His ankle was now throbbing, but he'd become rather accomplished at ignoring the pain.

"What are you doing on the floor?" Min leaned forward as if she meant to help him back onto the seat.

Evan held up his hand. "One moment. I need to ask you something. This is not the location I'd imagined, but I don't want to wait." He pulled his great-grandmother's ring from his coat and took Min's hand.

"Lady Minerva," he started.

She tugged her hand away. "Not yet. I need to know that you will be honest with me at all times, no matter what. And that you will do your best to keep chaos and scandal away. I've had enough to last me a lifetime."

Evan took a deep breath. "I know you have, and I'm so sorry that I nearly dragged you into my problems—which are completely resolved now, by the way. I want you to know that your happiness will forever be my primary goal. When I wake up in the morning, my first thought will be how I am going to make you happy today, and my last thought before I go to sleep will be to plan how to make you happy tomorrow."

"All I've ever wanted is a partner I love and who will love me in return, someone who will see marriage the way I do—something to be cherished and honored. I know that's a great deal to expect and more than most gentlemen would probably want. But I held out hope that the right man was out there."

"I am that man!" Evan said with a grin. "I am *your* man."

Min smiled, joy lighting her incredible eyes, making them look like silver. "I knew that the moment we kissed. Perhaps before, but that sealed it. I realize now that the friendship we shared and built upon at Longleat is why I feel so safe with you—why I fell in love with you. It could never have been anyone else."

"I feel the same. We were meant to be." He was desperate to put the ring on her finger. "May I continue now?"

"Oh yes." She presented her hand to him with a giggle.

Evan took her hand and looked into her eyes. "Min, I

cannot imagine my life without you in it. I don't want to endure another day when I don't see you. I knew that before I went to London, but being away from you the past few days has clarified the matter. I love you beyond reason, and I want to spend my life showing you how much." He took a short breath and smiled. "Will you be my wife?" He held up the sapphire ring in his other hand.

Tears glimmered in Min's eyes while her answering smile was wider than he'd ever seen before. "You have a ring?"

"It belonged to my great-grandmother. My mother hoped I would present it to my wife as a betrothal ring, which I just learned today in fact. I think it's perfect because it is the exact color of the forget-me-nots you gave me."

"*Evan.*" She sniffed and moved toward him.

"Wait! You have to answer me first."

"Of course. Yes. Yes. Yes. Forever yes."

Evan slipped the ring onto her finger and prayed it would fit. Miraculously, it did.

Min gazed at the sapphire glinting on her pale hand. "It's perfect." She looked at him, her eyes brimming with emotion. "I hoped and prayed I would find someone like you, but I feared I wouldn't. I confess I'm still a little afraid that things may change."

"They won't," Evan said fiercely. "My love for you is stronger than anything I have ever known. It will not waver."

"Then we shall be fortunate as we weather life's challenges, for I love you so very much. No other man has ever seen me for who I am or treated me as anyone other than Henlow's daughter or Shefford's sister. And today you saved me. Now, will you please sit beside me?" She patted the seat expectantly.

Evan laughed as he vaulted himself back up to the seat. He immediately stretched his left leg out. "It's good you're on my right side," he said as he turned his head toward her.

She put her hand on his cheek and kissed him. It was several minutes before she left him with a sigh, then snuggled against his side. Holding out her hand, she admired the ring. "This belonged to your great-grandmother and was intended for me—your betrothed—and just happened to be the color of the forget-me-nots. It seems we *were* destined to be."

"Absolutely." Evan knew it in his soul, but proof was nice too. He kissed her temple and smiled. "When we arrive in Bath, I want to speak with your father immediately."

"You don't need to ask his permission to marry me," Min said.

"That is not why I wish to see him. I'm going to ensure he doesn't proceed with his plans to divorce your mother."

Min sat up and angled herself to face him. "What makes you think you can talk him out of it?"

"My father and I successfully persuaded Sir Abraham not to divorce his wife," Evan explained. "I am hopeful I can convince your father to do the same."

"You truly did resolve everything?"

"With my father's help." Evan explained how he'd told Sir Abraham the truth about his wife's lover and convinced him not to proceed with a divorce. He also shared that Roger would be leaving London.

Min's brow pleated. "I'm sorry your friend has to leave London, but hopefully he's learned from his roguish behavior."

"I'm sure he has. I know I have. This entire affair— perhaps that is a poor choice of word," he said with a grimace. "This entire situation has shown me how I truly am. I have gone about finding my place in the wrong way. Being a rogue did not fulfill me. I have found where I belong—with you."

"We've yet to take our vows, but I will be with you in

good times and bad," Min said. "I believe I've already demonstrated that I will stand by you in sickness as well as health."

Evan laughed and kissed her again. "You have indeed. I will be forever grateful that I sprained my ankle."

Her gaze held his. "I do love you—especially for wanting to try to stop my father. I am not sure you will be successful, however."

"Perhaps, but I have to try. I learned from my own mistake with the Mrs. Dalton matter that to not consider how my actions would affect my family was the height of selfishness. And as my father and I worked to dissuade Sir Abraham from his plans, I saw how I could try to convince your father in the same manner. Just as Sir Abraham ultimately didn't want to negatively affect his children, so your father must."

"It sounds as though you will make an excellent argument," Min said. "But don't underestimate his desire to punish my mother. I think everyone learning the truth about Ellis has made him see just how much he has suffered from my mother and for how long."

Evan gave her a dark look. "I can completely understand his need to hold your mother to account for her actions. Perhaps we will find common ground on that front. I have to think that because she orchestrated your kidnapping, she will be publicly shunned."

"That would mean making the details of what happened today known—including that you rescued me and we've been alone together." She glanced at the ring on her finger. "Though, I suppose that hardly matters since we will marry. My mother would say it would cast a dark cloud." Min rolled her eyes.

"Your mother was content for your marriage to begin with a gossip-inducing altercation in the park and a kidnapping. This situation is slightly brighter," he said sardonically.

"Still, I think it's best if we move on. No scandal, no turmoil. You've endured enough of that."

Her gaze warmed with love. "Thank you. I know it will be difficult for you to let Spilsby roam free. It will for me too, particularly since I threatened him with prosecution, and he had the audacity to tell me he would be fine because he's a viscount now." She made a face of disgust.

"I have faith Spilsby will get what is coming to him—one way or another. And I will hope that we will be there to see it." He gave her an eager smile. "Now, do tell me how you struck Spilsby at the gardens earlier. Explain it slowly and in great detail."

Min laughed and did as he asked. Then he kissed her again, which led to an immensely enjoyable journey to Bath.

$\mathcal{B}$y the time they reached Bath in the evening, Min wanted nothing more than to nap. She was exhausted by the events of the day, most pleasantly so because of the delightful trip with her new betrothed.

Min could hardly believe all that had happened. Or how happy she was.

They'd taken Merlin to the mews straightaway so Evan could make sure his beloved horse was cared for by the grooms. Once he was unsaddled, brushed, and happily snacking on an apple, Evan tore himself away and they made their way to Min's father's house in Catharine Place. Evan had sent a groom to exchange his riding boots for slippers and to fetch his walking stick.

Jurgens greeted them at the door with an expression of relief. "I'm so glad to see you are all right, Lady Minerva. I will tell your father you've arrived."

However, before the butler could even leave the entrance hall, the duke came running in. "Minnie, my dearest!" He scooped her up against him and hugged her tightly.

Min returned his embrace for a long moment. She knew without a doubt he'd had nothing to do with her kidnapping.

When they parted, the duke looked to Evan, who, despite having his walking stick, was listing slightly to his right. "I can't thank you enough for rescuing my daughter, Mr. Price."

He held his hand out, and Evan shook it.

"I take it Her Grace's butler explained to you what happened?" Evan asked.

"He did indeed." The duke shifted his focus to Min, his expression turning dour. "I have already had words with your mother. Rather, I should describe it as an argument." He shook his head. "I still can't believe she would arrange to have her own daughter kidnapped, though she did not care for me using that term."

Min scowled. "Perhaps not, but that's precisely what she did."

"What of Spilsby?" her father asked.

"We left him by the road somewhere on the way to Bristol." Min sent an appreciative look toward Evan.

"You just left him there?" her father asked with a bit of frustration.

"I wasn't going to bring him back with us," Evan said.

Min didn't want her father to think they'd kindly set the bounder loose. "Papa, you'll be pleased to hear that Evan threw him from the coach and hit him several times, I think —I can't exactly recall.

"That *is* satisfying." He smiled at Evan. "Thank you, Price."

"I may also have pointed my pistol in his face," Evan noted.

Min's father's eyes narrowed. "I will ensure he pays for kidnapping you."

"Papa, I would prefer to move on from the entire matter. I don't want more scandal."

The duke's face flushed. "We can't let him get away with kidnapping you."

"You must respect your daughter's wishes," Evan said firmly. "She doesn't want any more chaos, particularly with what you have planned."

There was a moment of hesitation in which the duke appeared conflicted. He fixed his gaze on Min. "Spilsby didn't hurt you, did he? I won't be able to ignore that."

"No, his intent was just to force a marriage by ruining my reputation."

"I would have called him out," Evan said.

"I have heard of your prowess with a pistol and blade," Min's father said with a nod. "Perhaps you'll have reason to yet." He looked back at Min. "But your reputation may be tainted if anyone knows what happened."

"I doubt that will happen," Min said. "In any case, I am now betrothed and will be married with due haste." She smiled at Evan.

"Is that so?" Her father blinked as he regarded them both.

Min held up her hand and flashed her betrothal ring at her father. "Please say you're glad. I have never been happier."

"If this is what you want, how can I be anything but delighted?" her father asked with a grin before fixing a stern look on Evan. "Though if you don't treat her well, you will have me to answer to. And don't think I'm not aware of the irony of me making demands on anyone regarding their marriage. It is because of my behavior that I wish to ensure my daughter's husband is above reproach because that's what she deserves."

Evan inclined his head. "I couldn't agree more."

"I'm well aware of the mistakes I've made," Min's father continued. "But the two of you are already in a much better position than I have ever been. You both love each other."

"We do indeed." Evan spoke with a confidence that made

Min's heart flip. Her love for him seemed to increase moment by moment.

"Then I can't ask for anything more," the duke said.

"I, however, have something to ask of you." Evan flicked a glance at Min.

"Come, Papa, let us go to your study or the drawing room," Min suggested.

"The study will do." Her father gestured for them to precede him.

Min took Evan's arm so he could lean on her a bit as they made their way to the study. "You must sit," she said to Evan, guiding him to a chair.

"I'm disappointed there is no settee so we may sit next to one another," he said softly, with a mock pout.

Min flashed him a brief smile. "You've sat by me enough today, haven't you?"

"Never," he whispered with seductive promise darkening his gaze.

Min took a chair near Evan's, and her father sat opposite them.

The duke sent Evan an expectant look. "What is it you wish to ask? I'm sure you'll find Min's dowry is most agreeable."

Evan waved his hand. "It's not about that. I ask that you not proceed with divorcing Her Grace. You must understand that doing so will only have negative effects on your children —and on Ellis, who certainly doesn't deserve any more grief."

A pained expression overtook the duke's face. He briefly looked down at the floor. "I have considered this, so please know that I haven't made this decision lightly."

"I understand, Papa," Min said. "But you *must* rethink this. Like it or not, there are some who already think poorly of Sheff because of whom he married, and our mother certainly hasn't helped with things she has surely said about Jo. I can only imagine the sentiments she's expressed to her friends and the gossips of the ton. But most of all, you must think of Ellis," Min pleaded. "She doesn't deserve further turmoil, and if you bring a suit against her father, it will only make matters worse."

Her father's brow was deeply creased. "I know that, and it did give me pause. However, I have since learned that your mother has another lover, one who is far more recent. In fact, they continue to see each other. He lives here in Bath."

Min sucked in a breath. She should not have been surprised.

The duke's gray-blue gaze hardened. "I'm planning to sue him instead."

Min wasn't sure they'd be able to talk him out of it now. She sagged against the chair and looked over at Evan, who was watching her.

His jaw tightened, and he shifted his attention to the duke. "Please don't do that. What will be the benefit?"

"I will no longer be married to her," the duke replied simply. "Nothing will bring me greater joy."

Evan's expression settled into a near scowl. "Not even the peace and happiness of your children?"

Min's father flinched. "Of course, their happiness means everything to me, but I have denied my own for far too long. Now that I have someone whom I love, I want to be with her in all the ways that matter, including in the eyes of the law and the church. Surely you can both understand that?"

Min's heart broke for her father. It was hard to argue against that, especially now that she knew how it felt to be truly, madly, and deeply in love. The thought of not being able to become Evan's wife cut into her and threatened to steal her breath. "Papa, I know we're asking you to sacrifice what you want, and you have already paid a great price for marrying our mother. Yet, if you hadn't, Sheff and I would not exist. So there is something good that came of it, isn't there?"

The duke looked away as he nodded.

"It's time to end this cycle of punishment and suffering in our family," Min said. She suddenly saw her life and her family in shocking clarity. Her mother broke her father's heart. He punished her by having affairs. She retaliated by having affairs. He struck back by bringing her illegitimate child into the household. And her mother responded by treating Ellis horribly. "You and Mother have waged a war for nearly thirty years. I understand you wanting to end it, but you can do that without a divorce. A divorce would be your final punishment, but what you—and Mother—have failed to understand is that every battle you've waged has had devastating consequences for me, Sheff, and Ellis. Despite that, Sheff is happily married with a child on the way. And I am on the verge of marrying the man I love. Ellis now knows the truth and can pursue a life *she* wants instead of what has been dictated for her. Please don't rob us of the happiness and peace we all deserve."

Her father blanched. He wiped his hand over his mouth. "I hadn't thought of it that way." He was silent a long moment before nodding vaguely. "We haven't been good parents. I don't want to ruin your happiness. You're right that you, Sheff, and Ellis deserve that. It's time to end the war."

Min hated that he looked defeated. "You aren't losing, Papa," she said softly. "You have Mrs. Welbeck and the love you share. Mother has bitterness, and none of her children want anything to do with her. Please let joy heal you. We can all move on from this."

Her father gave her a weak smile, but his eyes were bright —with tears and with pride. "How are you so much wiser than me? I'm happier than I can say that you've found love and your brother has done the same. I would ask if there's anything I can do for you, but I doubt there is."

"The thing I want most is for Ellis to be at my wedding," Min said. "She has not responded to any of my letters that you forwarded. Can you inform her that I am betrothed and would like her to be with me at the wedding? I don't know where she is, but we're planning to marry in London as soon as Evan can obtain a special license."

The duke hesitated before saying, "I can tell you that Ellis is also in London."

Min's chest tightened as emotion washed over her. At least she knew where Ellis was.

"But don't ask me for her address," her father said, before Min could utter the words. "I will convey your invitation, and it will be up to her if she attends."

"Does she blame me in some way?" Min asked.

"Of course not, dear. She's just a wounded bird at the moment, and, like me, apparently, she needs time to heal."

Min nodded as Evan reached over and took her hand. She squeezed him, grateful for his presence and support.

"When should we adjourn to London?" the duke asked.

"The day after tomorrow," Min replied at the same time Evan said, "Tomorrow."

Her father laughed as Min shook her head at Evan. "You need a day of rest after today's upheaval."

"But I want to marry as soon as possible," Evan said, his eyes dimming with disappointment.

The duke smiled at them. "I will leave for London in the morning and see about obtaining the license for you."

Min's heart leapt. "Thank you, Papa."

Evan sent her father a wry glance. "I suppose your position does have more weight than mine."

"Even so, I believe you could obtain it on your own," the

duke said with a shrug. "My involvement will hasten things, which it sounds like you both want."

"You don't mind that I stay here, do you, Papa?" Min asked. She'd considered staying with Pandora as she'd originally planned, but her father's house was much closer to Evan, and that was preferable.

"Of course not, Minnie. You are always welcome anywhere I am, as are you, Price."

"Evan, Your Grace," Evan replied.

"Henlow," her father said. "We are family now."

Min stood, and the men rose with her. She went to give her father a hug. He held her tightly and kissed her brow. When they parted, he sniffed.

She was so grateful he'd listened to reason. "I'm going to walk Evan home now."

The duke clasped Evan's hand once more. Min took Evan's arm, and they left the house.

As they walked to his mother's, Evan glanced over at Min. "That went even better than I expected. Your argument was most persuasive."

"You inspired me," she said with a smile, though her heart felt a little heavy.

"I sense a bit of sadness in you just now." His brow was furrowed as he regarded her.

"I miss Ellis so much. I'm sad she's not here to share our good news and that she may not be with me when we marry. On the rare occasions when I did imagine my wedding at some point in the future, I expected she would be at my side. I suppose that was selfish of me to think that, as my companion, she would always be beside me. She has her own life to live."

"I don't think that was selfish of you at all. Just as I don't believe you expected her to do anything as your companion." He stopped just before they reached his mother's house and turned to face her, taking her hands. "Ellis is like a sister to you, yes?"

Min nodded.

"Then, of course, you would expect she would be at your wedding and by your side. If she isn't there physically, you must believe she is with you in spirit. As your father said, she needs to heal."

"I know," Min whispered. "It's just hard, and I'm not very patient."

"You demonstrated that quite adequately in the coach earlier," he remarked with an arched brow.

Min giggled. "Don't talk about that here." She glanced around the square.

"Is it unseemly?" He waggled his brows at her.

"No, it's arousing." She enjoyed the flare of desire that sparked his gaze.

"Just wait until we're married," he murmured.

She gave him her sauciest stare. "I sincerely hope I don't have to."

EPILOGUE

*M*in and Evan's wedding day was unique in that the bride's mother was absent due to "illness." In truth, she had not been included in their plans.

Jo hosted the wedding breakfast at Henlow House. It was her first official duty as the Countess of Shefford. Min had never been happier.

And yet there was a hole in Min's heart because Ellis wasn't there either. She'd finally written, at least, but it had been to politely decline the invitation to the wedding. She just wasn't ready to see everyone, and that included her two half sisters. Persey had stood up with Min, and now they were gathered with the rest of the Rogue Rules Club in the library at Henlow House.

Min swallowed past the lump in her throat as Ellis's absence now seemed most keen. They were not the full club without her. Even Iona was present. She was in London visiting her sister, Lady Kathleen, and Min had been delighted to invite her today. The other members of the club had greeted—and accepted—her warmly.

Pandora sat beside Min on the settee. She'd journeyed

from Bath to attend the wedding and to visit her sister and her family. And to present what was, by now, a tradition when one of their club married: an embroidered copy of the rogue rules.

Handing Min the wrapped package, Pandora smirked. "I'm sure you know what this is."

"I think I do," Min replied with a laugh. She opened the package and gasped. The embroidery included stitched forget-me-nots and pink roses. Min had told Pandora the story of the pink dungeon and Evan's penchant for blue and brown.

"I love it. How ever did you embroider this so quickly?" Min asked.

"I confess I started it before Evan proposed." Pandora shrugged. "Even if you didn't marry, I thought someone else might. I added the flowers after you became betrothed."

There weren't many "someones" left.

"Do you include yourself in that number?" Tamsin, Baroness Droxford, asked with a sly smile.

"Absolutely *not*," Pandora said with a firm shake of her head.

"That leaves our newest member," Persey noted. They all turned their heads toward Iona, who was seated in a chair.

Iona's eyes widened slightly. "I expect I will marry, but I'm in no hurry. Though, if my mother has anything to say about it, I will be wed by spring."

"Before the London Season?" Gwen, Min's new sister-in-law, asked.

"I am not planning on participating in the Season," Iona said. "I don't feel as though I belong."

"But your brother is an earl," Tamsin said, her brow creasing.

"My *half* brother. My father was his father's steward.

Some people can't see past that. *And* we're Irish," Iona added with a wry tilt of her brow.

Jo gave her an understanding nod. "I don't blame you. People can be awful."

"If anyone is rude to you, I hope you'll tell me," Min said fiercely. "I will not tolerate anyone who is cruel."

"We will all look out for one another," Persey said. She looked to Iona. "If you do have a Season, we'll make sure it's splendid."

"That's kind of you." Iona smiled. "If I am married before next August, I may not be able to join you all in Weston, and I am looking forward to that more than anything."

"Do *not* marry a man who won't allow you to spend your summer holiday in Weston," Persey said vehemently.

"Is that a new rogue rule?" Iona asked.

"No, it's just good advice," Jo replied, to which Persey nodded in agreement.

"I'm glad we'll all be in Weston together," Gwen said with a smile. "I know it will become challenging as our families grow." She gently touched her midsection, and there were gasps and smiles around the room.

"Are you expecting too?" Tamsin asked.

Gwen nodded. "It turns out my illness was for a specific reason."

"Somerton must be thrilled," Min said with a grin. "I certainly am. I'm to be an aunt two times over next year." Ellis would be an aunt too, for Jo was her half sister. "I do hope Ellis comes to Weston." Min didn't think they could assume she would. She'd said in her letter that she was determining her path in life and wasn't yet sure what it would be.

Min's statement sobered everyone.

"She'll come around," Persey said softly. "We'll just be here for her until she's ready to share her plans."

The lump re-formed in Min's throat, so she nodded. She

did not like being melancholy on what should be the happiest day of her life so far. Shaking her doldrums away, she looked back down at the embroidered rogue rules in her lap. She still couldn't quite believe she'd married her very own rogue.

"What do you suppose it says about us that we've all married reformed rogues?" she asked.

This was met with laughter.

Pandora looked to Iona. "It's up to you to marry a nonrogue."

"Perhaps it will be you," Iona said. "If anyone deserves that, you do." She knew all about Pandora's past with Bane and the origin of the Rogue Rules Club.

"As I said earlier, absolutely *not*. I don't care if he's the nonroguiest rogue who ever lived. I have come to treasure my independence. And I've a meeting with the publisher for my novel next week. I sent a note when I arrived in town, and they invited me to meet with them."

"That's wonderful!" Min gushed as the others did the same.

"Will you be publishing with your name?" Tamsin asked.

Pandora shook her head. "No, I shall be anonymous. I think my name has seen enough notoriety."

Persey looked at her sister with immense pride. "Well, we will all know who the author is, and we could not be prouder."

They visited for a short while before returning to the drawing room. Guests began to depart, and when, at last, Min and Evan were alone, she collapsed on a settee. Kicking off her slippers, she put her feet up on the cushions.

Evan lifted her legs and slid beneath them. He massaged her feet, and Min let out a soft sigh of pleasure.

"Careful, Mrs. Price." Though she was still Lady Minerva, she'd told Evan when he'd teasingly called her that earlier that she liked it. It showed that she was definitively his, and that made her giddy. "You keep making sounds like that, and I can't be responsible for my actions." He gave her a wicked leer.

Min's heart flipped. The way he looked at her never failed to stir her emotions as well as her desire. She hoped it would always be thus, and—perhaps surprisingly—truly believed it would.

"Our chamber isn't far." She moved her foot to gently caress his groin.

Evan groaned. "The things you do, my wife. I look forward to when we have our own home."

"Soon, my love." In fact, they planned to purchase one nearby on Duke Street. Evan had been hesitant at first because it was expensive, but they could afford it with Min's dowry. "Thank you again for agreeing to the house on Duke Street."

"I suppose I never imagined I'd be living in Mayfair, married to the daughter of a duke." His hands moved up beneath her skirts from her foot to her ankle, and one traveled even farther toward her knee.

"I never imagined I'd marry a rogue." Min became very aware of his wandering hand, and her body began to heat. "You're certain you don't mind hanging my new embroidery in our bedchamber?"

"Absolutely not. Between the forget-me-nots and the pink roses, it is a wonderful reminder of how we fell in love." His hand was now on her thigh, and he'd scooted himself over so that her backside was pressed against the side of his thigh.

"Should we adjourn to the bedchamber?" Min suggested as his fingers found their way to her sex. She parted her legs, inviting him to continue despite her question.

"We probably should," he murmured. But he stroked her folds and teased her clitoris in a breathtaking assault.

"Though, there's a risk in staying here that is arousing, is there not? Anyone could walk in." He thrust his finger into her sex.

Min clenched her jaw to keep from moaning. She moved her hips against his hand and closed her eyes as she leaned her head back on the arm of the settee. "You are very naughty, Mr. Price." She gasped as he found that delightful spot deep inside her sex that made her quiver.

He suddenly removed his hand and pulled her up. "I'm afraid there are too many naughty things I wish to do. This risky location simply won't do." He kissed her, long and deep, until her body thrummed with desire.

When the kiss ended, he did not move. She opened her eyes and saw him looking at her. He was so close—their lips almost touching—that she could see all the golden flecks in his dark eyes that made them sparkle.

"I love you, Min," he breathed, a smile lifting his lips.

Another lump formed briefly in her throat. Apparently, today was a day for emotions. "I love you." She caressed his cheek. "I can't believe how lucky we are, that our friendship became so much more."

"Can I tell you that I hated you calling yourself my 'sister-friend'?" He made a face.

Min laughed. "Why?"

"Because I knew even then that to describe you as anything sisterly was an abomination. My feelings for you are not brotherly. They are wholly primal and completely focused on mating—in every way. You are my partner in all things, my light in this life, and my love for all time."

A shiver danced up Min's spine, followed by a warm suffusing of joy through every part of her. This was what she'd dared to want. "You have made all my dreams come true, Evan."

He kissed her again before standing and sweeping her into his arms. "I never plan to stop."

Join Ellis in London as she accepts a job as a secretary—as a man—for the Marquess of Keele, a widower who doesn't believe he can find happy ever after a second time. But when their wounded hearts meet and unexpected sparks fly, can they take the risk of falling in love?
Don't miss the next Rogue Rules book, SINCE THE MARQUESS DEMANDS.

Would you like to know when my next book is available and to hear about sales and deals? **Sign up for my VIP newsletter** which is the only place you can get bonus books and material such as the short prequel to the Phoenix Club series, INVITATION, and the exciting prequel to Legendary Rogues, THE LEGEND OF A ROGUE.

Join me on social media!

Facebook: https://facebook.com/DarcyBurkeFans
Instagram at darcyburkeauthor
Pinterest at darcyburkewrite

And follow me on Bookbub to receive updates on pre-orders, new releases, and deals!

Need more Regency romance? Check out my other historical series:

The Phoenix Club

Society's most exclusive invitation...

Welcome to the Phoenix Club, where London's most audacious, disreputable, and intriguing ladies and gentlemen find scandal, redemption, and second chances.

Matchmaking Chronicles

The course of true love never runs smooth. Sometimes a little matchmaking is required. When couples meet at a house party, provocative flirtation, secret rendezvous, and falling in love abound!

The Untouchables

Swoon over twelve of Society's most eligible and elusive bachelor peers and the bluestockings, wallflowers, and outcasts who bring them to their knees!

The Untouchables: The Spitfire Society

Meet the smart, independent women who've decided they don't need Society's rules, their families' expectations, or, most importantly, a husband. But just because they don't need a man doesn't mean they might not *want* one...

The Untouchables: The Pretenders

Set in the captivating world of The Untouchables, follow the saga of a trio of siblings who excel at being something they're not. Can a dauntless Bow Street Runner, a devastated viscount, and a disillusioned Society miss unravel their secrets?

Marrywell Brides

Come to Marrywell, England where the annual May Day Matchmaking Festival has been bringing hopeful romantics together for hundreds of years. The dukes and rogues of the

Regency will meet their matches with spirited and captivating ladies who may very well steal their hearts.

Wicked Dukes Club
Six books written by me and my BFF, NYT Bestselling Author Erica Ridley. Meet the unforgettable men of London's most notorious tavern, The Wicked Duke. Seductively handsome, with charm and wit to spare, one night with these rakes and rogues will never be enough...

Love is All Around
Heartwarming Regency-set retellings of classic Christmas stories (written after the Regency!) featuring a cozy village, three siblings, and the best gift of all: love.

Secrets and Scandals
Six epic stories set in London's glittering ballrooms and England's lush countryside.

Legendary Rogues
Five intrepid heroines and adventurous heroes embark on exciting quests across the Georgian Highlands and Regency England and Wales!

If you like contemporary romance, I hope you'll check out my **Ribbon Ridge** series available from Avon Impulse, and the continuation of Ribbon Ridge in **So Hot**.

I hope you'll consider leaving a review at your favorite online vendor or networking site!

I appreciate my readers so much. Thank you, thank you, *thank you.*

ALSO BY DARCY BURKE

Historical Romance

Rogue Rules
If the Duke Dares
Because the Baron Broods
When the Viscount Seduces
As the Earl Likes
Until the Rake Surrenders
Since the Marquess Demands
What the Scoundrel Desires
How the Devil Sins

The Phoenix Club
Improper
Impassioned
Intolerable
Indecent
Impossible
Irresistible
Impeccable
Insatiable

Marrywell Brides
Beguiling the Duke
Romancing the Heiress
Matching the Marquess

A Rogue to Ruin

Love is All Around
(A Regency Holiday Trilogy)
The Red Hot Earl
The Gift of the Marquess
Joy to the Duke

Wicked Dukes Club
One Night for Seduction by Erica Ridley
One Night of Surrender by Darcy Burke
One Night of Passion by Erica Ridley
One Night of Scandal by Darcy Burke
One Night to Remember by Erica Ridley
One Night of Temptation by Darcy Burke

Secrets and Scandals
Her Wicked Ways
His Wicked Heart
To Seduce a Scoundrel
To Love a Thief (a novella)
Never Love a Scoundrel
Scoundrel Ever After

Legendary Rogues
Lady of Desire
Romancing the Earl
Lord of Fortune
Captivating the Scoundrel

Historical Mystery

ABOUT THE AUTHOR

Darcy Burke is the USA Today Bestselling Author of sexy, emotional historical and contemporary romance. Darcy wrote her first book at age 11, a happily ever after about a swan addicted to magic and the female swan who loved him, with exceedingly poor illustrations. Join her Reader Club newsletter for the latest updates from Darcy.

A native Oregonian, Darcy lives on the edge of wine country with her guitar-strumming husband, incredibly talented artist daughter, and imaginative, Japanese-speaking son who will almost certainly out-write her one day (that may be tomorrow). They're a crazy cat family with two Bengal cats, a small, fame-seeking cat named after a fruit, an older rescue Maine Coon with attitude to spare, an adorable former stray who wandered onto their deck and into their hearts, and two bonded boys who used to belong to (separate) neighbors but chose them instead. You can find Darcy in her comfy writing chair balancing her laptop and a cat or three, attempting yoga, folding laundry (which she loves), or wildlife spotting and playing games with her family. She loves traveling to the UK and visiting her cousins in Denmark. Visit Darcy online at www.darcyburke.com and follow her on social media.

facebook.com/DarcyBurkeFans

instagram.com/darcyburkeauthor

pinterest.com/darcyburkewrites

goodreads.com/darcyburke

bookbub.com/authors/darcy-burke

amazon.com/author/darcyburke

threads.net/@darcyburkeauthor

tiktok.com/@darcyburkeauthor